THE REBOOT

NEBULA CHRONICLES

ANAND ARORA

INDIA • SINGAPORE • MALAYSIA

ISBN 979-8-88704-928-1

Dedicated to

PHAM, KAPS and Isaac Asimov

Contents

Acknowledgements *7*

Chapter 1 Routine as Usual – or is it? 9

Chapter 2 It's not Just a Job for Me 27

Chapter 3 I use Emotion for the Many and Reserve Reasons for the Few – Adolf Hitler. 44

Chapter 4 The Usuals: Issues and Stuff 58

Chapter 5 Everything is Alright! 73

Chapter 6 Just Hope we are all Wrong! 86

Chapter 7 It Breaks Out 99

Chapter 8 We Call it 'The Kraal' 112

Chapter 9 But for the Outside World 128

Chapter 10 Fair or Unfair: Does it Matter? 144

Chapter 11 Those Slimy Loose Ends 159

Chapter 12 Jared Lincolns Story 174

Chapter 13 You and What Army? 191

Chapter 14 Nobody Speaks, Nobody gets Choked 205

Chapter 15 Playing God for Everyone 219

Chapter 16 Oh Captain, My Captain 234

Chapter 17 Les carrottes sont Cuites
(The Carrots are Cooked!) 251

Chapter 18 If you Just Smile. 271

Chapter 19 That's What Makes you that Guy! 285

Chapter 20 Speech, Speech, Speech, Speech! 300

Acknowledgements

I have always been inspired by many stories since my childhood. People who know me the best have understood by now that I live in two worlds – one that is visible to the naked eye, which we call the real world, and the other that is invisible yet fabricated by your imagination, dreams, and vision. To me, both are real, with me controlling the latter and me often getting controlled by the former.

This is my attempt to flee from the control, the visible world has on me. I would like to present my first story to the world. A story, I have lived in my invisible world as a spectator (and not as a character myself).

There is a long list of people responsible for helping me find true inspiration, wisdom, motivation, discipline, and confidence to produce this piece of work.

Thank You, Almighty God, for giving me a chance to be human and be with the people I adore.

My parents, for their unconditional love and support for making me who I am today.

My daughter, Prisha, with whom I had many discussions about this story, events and characters in the book. She has been my cheerleader, motivation, and first editor for this book.

My son Medhansh, who comes up with something startling, young, fresh and a joyful fact every time I converse with him. You are simply the best.

My wife Himani, for being a strong pillar of existence in my life and maintaining a sense of sanity in a life governed by fuzzy logic.

My brother Parag, for enthusing me with motivation, hope, and being my failsafe in life.

To all the relatives and friends who helped me boost my self-confidence from time to time and being patient as well as supportive during the journey of producing this book.

And above all, thank you, Isaac Asimov, for writing the legendary "Foundation Series", which inspired me to the core and helped me bring out this book.

In the end, thanks to Notion Press for your support in publishing this book.

Chapter 1

Routine as Usual – or is it?

'Nebula,' as they call her, was the most spectacular innovation in the history of humanity. Ever since humans evolved, one question has been a daunting one for thinkers and scientists of society. It is – who is out there in the sky above? Many started with religious beliefs, then came the cult of art forms like Astrology, and then the leading theoretical physicists arrived who questioned everything. The rationalists took this one step ahead into an actual experiment, and the world of space technology was born.

4 June 2031, Belgrade, Serbia, 0900 AM

It's 9 AM in Belgrade. A black Volkswagen SUV is driving across the Ada Bridge over the River Sava. Driving the same is Jovan Novsky, Chief R&D scientist of Pioneer Kvalitat, one of the leading global manufacturers of space and defence equipment, globally managed by the CEO, Polsky Bazic.

He is a bit cheerful – Mornings are always like that with his routine of dropping Alexei and Maxim, his kids, to the school en route to his office. However, this time, the kids are fighting for another bet they had in the evening over the last night's game of Polaris90, the world's leading online gaming championship. Sadly, they could not watch the game, as the gaming event starts at 00:00 GMT, which is late for the kids to be awake (i.e., 01:30 am in Belgrade) and goes up to 5 hours.

Last night's game was eventful – Brazil vs France, the two gaming legendary teams in the world. The kids betted on different groups for 1000 tokens to be exchanged online for Polaris90 merchandise.

"Alexei, always listen to the big bro. He knows more about Polaris than any other boy in the town, bruv. You can't defeat TeeKay at all – France stood no choice. So pay-up time this evening... Haha," boasts Maxim, the 13-year-old boy and elder son of Novsky.

The little 9-year-old Alexei was sulky but undefeated in his attitude and said nothing.

"Come on, bro. A bet is a bet. You will pay up tonight!" says Maxim.

"Maxim, you got it this time. But it's so unfair, Dad! It was not me betting; it was you. Why did you tell me to bet on France? You know TeeKay never gets eliminated before 90 minutes, and by that time, he had already destroyed half the empire. Dad, why, why would you convince me to go against TeeKay?" says Alexei in a sad voice.

Novsky laughs and tells Alexei, "Son, take chances and wish for the impossible to happen. That is life, Alexei. Hope! Hope for the weak to be strong. Hope for the losers to become winners. Hope for...."

Maxim laughs in-between. "Hope that one day Alexei will win a bet against Maxim. If that happens, it would be 1 in 100. Of course, by that time, he would have lost – 100,000 tokens for a win of 1000 tokens. Fair Dad Fair –Alexei, please hope, bro!" he jokes again with sarcasm.

Alexei yells, "Dad!!!"

Novsky looks in the rear mirror toward Maxim and says sternly, "Maxim, now come on! Leave it this time!"

The car has now slowed down– School Area speed limit!

Novsky tells the boys, "Boys, a game is to enjoy and learn, not to capture any gains or feel sad for losses. Try to learn from the players what went wrong in Brazil. Now, come on, cheer up. It's your turn to scoot off now."

Alexei and Maxim both say in unison, "Bye, Dad. See you in the evening."

"Bye, my boys. Now cheer up Alexei– Big day ahead," says Novsky as the kids get out of the car into the crowd entering the school.

Novsky looks at them going into the school and smiles, "What a generation!" he thinks, "Would be interesting to see how they shape the next 60 years!" He drives to the office.

4 June 2031, Pioneer Kvalitat Office, Belgrade, 03:00 PM

Jovan Novsky is waiting in the CEO's chambers. He is sitting on a lounge chair waiting for his boss, who is walking outside the room and speaking on his cell phone. Jovan could catch bits and pieces of the conversation through the not-so-thick walls of the CEO chambers.

It doesn't take long for Jovan to figure out that he is on a call with Mr. Mashkov, the Russian president, to discuss the recent army shipments.

The top army brass had raised their suspicion over the quality of the latest design, 'Bazic 1201,' named after the CEO (and the cofounder).

Jovan thought: Assuming you are a Kalashnikov is one thing, but acting in front of others is a sick thing to do, Polsky.

He suddenly remembers the 2020 movie 'Kalashnikov AK47', which was a sensation in the Russian land. It was the biography of Mr. Kalashnikov and his legendary adventure of creating the most high-quality assault rifle the world had seen in the 20th century. Well, Polsky Bazic hoped his new creation would change the 21st.

The latest German technologies in the Supersonic Rifles had already wooed away the armies of many renowned nations like the USA, India, the UK, and China. Not only that, they were even causing whispering whirlpools inside the Russian Military, and that meant a tremendous loss in business for Bazic.

In reality, the Bazic series could not stand a chance against German technology, yet they allowed Kvalitat to supply arms + ammunition for the first time to the Russian military. That was mainly because of the personal relationship, Bazic, the CEO, had with the Russian president.

However, 99% of Kvalitat's business had supplied surveillance and space technology defence equipment to multiple nations. Space had been only in the hands of exploration agencies like NASA, ISRO etc., for a century, but post-2025, the corporate sector steered the advancement in space technologies.

The coming era is going to need not just exploration but also probably a Space War between either the nations of mankind or even beyond (early signs of which were observed in the 2020s).

Not only did Kvalitat build ballistic missiles for space defence but also leveraged the technologies such as high-speed power satellites, as well as build space stations for the nations.

Jovan looks around the room to distract himself. The interiors of the CEO chambers were classic. At the head-start of the room, there was a luxurious silver-coated wooden fabric and a leather 3+1 seater sofa-set on which Jovan sat opposite a centre table, glancing at the statue of Serbian independence in front of him.

In the room, one could see wooden panels on the wall with antique dimly lighted lamps pointed towards paintings hung on the wall. Amongst those was a group photograph of a couple of army soldiers, along with an older man at the centre, whom Novsky assumed was Bazic Sr.

Then there were photographs of space missions, missiles, and a couple of pictures of Polsky Bazic and some diplomats, including Serbian, Russian and even Indian political leaders. The highlight, however, was the CEO's chair and table at the end of the room. This was a classic antique wooden office-table set, with handmade gold foil wood carving and leather that appeared to be of high quality and Italian import. The room must be 2000 sq. ft in size with a lot of space to give a feel of tranquillity and luxury.

While in his thoughts, his cell buzzed and lit up with a text from Albina. She was busy with her project today and wanted

Novsky to get some stuff during his return. The kids will come home with their neighbour-friend today. 'Managing two kids and working alongside them isn't easy. But good that they blessed us with community support,' he thought.

Suddenly the door opened, and a tall man who looked fresh and young, although Novsky knew he was 55 years old, entered alongside a blonde woman in her 30s, Ms. Natasha, a model-looking woman who was Bazic's secretary.

She keeps the files and his laptop on the table and proceeds towards the exit. Bazic smiles at Novsky and asks him to join him at his mahogany table. Bazic takes the chief seat, and Novsky sits opposite with a sigh.

Bazic asks, "What's the matter, Jovan? You don't look enthused today?"

Novsky replies, "Nothing, boss. The morning chores and the day's plan are clogging my mind."

Bazic enquires, "How are Albina and the kids? I told you last month about taking a vacation, Novsky! This entire workload and family responsibility take a toll on even the fiercest soldiers."

Novsky shrugs. "It's okay, boss. Need to finish this sprint of activities before the new update on NEBULA is released. I might take them out for a while."

Bazic smiles and asks, "So, how is the Board of Director presentation shaping up? Are you ready to show me a version of the same?"

Novsky gesticulates and says, "Boss, I know I was supposed to land the deck in your mail last evening. But, give me 3 to 4 days more for the same. The new engine automation sequence software patch is ready to be released for ARK2135, and I was engaged in the sprint for the same."

Bazic now looks a bit irritated and, with his hands flying in the air, says, "Novsky, the delay is one thing I would have been OK with if it was related to the data for presentation work. But you are bold enough to admit you are working on the ARK2135 update project at top priority.

"What did we discuss? Keep working on it, but as soon as a priority one business comes back in, we put a hold on it for some time. Even SERB-SPACE, ROSCOSMOS and ISRO are all aligned with this!"

"Boss, I understand your frustration. But try to understand us here! Once we start the sprint, it is not very motivating to distract ourselves from the development activity and move towards something else. I did not allocate any resources in the ppt. But, give me 3 days. I will get to it."

Bazic retorts, "Novsky, this ppt is not it. I have been sensing a pattern of distraction in you for a couple of months. Tell me if something is bothering you?"

Novsky says, "Nothing, boss. It is just that after the NEBULA launch, we started focussing on the least important items like the ballistic projects and business updates. However, the next big thing on our plate is ARK, which the BOD members are not that excited about. It can be a big project. We hired so many experts during NEBULA times, giving them hope that bigger and far more important projects are in the row, and now suddenly they work for college intern level projects."

"Novsky, don't be a child. Come on. You are a senior member of the firm. Act like one! The project is a show-off only. What do you think? Is the prophecy coming true? World end and all – Noah's Arc and stuff! Let us be practical. It is a good backup strategy. But I am not interested in my lifetime to see the security patches for the dumbest software in ARK. I am keeping the project alive only because I believe in you and told you that this would be your so-called 'Research Backup Project' if nothing is on your plate. Stop working on the software and get me a fact-oiled, chart-laced pitch deck!"

"Sure thing, Boss. I have something to ask, sir. Have we been able to get the contract on the Version 2 for Ryan Jettie?" (He was referring to the famous Ryan Bomb installed on NEBULA)

"Not yet, Novsky. You know how these deals work. One politico leverages another, and then multiple firms like us settle for small pieces of each these days. However, the discussion has progressed to a good stage. Maybe in the next W-BATCO, we will demo something."

W-BATCO was one of the most renowned weapon expos in the world. Novsky gets up, humming slowly and leaves the desk.

"And Novsky," Bazic says.

"Yes, sir?"

"Take a 2-week break from this ARK thing now. I have something lined up for you in New Delhi. Want to catch up with your old friend Sharma?" Bazic teases him.

Novsky shakes his head and grins. "Oh no, Boss. Not again!"

4 June 2031, Prime 1 Office, Lodhi Gardens, New Delhi 0700 pm IST

Ranjan Sharma was about to pack his laptop and briefcase when he heard a knock on his cabin. Mahavir enters and says, "Leaving?"

"Yes, Mahavir. Done for the day. What about you? Are you heading for any gala dinner tonight?" Ranjan mocks, looking at the flamboyant TUX Mahavir is sporting.

"Yes, you know how it is on Fridays for me. Another celeb's birthday, a couple of politicos and biz guys, but am largely in for the free booze and pasta as you know me."

"A skilled actor, you are Mahavir! I know this is a shadow excuse for some biz-deal or consulting assignment you will get," Ranjan teases.

Ranjan Sharma, the 52-year-old scientist and CTO/Head-Engineering in Prime 1, had a friendly rapport with his boss, the flamboyant 57-year-old Mahavir Singh, a second-generation entrepreneur in the Singh family who profited out of Defence deals primarily attributed to the army contracts, Sr. Singh (Mahavir's father) had.

Mahavir's grandfather was once a deputy general and retired with pride from the Indian Armed Forces. Then, his father started his defence consulting business handling the IT infrastructure first and later moved swiftly towards arms/ ammunition and beyond.

The second generation of Prime1 owner, Mahavir Singh, now commanded control in defence contracts and had a breakthrough working with ISRO in the NEBULA project. This project put PRIME-1 at the top of the corporate world and Mahavir, one of the wealthiest persons in the country. Ranjan was the mastermind behind the NEBULA project from the idea to execution. This made him a top-notch scientist in the world.

Mahavir was exceedingly fond of Ranjan and considered him his most important asset, allowing him to operate independently across many projects. The rapport was of a friendship only between the boss and subordinate.

Mahavir walks to Ranjan's desk, helps him place his notebooks and laptop charger in his bag and says, "My friend, you know me better than anyone. There is not a single politico deal that goes without booze these days. You gotta get these guys to relax and make them feel at ease about the business stuff. Is there a better way to spill the beans of mutual benefits without having a glass of McLeish 16 YO?"

Ranjan smiles. "You would know, my friend. My brain is 80% occupied with my work and the new technologies. Nidhi, Rajat and Zoya hijack the rest of it. Happy to stick to this circle of life only, mate."

Mahavir laughs and pats him on his back, "See you Monday. Have a pleasant weekend, mate!"

Ranjan smiles and looks straight into Mahavir's eyes, saying, "Mahavir, I have been meaning to discuss something with you lately."

"I know. You are uncomfortable with Kvalitat people, right?"

"It is not the question of comfort, Mahavir. You know how Prime-1 works with absolute rigour and speed in all our projects. We have put this firm on a Fortune 500 stack because of it. However, relying on Kvalitat for the ARK project has demotivated our team. Their updates are way too slow, and an approval request from their boss, Bazic, precedes every discussion. I feel that Novsky also doesn't like working with Prime-1 on this upgrade. He leaves no stone unturned to claim every release as his own personal victory, rather than attributing it to the mutual teamwork of both organisations. This attitude isn't healthy for the partnership. I know we have the upper hand on the project as this is an ISRO-led project, and we are their prime partners. I can line up an EU firm I connected with last year during a seminar I attended in London. All you need to do is give me a nod to at least kick-start the discussion on commercials and deliverables. We can get the patches and AI modules delivered much faster."

"Ranjan, you don't understand. It's not about delivery time or commercials on this. The entire thing is a complex matter to discuss, but trust me, the deal goes to the very top. If we want SERB-SPACE, ROSCOSMOS and ISRO to stick together on this agenda, we should act like professionals. And Bazic is a friend, and I trust him for more than the ARK project. Do you know last month, he put in a word in ROSCOSMOS for Prime-1 to handle the latest machinery replacement for their

RosCom Sat-2039 project? The project itself will be $500 Million, if not less. I am impatient for this closure. Even, it would be a good bump up on the team and thrill managing a new satellite launch." he pauses and then adds, "And the ARK project? Are you kidding me? You know, it is like a Science Fair exhibition of ISRO and ROSCOSMOS in which we participate. I don't understand why you scientists take science fiction so seriously, mate!" he mocks.

Ranjan realises there is no need to argue over this as he sensed the association with Kvalitat was beyond the professional level. Also, he had noticed in the past that there had been multiple visits by Bazic to Delhi and Mahavir to Belgrade, many occupied by their family members. So, after wishing Mahavir for the evening, he gets into his car, a 10-year-old Mercedes E class and drives towards Saket back to his home.

Sharma recalled his last call with Novsky a couple of months ago. It was a conference call organised by Srini from ISRO over the NEBULA 2024 project. There had been a bug in data collection from the NEBULA, and it had carried a lot of noise lately in the last few months. The three experts' masterminding projects collectively led the bug resolution with their teams.

Sharma remembered his altercation with Novsky over the same a couple of days ago.

Srini was unhappy that day. ISRO had been a significant client for both Sharma and Novsky, and Srini was one of the best minds to work with. Usually, Srini would get along well with both of them, but he was exceedingly impatient that day.

"Ranjan, you mentioned the new patch upgrade will definitely work in this case, and today you are telling me that the simulation says it failed!"

"Srini, come on. It happens. You are a scientist yourself! Not all experiments succeed. This is a scenario testing, not the final solution implementation. So you have got to be patient!"

"My friend, there is no time for being patient. If this continues, God knows how much precious data we will lose. I don't want to be responsible for answering questions related to incorrect predictions about weather or storms because we had a discrete, not continuous, flow of data. We need a fix, and that has to happen now!"

"I know, but it is not entirely in my hands. We are all working together on this one. And honestly, I am not getting much support here because we don't have the mainframe software access that Mr. Novsky has. Without that, we are just shooting blinds and praying that we hit the bulls-eye."

Novsky interrupts: "Ranjan, I don't think this is the time for the blame game. We could say the same about you. We have checked the mainframe software upgrade multiple times, and I don't think that's where the error is from. There could be many other reasons here. Hardware, software, your Astros sleeping in the NEBULA, who knows!"

Ranjan was somewhat exasperated. "Novsky, I am going all-in for my request this time. Srini, we want the mainframe login access. I know about the agreement, but these are special cases when both the firms need to work together. It would make things easier if we had access to the peripheral source code. I have repeated this many times by now."

Novsky shakes his head. "Simply not possible, sir. We took a long time to develop this technology, and it is also used by other organisations."

Srini, raising his voice, "Guys, for God's sake, stop arguing. I am not here as a corporate liaison for your companies. I need this fixed within a week. Please sort it out. Now I am getting off the call, but you guys, please continue and sort the plan out," Srini says and disconnects.

Novsky and Ranjan were the only two people remaining on the call.

Novsky says, "Ranjan, you should not be that direct with a client. This matter is between our firms, and we should not make Srini privy to these discussions. It's bad for both of our firm's reputations."

Ranjan is irritated. "Mr. Novsky, you can play all the good you can. But here we are working day and night, finding out a problem that most probably is in the mainframe source code. I feel I am wasting the precious time of my resources finding a needle in a haystack that my neighbour bought."

"Who said R&D was fun, eh?" Novsky says with a mocking smile.

"Is there anything important from your side? Anything of significant value for NEBULA?"

"Hey Ranjan, take it cool, Da. I am a friend, remember? We made this thing a few years ago. Piece of cake, if we get together on this. Do one thing. Come here for some time. We're gonna find it together. And Vodka is on me for all the days you are here,"

"Goodbye, Novsky. Most irritating, this conversation has been. As usual, you have been nothing but simply uncooperative." Ranjan disconnects the call.

Ranjan collects his thoughts and cannot understand what causes his frustration with Novsky. They both launched NEBULA together and once were good friends during the project. However, Novsky had been a showoff and started taking much credit for the project, which they both deserved. Their CEOs were mainly concerned with the payouts, while these scientists craved recognition. He needed to be careful around Novsky for sure. ARK project won't be another opportunity for Novsky to take the limelight. This time, Ranjan has to prevail. After all, this was probably the last project he would ever work on in his life before retirement.

Today, Sharma is definitely not in a mood to recall Nebula's political games between the firms while everyone tries to take claims to the highest stakes as much as possible. As he reaches his building, he drives to the basement to park his car while lost in his thoughts. He stayed on the 6th floor of the building, but he preferred to take the stairs. In this job, there is rarely any time for the luxury of gyms/other exercises. So, he manages with whatever he can to stay in his current shape, less diet, walk while talking, take stairs, etc. After all, he had diabetes and had to take care of his health more at this age.

Panting, he presses the doorbell to his apartment. Nidhi, his wife, opens the door and greets Ranjan with a smile and a hug. Nidhi is a senior lecturer at Delhi University and teaches Ancient History to graduate students.

Ranjan reciprocates, but Nidhi knows the smile is fake. Her husband is physically present but mentally engaged in something related to his work. It's something she was used to.

Ranjan asks Nidhi about Rajat, his son, a 27-year-old software engineer working for the firm BRAINPHY12. The firm had products and services in the advanced AI-ML algorithms with associations in multiple industries, including manufacturing, high-tech, digital startups and even space-tech. Nidhi mentions Rajat was partying with his colleagues and probably come late. She asks Ranjan to call Zoya, his daughter, 22-year-old, who was travelling for an expedition, part of her work.

After dinner, Ranjan relaxes in his study and reads an e-book. After that, he checks his inbox and finds, amongst many emails, something titled 'Urgent: Major D-Trans error in Nebula's Feed.'

Ranjan sighs. For now, it would be another week or two engaged with ISRO over troubleshooting some bug that something not designed perfectly might cause. More blame-games with Novsky, it means.

With a yawn, he opens the email casually and reads it.

From: srini@codex12.com

To: sharma.r@prime-engg.com, jovan.novsky@kwalitatp.com

Cc: mahavir@prime-engg.com, bazic@kwalitatp.com, muraly.t.swamy@codex12.com, engg.bharat@gov.tech.in

Date: June 04, 2031 Friday 11:15:12 PM IST

Subject: Urgent: Major D-Trans error in Nebula's feed

Ranjan, Novsky,

I would like to point out a concern. There is the latest data dispatch stream from Nebula that is throwing significant errors. We have tallied the same with our core-SAT feed for double-checking, and the data, so to speak, is not exactly a perfect match!

However, our core-SAT is not calibrated to measure and transmit the data in question. For such events, the only reliable data source is NEBULA as primary. We will calibrate our core-SAT firmware and request people on the deck to rerun the manual measurements. But meanwhile, we would like you to look into the matter with seriousness.

I have attached the variable velocity profile (VVP) and the light transmission data (LTD) for an external space asset under the question. We would run more measurements to confirm the error in the data; however, we are fairly confident that the scanners of NEBULA need to be calibrated. Really hope it's the software!

Our core team has tried everything today to find the bug, but without success.

We request your physical presence in ISRO Bengaluru for this troubleshooting exercise. We would, in the meantime, work on the calibration of our core-SAT till you guys come.

Since the matter is highly sensitive, I request you not to send any subordinates but yourself. Have marked Mr. Mahavir and Mr. Bazic in the email as well. I hope you guys will provide priority support to attend to this problem.

I have already briefed Anu, who will arrange your travel and accommodation based on your travel plan (which I hope can be this week, preferably in a day or two).

Regards,

Srini

Sharma sighed again. Srini had marked all the bigshots in the email. Mahavir, Bazic and even Muraly and Bharat. Muraly was Srini's boss and ISRO's head, a powerful position in these times and a very close confidante of the current Prime Minister. Bharat is a Chief Engineer in the New Technological Breakthrough department within Indian Engineering Services. He is again an influential person with his reach in getting new projects approved or scrutinising the existing ones.

So they had raised the stakes. This can't be a simple matter. Only one way to find out.

Pack your bags!

Chapter 2

It's not Just a Job for Me

Nebula Diaries project was kick-started in 2025 with the launch of a massive space shuttle known as NEBULA. They launched the project intending to understand the solar system and beyond. However, the scientists added another layer to it: a Data Analytics Module transforming into an AI Decision Making Algorithm. They were wise enough to let the control of actions post a decision recommendation to human authorities, or it would have been chaos in such a connected world.

The resulting project was named The ARK. They built tiny spaceships with the same name, 'ARK'. They would create these with a purpose to supply the brain of NEBULA, i.e., the real human beings. The ARK would act as a space shuttle and become even a residential pod inside NEBULA once docked. NEBULA would then serve as an external environment for the ARK. One could joke that the ARK was the brainchild of Nebula. The Noah's Arc story, where it was postulated that humans should be prepared for the eventual catastrophe around the earth, inspired the ARK. These ARKs would be able to transport its significant population away from the planet into a secure, self-sustaining hub. These independent hubs would be massive space stations, the size of a small city, where chunks of humans can live.

They would design the hubs so that all activities related to human beings inside the hub should be autonomous and rely on no external stimuli. Such activities could include agriculture, availability of water through an initial reservoir being recycled again and again, proper air inside the chamber (recycled as well), autonomous power generation (not relying on any fuel but an internal process that could be hydro or nuclear), etc. NEBULA was one of the first small hubs launched in 2025 and positioned outside the solar system.

However, NEBULA was not self-sustaining. It had provisions, facilities, power etc., to support around 100,000 human beings for 50 years or more. They did this to support the astronomers, scientists and even space rangers. The plan was to send occasional fuel and rationing ships to them every decade. ARK was a project that was chartered to send these humans to NEBULA. The first ARK was supposed to be ready and deployed by 2030; however, there was a bureaucratic delay as post NEBULA launch, the entire focus shifted towards understanding the solar systems through NEBULA's readings generated via auto-bots scanning the solar system.

The plan was to create 10 ARKs per NEBULA by 2135, 100 years from now. Till then, upgrades, patches and developments will be done on NEBULA itself. By 2135, they intended to transport the first 100,000 humans to NEBULA for a self-sustaining life. These humans will be volunteers and become the first space population of human beings.

Around this time, more NEBULAs will be created, and subsequently, in the next 200 to 300 years, a significant percentage of the earth's population will live in space or on a planet that could give them life. Of course, by that time, the earth will become another tourist destination, and the offload of the population from earth would provide breathing space for the planet to recuperate from its losses (in flora, fauna, molten ice and fresh air).

The first ARK was ready by 2030, but they put the launch on hold for a few reasons. The two principal scientists leading these projects' conception, design and control were the stellar scientific resources of two major corporates, Kvalitat and Prime 1, named Sharma and Novsky.

05-June 2031 Saturday, New Delhi, 0800 AM IST

Sharma is rushing from the bedroom to the living room to the kitchen. Last night's email had caused a frenzy amongst PRIME-1, and the call following the email from Mahavir showed a sense of urgency. He had to travel to ISRO in the first half itself. All his arrangements have been coordinated already. He knew the complexities associated with his job, mainly when one dealt with sophisticated technologies like Space-Tech.

After all, it was Rocket Science!

The email had been a sort of bombshell for everyone. In the past, most of the tech issues were resolved on emails, screen shares, calls etc., but any request for urgent travel to ISRO was rarely made.

Sharma is calculating many scenarios that could have happened. While lost in his thoughts during the packing, he was shoving his clothes, utility bag, travel stuff etc., in his suitcase. He feels disappointed to waste time on such trivial issues raised by Srini. He doesn't want this to happen.

Distracting himself from his core passion, which is working on the ARK project, and instead of working on some repair and maintenance stuff, was the last thing he wanted himself to be involved in. But a lot of money was spent on Nebula already. Even the least trivial issues in the system had to be dealt with urgently. After all, NEBULA was Sharma's creation as he led the entire project along with Novsky.

Nidhi enters his room, carrying his ironed suit and hangs it on the coat hanger nearby. She sits down, staring at Sharma, preoccupied, finger on his cheeks, lost in his thoughts when she speaks.

"You have got to talk to Rajat, Ranjan! Don't be a self-consumed father." Nidhi says.

"Nidhi, I know what you mean. I will speak to him. I have acted stupidly in the last few days. But, I am also trying to come to terms with it now. It's just that this job doesn't give me breathing time for anything these days."

Nidhi grins and asks, "These days?"

"Alright, all the days since I joined or married you. Are you happy? Another score for Nidhi. The tally is 100 to 1 on Nidhi to Ranjan, alright? Thanks for ironing the suit, girl! Tell me, have you made any sandwich for me, or should I go ahead with the Muesli in milk today as well?" Ranjan mocks with a sheepish smile.

Nidhi comes close to him and puts her arms over his shoulder. With a pleasant smile, she says, "My dear, irritating husband! Everything is cooked, and even your favourite Kathi Roll stuffed with many junks you like is packed. Now listen to me!

I have been worried about you. The Nebula project has taken a toll on you these past few years. It has been 12 years already that you have been on this project.

You have done a stellar job. As you hand over the things to the new generation, it's time to focus on yourself. Mahavir has told you many times to take vacations. What is it with this job now when you told me 7 years ago that the Nebula launch was your life's purpose? And now that is done. Enjoy the rest of the time with us. You can take up retirement already. We have enough money for 2 generations owing to the bonuses you have earned over the past years. Come on. I need my husband all the time with me now."

Sharma smiles, holds Nidhi's hands, and says, "Honey, you know how important my work is for man-kind. And I'm blessed to have you and my kids who understand this. I miss the domestic bliss, love, and warmth of my family. Truth be told, every time I get one of those little family moments, I feel blessed and cherished. But, I can't get that enough as I need to return to my real purpose, which you know.

Now, come on, and be a sport! You are the wife of a man trying to make a difference with his work. And by the way, you never spoke about retirement and the boring stuff. Just tell me, what is bothering you these days?"

Nidhi presses her lips and speaks, "Ranjan, I feel you and Rajat are drifting apart because of your work and the differences in your thinking. I always imagined you and him getting along well and pursuing common things together. Now you know Rajat has a singular goal and can't confine himself to the bureaucratic ways of working, which you must do because your biggest client is ISRO."

"Rajat always wanted you to join his firm as his boss and would be pleased to have an expert like you over there. He has often asked me to convince you to take over the CTO position in BRAINPHY12. It is his dream to learn from his father. Think about it. I am not saying to join Rajat's firm only.

If not BRAINPHY, there is something else you can do. I know you both very well. The way into your hearts is through your work. You should work something together to re-establish your relationship with him."

Ranjan replies, "I know, honey. I know! Believe it or not, Rajat and I will work on something together once the ARK project is over. Today, I asked Raju (Rajat) to drop me at the airport as I just wanted to catch up with him. I look forward to talking to him too. Trust me, there is no love lost! It's just we both have different ways of working now."

Nidhi smiles and then holds his hands. "I know, love! We are blessed to have a husband and father like you! You do a lot of work alone at your end, not only for us but for humanity. We are all so proud of you, and there is nothing more we could have asked for in life than someone like you as the head of the family. But I worry about you.

"How much you hold inside you, the stress of work and occasionally personal issues! Besides, you don't speak these days about anything that bothers you. You are always lost in thought, calls or reading work. And trust me, rather than feeling left out or angry with your busy schedule, I admire you. I can handle anything when you are here.

"I am worried that there is something deeper inside you, a void you are not sharing with me. So for God's sake, try to connect as much as possible with Zoya and Rajat, as I don't want them to drift away from you. You and I are inseparable, whatever may come."

Ranjan looks at her, kisses her forehead, and says, "This and forever...."

On the way to the airport in the car, Ranjan and Rajat were silent for the first few minutes. Finally, Ranjan breaks the silence and says, "How is it going, son?"

"You know, Dad, when you sign up for a start-up firm like BRAINPHY12, it's all hands on deck. But yea, overall, it's good. I am learning a lot!"

Ranjan says, "That's good. What are you working on these days?"

"Oh, you are going to love it. We are building a VVC AI Tutor profile for one of our clients in the US. They are the world's renowned education institute in engineering."

"What is VVC?"

"Dad, it's Virtual Video Conference AI Tutor and not Variable Velocity Profile. Yea, I know your abbreviations, Dad!

Basically, it's a virtual video-based robot that looks like a human, talks like us, and delivers a complete video lecture online to the students of our clients. The algorithms and logics are wired and coded to make it appear like a complete expert tutor."

"Wow. What will happen to the real tutors now?"

Rajat laughs and replies, "Well, Dad, they would have a hard time in the market now. But they are still important in this entirely new scheme of things. They are the ones who will train the AI logic, algorithms, and these robots now. We are kind of making their work easier and more impactful. Imagine every professor having multiple virtual AI profiles focusing more on deeper research and analytics of students' performance rather than just doing the daily mundane lecture delivery."

Ranjan smiled. He knew his son had always stood for a greater good and was passionate about solving human problems rather than just making money like other entrepreneurs.

Rajat asks, "So, Dad. What is this super 007 secret work you are headed to?"

Ranjan winks and replies, "You know, son. I can tell you, but then I have to…."

Rajat says, "Old man? You are going to take me down? What about your breathlessness? With the first punch, I am going to land on you?" he punches his dad's shoulder teasingly.

They both share a hearty laugh. They are about to arrive at the airport. Rajat breaks the big question. "Dad?"

"Yes, son?"

"I was wondering if maa spoke to you about the role I wanted to discuss with you in BRAINPHY12?"

"Ya son, she did. And to be honest, I appreciate you bringing that up with your mother. It's just that I need to finish some things that I started here at PRIME and can't detach myself from these projects. This is everything I stand for. And you understand it much better, how much it means for a scientific man to see his creation go to the final stages."

"I know, Dad. But you work in space projects with a horizon of impact that exceeds 100 years beyond my lifetime. Don't you want to work on something you could see benefiting mankind immediately? Also, you have done enough, Dad. And I have seen you struggling with bureaucratic ways these people work. How many times were you close to getting awesome ideas executed in Nebula? For example, that climate predictor you spoke about, that asteroid catcher project, the extra-terrestrial intelligence project, and so on. I used to see that look of a sci-fi-fed kid in your eyes since childhood, and now you are tuned in to the ways of working of governments and organisations all towards personal profits of certain industrialists and power-up for politicians. Dad, come join us and be free to execute whatever you like. It's a golden chance during this phase of your career."

"Son, trust me. Beyond all that you mentioned, there is another motivation for me to join BRAINPHY12: which is to work with you and be closer to you. But you must give me a few more years here, as I don't think anyone else can steer these things. Even though that idiot vodka-drinking hippie Novsky believes he calls the shots, it's through me the real action happens," says Ranjan.

"Ha-ha! Dad, you and your Novsky! It's ok. Have all the fun you can have here. Come on here. Give me a hug. Your pillar is on the left. I will also be scooting off for an important meeting," says Rajat.

Ranjan hugs Rajat and says, "Sure, son. I know where you are heading. Is she waiting already?" he winks at him.

"Well, how do you know, Dad?" Rajat grins.

"Come on, I was 27 once upon a time as well, boy. Give my regards to Shreya. Also, tell her to ask her father not to give a tough time to her to-be father-in-law," says Ranjan with a wink.

"Ha-ha, only if I was not dating your boss's daughter. Dad, you know how Shreya and Mahavir uncle are! Holiday –father-daughter pair, ya?" says Rajat.

Sharma smiles, "See you, son! Keep rocking!"

Sharma enters the airport and checks past the security clearance. Having checked in his bags, he walked towards his favourite international lounge as his flight was delayed. At the lounge entrance, a familiar Serbian face, Jovan Novsky, greets him.

Novsky smiles and gives Ranjan a big hug in front of everyone. Ranjan, feeling awkward, reciprocates with a smile. They decide to have some snacks in the lounge and sit together.

Ranjan orders his usual, a black coffee with some cookies. While his Serbian friend orders a drink along with some snacks. Ranjan sits opposite Novsky as he looks at the Serbian, who is having alcohol in the morning.

Novsky, "It's not bad, this Indian whiskey, Mr. Sharma!"

Sharma is undisturbed.

"Why do they call it whiskey, I wonder? Do you know whiskey means 'water of life,' a Gaelic word 'uski'? Speaking of that, do you know Gaelic – an odd language of Scottish origin?"

Sharma interrupted, "Is there anything you want to talk about, Novsky?"

Novsky, "Yea, Sharma. Why do you hate me, man? I mean, whenever I talk to you, I feel you hold a grudge? Come on, tell me what it is?"

"I don't hate you, man. I just don't like you a lot, and there are a lot of differences. Besides, I don't drink in the morning. So stop talking about whiskey." Sharma gulps down a glass of water while not looking at Novsky.

Novsky smiles and then sinks back in his chair and says, "Don't you feel all this is so dull, Sharma? This world of nulls, roaming around us, not understanding what's going on, lost in their own world in their minor problems. While men like you and I create a haven for them beyond this planet." He leans closer to Sharma and says, "Don't you think you and I are a rare species with an intellect given to us for delivering goodness to mankind? We make quite a pair, don't we?"

Sharma replies in a bored voice with his eyes on his phone, "If you say so."

Novsky doesn't seem to get the message. "Now this space problem we have got ourselves into. Do you think we relate it to some sensor malfunction on Nebula, something you guys were supposed to look into?" he says with a smile as he puts his glass down.

Sharma realises Novsky is indirectly blaming PRIME-1 for the issue as Sharma and his team installed the sensors. He gets up as he hears the boarding announcement.

He ignores the comment and says, "Alright, time to go. Also, if you bring up this discussion with Srini without examining the facts, I am not cooperating with you anymore."

Novsky laughs, puts his drink down, grabs his bags and says, "My friend Ranjan, Da. Come on, have the heart to laugh."

Same time, Cafe Brownstone, Gurgaon, India

Shreya is busy looking at the screen of her new translucent phone-shaped metamorphosed laptop and going through her feed. Rajat is sitting opposite, enjoying his coffee, and lost in his thoughts.

"When was the last time you enjoyed eating, Rajat?" Shreya asked.

"What do you mean? I just finished my breakfast," Rajat says.

"You mean you just chewed and swallowed something you ordered? No comments on how it tasted! You didn't even look at it. I guess this has been the same for a long time now. What's the matter with you?" Shreya asks.

"You are right, Shreya. My mind has been swayed away for a long time now, ever since I joined BRAINPHY12. Dad hasn't been the same as well. I know it disappointed him when I turned down the offer your dad gave me to work for your firm," says Rajat.

"And, did you turn down the offer because of me or your dad?" Shreya asks, realising that maybe Rajat might not want to work in the company of his girlfriend's father or under the tutelage of his father.

"No. Why would I do that? Mahavir uncle had been kind to offer me a senior tech role, which is way up the food chain for a fresher like me. But I knew I wasn't ready for it yet. My intention was always to learn something from the ground. Plus, I like BRAINPHY12 culture. It was just a match for my persona and working style. But you know it! As you understand me well now. I just wish Dad could too. He still feels I don't consider his work is of notable importance, maybe."

"And, do you?" asks Shreya.

"No, on the contrary, I am proud of what he did all these years. You know all about it. You have been telling me about my dad's progress with pride. I could see the glow in your eyes whenever you talked about my father's work in PRIME-1. I know that even Mahavir uncle appreciates him more. It's all good. It's just that I don't feel like being there."

"Rajat, you are overthinking, babe! Yes, I am fond of Ranjan uncle. He has been like a sci-fi hero since I was a little kid. He would surprise us with stories that were way too fictional, yet he would reason with us on the concepts behind them. I work with him as I head the Public communications in Prime-1. I know everything he does, and it makes me feel proud of him, more so when I think of it also from our relationship point of view. After all, he is going to be my dad as well," she says with a smile and continues, "I have had lunch table discussions with him about you, and yes, he had mentioned it several times that he wanted you to be on PRIME-1. But trust me, he doesn't feel bad about you working for BRAINPHY. As a matter of fact, last week only, he was telling me about the project you are working on with excitement."

Rajat looks at Shreya and holds her hands, "Hmm. Guess he never told me about that. I really want to work with him. Do you know my bosses are such huge fans of Dad? They even asked me to talk to him about leading the tech department of BRAINPHY12. I told him because I am excited to be mentored by him daily; however, I feel his heart is in PRIME-1 only."

Shreya pushes his shoulder with a laugh, "Oh, so you are now poaching your girlfriend's company's CTO? Want to hang me out dry with my will, do you? Without him, PRIME-1 doesn't have any future, sweetheart!"

"Come on, Shreya!"

"Kidding, but he won't leave! You should not ask him to. His heart is stuck in NEBULA. Your Mom should be jealous of it," Shreya winks while saying this.

"I know, Shreya. Tell me something. Have you found anything unusual about my dad? He has been very different in the past few months. Like he rarely carries a smile these days," says Rajat.

"No. Not that I have noticed Rajat. But is that the reason for you to broach the topic of the BRAINPHY12 job with him? Rajat, trust me, if I know uncle is stressed or wants out, I would be the first one on his side to persuade him to go. When you told me about his dream of becoming an author and writing a book on The World Scientific History, I was moved. I think after PRIME, he should follow his passion. But if the time for that is soon, then I'm more than happy to oblige," says Shreya, the Chief Communication Officer and the largest shareholder of PRIME-1 after Mahavir.

Same time (on the flight)

On the flight, Sharma plays with his phone before the pre-boarding announcements. He glances at the social handle of Zoya, his daughter doing a photo shoot of wild animals in Bannerghatta National Park in Bengaluru. After a few minutes to leave, he attempts to call Zoya, but she doesn't pick up the call.

'Probably busy with her camera as it's the best time to take morning shots,' thought Sharma.

Then he glances back at her social feeds, where she had added the pictures of Ranjan, Rajat, Nidhi and her in their home. They were celebrating Rajat's birthday a few weeks ago. After trying another failed call to Zoya, he sends her a text message about the flight plan.

He remembers his younger days when the kids would go to their primary classes in school, and he was one hot-shot scientist who worked overtime towards his life's dream project. During those days, he used to tell stories about the future of space exploration through his favourite science fiction books. A book that influenced Sharma the most was The Foundation by Isaac Asimov. He would translate The Foundation to both Zoya and Rajat in a fantasised kids-story format.

The entire idea of space exploration and civilisations across multiple planets seemed quite plausible to Sharma, as he was a believer in science. His passion was shared by Rajat, who would ask more profound questions about space exploration technologies. Rajat and Ranjan would discuss at length about scientists (both real and fictional stories), watch sci-fi movies and analyse them in the end.

Zoya used to be a pleasant company, for she would bring utter cuteness in little things in those moments like checking out what sort of clothes they were wearing, asking questions like 'Why are they not hungry, Dad. They have been running for quite a while?' and so on.

Sharma smiles as he starts thinking about Zoya, his younger child, who was the only one in the family with a love for the little things. She would have her room done creatively, full of paintings and pictures of animals. Her hobbies and profession were in complete synch. She was into Animal Photography, Creative Painting of fictional animal creatures, Video-documentaries etc. Sharma was proud of Zoya as he saw her deeper inclinations toward nature from the beginning. While thinking about Zoya, the rarest smile would be painted on Sharma's face and a zest of peace in her brain.

If Rajat was his hope, Nidhi his support, Zoya was the eternal peace of his life.

Three rows ahead, a Serbian is dozing off carelessly without any worry in his mind. Sharma looks at him with a frown, 'Of all the people in the world, I had to find myself in his company during the last years of my career.'

Before switching off his phone, Sharma stumbled upon news from his feed-cast that read:

"Major cargo carrier airlines crashed near Somalia in the Arabian Sea. Two people were reported dead, including the pilot and co-pilot. The airline, King's Special, is denying pilot error and assessing the situation; however, all indications are foul weather. The plane KSP412 was one of their finest designs and never had any such incident before."

Sharma sighs and rolls his eyes. Had to read about a plane crash just before the flight took off, and that, too, the thought of risking such a thing with a buffoon like Novsky on the plane. Don't want to die with him at least, he thinks and tries to doze off.

Chapter 3

I use Emotion for the Many and Reserve Reasons *for the Few – Adolf Hitler.*

The launch of NEBULA provided many technical challenges, including the damage to the vessel by heavy, high-speed objects like meteors. The core team had come up with an excellent solution. The team had sought counsel from NASA in this case. One of the expert consultants on NASA, known as Jan Ryan, developed an Artificial Intelligence Collision Prevention Control (AICPC) module on NEBULA that ran on the logic of pre-detecting the probability of colliding with an asteroid.

The sequence was:

- *High-speed specialised cameras around the NEBULA, always in the 'ON' mode.*
- *Detect the collision course probability using simulations 4 hrs in advance.*
- *Prepare the countermeasures post detection of probability.*
- *Detect the colliding object's speed, mass and impact analysis.*
- *Activate Ryan Bomb at The Optimum Displacement and time.*

Ryan Bomb was the real mastermind of Ryan and was deployed on Nebula with a unique release mechanism that can adjust the damage depending on the danger. J. Ryan was indeed a celebrity amongst the scientific community.

05-June 2031 Saturday, ISRO Headquarters, Bengaluru, 0930 AM IST

He was about to kick start his morning meeting when his secretary came in a hurry inside his cabin. She informed him they had asked him to urgently call the defence minister.

T Srinivasam, the Director, Special Ops of ISRO, is usually calm and methodical, fondly called by his peers as Srini. He politely asks his team of 4 engineers inside his cabin to excuse him for a while.

He had been leading the morning planning meeting for the bug resolution data to be shared with Sharma and Novsky later in the afternoon when they arrive. But when the second-in-command in the country's power-chain calls, you leave everything and attend that call.

Defence Minister S. Pillai (or Sundaram Pillai) had been the right hand of the current Prime Minister, Mr. Singh, for even the second term of his Governance. In his role as DM, he miraculously strengthened India's position against its enemy, primarily driven by his focus on steering R&D programs and associations with expert organisations such as Kvalitat and Prime-1.

The news in the morning was critical enough for the two to get into a call.

Srini says, "Good Morning, Sir! How can I be of service to you?"

The DM says, "The morning is not good, Srini! I take it you haven't seen the news, or you would not be that relaxed!"

Srini says, "What happened, sir? Yes, I have been busy in a few meetings since morning, and I have also learnt from you not to trust the news, sir!" he says while scrolling his phone and checking the latest news of concern. And then, immediately after saying this, registers the shock and says, "Oh Damn!"

The DM waits as he absorbs Srini's reactions and then speaks, "Yes! This happened this morning. The plane crashed, and the consignment was gone, along with human casualties. The Canadians are pissed too."

"How could this happen? Pilot error or a hit?" Srini asked.

The DM says, "We are investigating all possibilities right now, Srini. However, it's time to consider damage control. Our Canadian friends can't duplicate the consignment in a short time. I have learned from my sources that PRIME-1 and Kvalitat people make similar ballistic devices for some of their clients. Mahavir will come back with the proposal very soon. I suggest you have a call with both Bazic and Mahavir and try to get this done in a month. I don't want the project showcase to be disturbed, and the demo is in a few months only."

Srini says, "But sir. This project was important from the point of view of our Indo-Canadian treaty last year. Won't this impact our relations with the Canadians?"

"Don't worry, Srini. I already spoke to my counterpart in Canada. They understand we must go ahead with alternate sourcing possibilities. Although they want us to guarantee and bear some of the losses as we paid upfront. While that is something I am taking care of, you stop worrying about the politics and bureaucracy and go ahead with the work. And oh, also this time, they should transport the payload via road from the Russian facility of Kvalitat under top security," says the DM and disconnects the call.

Srini is lost in his thoughts. There is something not adding up here. Why did the DM mention top security?

Prime Office, New Delhi

The call was patched through the dialler 5 minutes ago, and the discussion started with a sombre mood owing to the shocking event of the morning that added to the loss of life of 2 gentlemen carrying the payload by air.

Srini urgently had a conference call with Polsky and Mahavir and communicated the situation as briefed by the DM. He had requested both to work out the Damage Control plan and expedite the required shipment through their networks/ internal sources as early as possible. After Srini, Polsky, and Mahavir disconnected the call, it reconnected back through a secured VPN password-protected call.

Polsky said, "Very shocking, Mr. Singh! Two lives gone, just like that. I have never been a fan of aviation technology breakthroughs happening recently. I always thought plane crashes were a 20th-century thing. And yet here we are in the 2030s, paying for the engineering errors in an industry deprived of innovation lately."

Mahavir says, "Agree, Polsky. What can I say? Lately, it is all about space exploration and ballistic engineering for battle station preparation only. Commercial aviation is the least of the worries for any R&D establishment worldwide. What do you now suggest we do?"

Polsky replies, "Much as I would have loved this not to come to us, on the bright side, I recognise it as a business opportunity. Now the price quote for the delivery should come from one of us and I suggest we agree on an aligned number. You and I know the discussion is only on the margin percentages between us. So what do you suggest? We do a 50% over the top against our usual 10%, considering that this is a non-negotiated territory for the Indian Government?"

"Polsky, no one in ISRO or Government has an actual idea about our costs of manufacture. Why only stick to 50? I say this is a one-time gift that comes once a year. Let's charge twice and put a 100% margin over our total costs. We will round up the books and show them as 10. You and I both know how we have done this in NEBULA!" Mahavir laughs.

Polsky laughs and replies, "Mahavir. I like you, man. Frankly, I was hoping you would say 200, but it's ok. My friend, for you, I will settle for just 100!"

Mahavir grins and says, "You pesky Serbian! I know you damn well, man. Now tell me the truth? Did you order this hit?"

Polsky speaks, "Oh no no. I have no clue how this crash happened? And frankly, I am sorry for the loss of life, Mahavir. I can't imagine someone could stoop so low to kill two human beings to get this contract fired from the Canadians when the obvious choice left is the backup from us both." he adds mockingly, "Now come on, tell me, did you do this?"

Mahavir says, "Well. No! I am delighted though about the business, my friend. I guess we should thank mother nature for causing this. After all, we are also God's children, right? Someone should take care of us as well. And you, Polsky, saying something like, stooping down to kill human beings! Huh?

"Need I remind you of Africa, my brother, where you gunned down a complete village to build your plant and drank their blood like a vampire? My friend, we are the true believers of Charles Darwin and are just following our duties. Ain't that right, Polsky?"

Polsky says, "Ya my friend ya… It is business 101 for me. And yes, what happened in Africa was a tragedy, but it was for a greater good, Da! Few got killed. So what? They were dying of poverty anyways. At least it paved the way to get 1000 people employed right who would have died of hunger, man. It is simple maths, man. I think I did a favour to the country."

Mahavir adds, "Well, one could say so. And that one would be me. So, for this contract, I suggest we get our teams to get on to the preparations."

Polsky retorts, "Yes, my friend. After all, the spare parts are for our baby, NEBULA's ARK only. Therefore, it is our right to develop the spares only. Mainly when the spares list includes Ryan Bomb, our favourite, eh?"

"Yes, God bless that scientist for giving us this invention. We are invincible in space because of Ryan Bomb, my friend. Let's get on to it. Sharma and Novsky would be excited to give the final upgraded ones on time. Time for them to get back on ARK for a little while."

"About that, Mahavir. I was reading the report by Novsky, and I realised the ARK demo is ready for showcase, and these people are just working on upgrades only to make it robust and do further testing. We have now predicted the 2130s to be a decade where it could possibly be needed. But I think once ISRO knows about the work's status, they will cancel our contract for 100 years on this project. I suggest we keep testing and upgrading the technology all the way down. This is our legacy that can be passed on to the next generations, man. You and I both know that ARK will never be needed, but governments would keep spending on this project for eternity, for this is the EARTH BACKUP AND RESCUE! Let's not get this off our hands, man!"

Mahavir nods: "I agree with you, Polsky. I have asked Sharma also to delay and slow down as much as possible. I told him to let the demo be made of pilot models, not the actual prototype. But Sharma and Novsky must compete against each other and do things well before time. Here, 100 years before it is needed. However, I am sure it would distract them long enough owing to all these new developments of the bug ISRO discovered.

Let us give the demo this time, but tell them to cut off with all the essential features that include hardware or software upgrades. Let them focus on the presentation elements and design only. But again, to keep the show going, let's bomb the test site valley with the Ryan Bomb and have some fun!" he says and laughs.

Polsky laughs with him. "Agree, my brother. Let us get our guys deeply swimming in the troubles of our day-to-day business. I suggest keeping them grounded and putting them into luxurious projects for some time. Your Sharma will retire in a few years, and Novsky is already gunning for bigger management roles and will soon be off technology. We will plan new guys who will stick to our agenda. So, it solves the problem!"

Mahavir agrees. "I like that, Polsky! Wonderful talk. See you later, old friend!"

When the call gets disconnected, Mahavir remembers the first time he met Polsky. It was December 2020, and the world was going through the recent shock of the Coronavirus Pandemic with a total lockdown in the entire world. It's times like this when world leaders think about the end of the world scenarios, otherwise known as ELEs (Extinction Level Events).

They hosted a secret conference in Serbia where delegates from various countries, including India, Russia, the USA, UK, Germany etc., were invited. The meeting was split into two agendas: the first one was the vaccine development and distribution programs worldwide. And the second hidden agenda was to discuss the potential future scenarios that would be critical for human life on this planet. There were no presentations for the second agenda, as it was an open table conference and a candid discussion on possibilities and further work required to come up with a proposal for the next meeting.

Mahavir remembers seeing a young man in his 40s, getting along with every world leader smoothly and steering his way through the billionaires and a few movie stars who were invited.

He comes closer to the young Polsky, holding a glass of Macallan and talking to one of the famous Russian actors. Mahavir introduces himself to both and engages in conversation with them.

10 minutes into the conversation, both Singh and Polsky realise they have way too much in common and take the subsequent discussion to the poolside, where a table for two is spread much away from the crowd. However, this date was not romantic but of mutual economic prosperity planning.

He remembered an extensive discussion with Polsky over the cinema, science fiction, and the latest tech innovations. One such debate was focused on two movies, 2012 and Geostorm, and how these movies had hidden potential ideas about what could be the future of humanity. Polsky firmly believed that human minds perceive fictional stories as an extension of their desires to see such imagination into reality. And it is all connected! Science fiction writers take extrapolative creativity into the recent and future developments of science and take a dip in their works, including books, screenplays and even movies.

Going by that logic, his assertion on the table was that both the movies 2012 and Geostorm have elements of truth with a probability of occurrence at least in a single-digit percentage, and it isn't futile an effort to start a backup plan for such consequences.

"Especially the Geostorm!" says Polsky.

Mahavir added, "I agree with you, Polsky. Climate changes and auto-up gradation of flora and fauna would lead to some sort of reset on our planet. Although sitting here like ducks, knowing nothing about what exists outside will not help us solve the real problem. Now, as I see and speak from an extensive benefit that I reap from the wisdom of one of my lead scientists in a theory that he shared with me, there are two angles to this earth problem.

First is that of an internal planetary nature, where a thorough understanding of our current planet would yield information that will help us create solutions to prevent disasters.

The second is that of an external space nature, where many untapped resources are available for our reach. These include minerals, fuels, food sources, nuclear sources, space if there are habitable planets, etc.

Now, to understand both problems together, the solution lies in SPACE technologies only. Often, the understanding of the planet is revealed by shining the light from the outside. You can't scan your leg while digging a hole inside your leg, right? It needs to be X-rayed from the outside. You understand what I am saying, Polsky? We need better X-rays to scan the earth from outside!"

Polsky smiles and says with a wink, "Yes, Mr. Singh. I think I am the one who will understand this better than anyone here."

Mahavir says, "I see your firm has ample expertise in space technology research and ballistic engineering capabilities as well. I have heard the news about you extensively discussing space exploration. Also, have heard how the ballistic technologies research by your firm is critical in terms of your space shuttle engine innovation program. I am a late entrant in this field but trust me, my capabilities in the Defence program and shaping of the Indian defence capabilities in the Ballistic Science field are none less than a passionate pioneer and, to some extent, even an inventor and a leader."

Polsky laughs and adds, "Mr. Singh. You don't have to say anything about your firm to me. I am a fanboy of PRIME-1 work, having read about you many times, and heard of you. Sometimes our firm has failed to file patents on various technologies that are the property of your firm and explored by you years before us. And I know about the lead scientist and the most respected space-tech expert, Ranjan Sharma, who works for you! Without any doubt, ballistics R&D is critical for space exploration. Needless to talk about, the historical examples include Sergei Korolov's Energia, the United States' ALBM project in the 1950s, the Polyus experiment, and my favourite Kvant-2, after which I named my company Kvalitat. Well, what can I say? I am thrilled at the thought of this conversation going ahead in some direction with you, Mr. Singh. How about we set up a longer appointment? Let's say we cancel the schedule for the next 2 days and lay the foundations of the world's future instead? I know a perfect spot, one of my villas built on the mountain Golija, near the town of Novi Pazar, a forgotten spectacle of the Ottoman empire."

Singh replies, "Golija sounds good, Polsky. It's been on my checklist for other reasons for a long time. So let's be students of the great Studenica for the next 2 days. I will have my scientists on standby for any call or query that will help shape our discussion."

Polsky replies with a broad smile: "One who admires the river Studenica, and the opportunity the river provides to the missionaries of change, deserves to own my villa rather than just stay in it!" He laughs, clinking the glass with a cheer to Singh.

Mahavir returns to his thoughts with a smile on his face. He and Polsky were alike. Both had this unique curiosity and passion to understand science like a child for fables and combine their fantasies to create realistic outcomes, yielding significant economic returns through their business acumen.

However, he is not very convinced of Polsky's response today. He feels something is amiss. This plane crash has led to many questions about who did it? Who would benefit from it, etc. He and Polsky need to be very careful to avoid getting bad press about them focusing their attention on getting this contract.

Singh had been evaluating a lot of options in terms of the PR story to the way they should handle this project. Suddenly, the door opens, and his secretary rushes in and tells Mahavir to check the news.

Mahavir switches on his television to hear the reporter saying, "Latest plane crash in the Arabian sea near Somalia has been declared a terrorist attack and not just an accident. A terror organisation that goes by the name of PUNSAM has taken up the responsibility for the attack. This is another attack by them in a similar fashion, by posting their Declaration of War document online on social media. Security agencies are currently…."

Mahavir switches off the television and checks his social media handle to see multiple updates on the PUNSAM's declaration. He can find the latest declaration document by PUNSAM, which states:

DECLARATION OF WAR

'I use emotion for the many and reserve reasons for the few.' – Adolf Hitler.

For years, powerful politicians and businessmen have used this planet's economic and scientific growth as an excuse to hide their nefarious actions and fool mankind. They are trying to hide their covert plans from the public. These people are mere acolytes of their predecessors, who established their authority by chicanery, not bravery. And who says things have changed, and the world is in a better place? It is a debacle hidden in the florid buildings and establishment that is as rotten as a fetid stench of human waste from inside. Our organisation must clean it from the inside, and we have taken another step today! The KSP412 that crashed today was carrying something for a mission we disapprove of. We took this step to warn a certain specific faction of people involved in the events causing natural imbalance to the planet and potential harm to mankind.

More such acts will occur until these world leaders act in good faith toward humanity, not themselves.

As usual, PUNSAM stands for:

"Longo vivas tempore humanity." (Long live the humanity)

Truly for mankind,

PUNSAM

Mahavir sighed. It's a pity that the space missions are now coming on the PUNSAM's radar. He texts the link to Polsky and asks him to call back. Time to take extra precautions for this consignment. Someone is watching them as it's clear PUNSAM is referring to the NEBULA-ARK project.

Chapter 4

The Usuals: Issues and Stuff

A secret treaty was conducted between a few governments of the countries that included India, the USA, Russia, Serbia, Germany and the UK. They concluded that independent efforts towards space domination would yield nothing impactful to the entire mankind. Hence, a syndicate was formed to unite all these nations collectively for the entire planet earth. The Unified Earth Space Discovery Agency (TUESDA) was formed. The current head of TUESDA was Mr. Bill Scott, from the United States with its head office in Washington DC, closer to the global political action. They decided the core research would be done by the US, manufactured by Russia/Serbia/Germany, and deployed or launched by India. India bagged the lead deploy site for TUESDA programs based on its successful deployment of missions such as MANGALYAAN at highly competitive costs. Project NEBULA was the first of its kind launched under the TUESDA program by ISRO, India. Srinivasan, head of ISRO, was extremely proud of the fact as he was on the launch committee. The launch of NEBULA was the testament to the success of TUESDA, and it prompted all the other powerful nations such as China, Korea, Japan, European Countries, LATAM, Australia etc., to join TUESDA.

ISRO HQ, Antariksha Bhawan, 1530 hrs, 05 June 2031

Srini, Sharma and Novsky, and 5 more engineers, are sitting in a conference room in the HQ of ISRO. (known as Antariksha Bhawan). The entire meeting is planned with only a few people aware of the topic.

Srini says, "Everyone, thanks for coming on such short notice. However, this matter, in the end, is critical and cannot wait. There is another small matter of an important consignment being bombed, something you have already heard in the news."

Novsky bends over Ranjan and whispers, "If the bombing is a small matter, then what is this weirdo hiding under the bush?" Ranjan shushes him and asks him to focus on Srini.

Srini continues, "So fellas, let's start with Problem number 1, the minor one to deal with, and I am sure we can resolve it straight with our seniors. Problem number 2 would require a bit of deep diving, and we will need to head out to the Lab after this."

"So, let's start with Problem Number 1. Terrorists blew apart a shipment carrying our essential raw material and equipment. Apparently, somehow, they figured out it was meant for ISRO and backed by the Indian Government. This has raised a lot of questions about our internal security as well. Now, I know that two gentlemen here, Mr. Novsky and Mr. Sharma, represent the two leading organisations in Space Tech Manufacturing and would have no problem re-arranging the same consignment again. We apologise that we didn't consider you on the vendor's priority list. Hell, you understand, with us Government agencies, we never put all our eggs in one basket!

To be transparent enough, our Canadian counterpart has refused to supply any further consignments from now on. Not only that, but they also believe we are a dangerous client to work for, as PUNSAM was targeting us. So, the entire association is now over. It is my request to you two gentlemen to work on the list of materials needed and supply us within 2 weeks at maximum," says Srini, handing them a confidential envelope with the list of materials.

Sharma replies, "Don't worry, Srini. This is a very unfortunate tragedy. However, I can assure you that PRIME won't even charge any extra markup on this one. We will supply asap."

Novsky also speaks, "Relax Da, Srini, my brother. You don't worry about anything now. Kvalitat and Prime are both on this one."

Srini nods and acknowledges both with thanks and proceeds, "That brings us to Problem Number 2. Something that is of the aggravating kind and a bit of an off-balancing nature. For that, however, I want both of you guys to follow me to the Lab in NRSC-N," he says, pointing to Sharma and Novsky.

NSRC stood for National Remote Sensing Centre and supported ISRO with the remote sensing capability, generating data products and analysing NEBULA's core data.

Sharma says, "That's it? You called us here for this only. And now we go to NRSC, you mean, Hyderabad?"

Srini says, "Forgot to mention. NRSC-N is the Bengaluru branch of the NRSC. What you are mentioning is the old NRSC that's still doing its work w.r.t remote sensing operations related to GIS, Image processing, aerial remote sensing etc. However, this branch was set up as a small office reporting directly to me and catering for the information received from NEBULA. I know you guys were not told much about it, and all we used to do was send you guys data related to your asks. However, the brains behind the data, analysis and decisions are the people from NRSC-N (or National Remote Sensing Centre – Nebula). And I called you here, as this is en route to the NSRC-N. Besides, lunch is better here in Antariksha Bhawan." He smiles as he says this.

Sharma smirks, "Surprise, Surprise, Novsky! And here we thought we knew all about our friends."

Srini laughs off the comment and says, "Believe me, you won't have time for any grudges once I show you what data we are handing."

After lunch, the trio gets outside the HQ office, bids the other team members goodbye, and gets into an electric car for a trip to NRSC-N. It takes them to a building. The same centre also houses ISITE (or ISRO Satelite Integration and Test Establishment). The entire premise is pretty green and is an environment that can stimulate free, creative thinking.

Sharma gets out of the car with the other two and stretches his arms around. It's been a tiring journey since morning. He looks at the building he has never been to, smiles and thinks, 'Governments and their budgets, still they can't construct a decent-looking building for such an esteemed organisation. No, they must go with the old architectural theme: White buildings, fewer glasses and more 20th-century appeal."

They all walk inside the new centre in the central control room. It all looks like an open office cum conference room where 10 engineers are sitting across in front of a row of computers, and there is a big screen that monitors the central dashboard of Nebula. After everyone is seated, Srini explains.

"The reason both of you, Mr. Sharma, and Mr. Novsky, are invited is to understand and make sense of some weird data that Nebula is throwing about an object. We believe this could be an error, and you guys could help us fix the issue so we can start getting the real data. Let me show you the data I am referring to."

With that, Srini opens up a chart of readings on the big screen.

"Have a look at this uncategorised object outside our solar system. The system is predicting a speed never ever observed for anything like this. Check this data of VVP (Variable velocity profile) for this object. The readings are very skewed, and the motion pattern of this object is curved. Either, this entire data is incorrect, and there is some issue with the calibration of our sensors. Or else, this thing has a mind of its own because we cannot predict the trajectory of this object. If the sensors are inaccurate, we cannot trust any data from Nebula, and the entire system goes for a toss. Let me also show you the next slide where we have the LTD, light transmission data, for the same. Same stuff!! Unusual, unreliable, and unrealistic readings. We have got to act now.

You can imagine the chaos in the global political machinery if this leaks out, right? All the long-term weather predictions, comet launches, hell, even the transmission data are wasted for the past 14 days. Needless to point out, serious implications for the future continuous model that are built on this data. I can't imagine the clean-up workload and massive resource pool diversion. Guys, the thought itself is giving me nightmares. Now you two geniuses designed the system, right? Why don't you look at the past data and make sense of it? Also, while you are at it, kindly draft the clean-up plan, please."

Srini stops as if to take a breath and is satisfied having spoken so much. And then, he takes a seat, sighs, and continues, "Also, there is a TUESDA meeting coming up end of this month. So, we got to fix everything before that."

They all look at the data and presentation for another few hours.

Novsky says, "Srini Da, me and Sharma disagree on most things except one. Nebula is the finest work we have produced in our lifetime. I doubt there would be an error in the satellite transmission data logic of Nebula. However, yes, sometimes the sensors or equipment malfunction. Remember, my friend, software lasts forever. You must keep replacing hardware all the time, just like PRIME does it with its employees." He laughs after completing his sentence.

Sharma looks at him with annoyance and then stares at Srini.

Srini says, "Novsky, my friend. There is no time for such debates about software vs hardware. God knows, last month, we debated on the same, and it was a collective patch upgrade error on both sides, remember? Now, this could be as small an issue as last month's or else it's goddamn science fiction. But, whatever it is. This time, I can't solve your internal disputes between Kvalitat and Prime, and I suggest you guys get along on this. The first step is to analyse the equipment and sensor data along with the software diagnostic status report for the past 2 months. Also, look at the science fiction data the sensors are throwing to determine what deviations we need to correct. I am sharing all this information with you on your encrypted emails today, and we should meet tomorrow to make some sense of it. Would appreciate it if you could skip the evening sightseeing and work on this as a priority. I know you two geniuses won't take many hours on this one."

Sharma says, "Srini, you don't have to worry. Even if there is an error in hardware or software, we will understand it and devise a correction plan tomorrow. Let's catch up tomorrow afternoon again on this one, and we both will present the plan collectively. I am not much of a sightseeing enthusiast, but a bit of evening rest would energise me well enough to work on this problem. So, will work in my hotel room tonight on this and wind up the remaining work in the morning before we catch up for the big meeting tomorrow afternoon. Sounds good?"

Novsky adds, "And my big brother has spoken for me as well, Da. What do you guys say in English? Ditto!" He smiles at Srini.

Srini says, "It's fine, guys. I leave it up to you now. But let's assemble here at 2.30 pm after lunch tomorrow and have the afternoon-evening session working on the correction plan."

With that, Srini bids goodbye to both. Sharma and Novsky get into their car en route to their hotel.

Marriott, Bengaluru, 8 pm

ISRO had booked both Sharma and Novsky in The Marriott hotel. Ranjan takes a bath, gets in his bathrobe, and pulls out his laptop after ordering his favourite North Indian thali. He checks his phone to see a few text messages from Novsky inviting him downstairs for some drinks in the bar but ignores it.

He video-calls Zoya, his daughter, a photographer cum influencer, who is currently in Kerela for some assignment.

Downstairs in Marriott, the pub is brimming with a cheerful crowd. Amidst them is a Serbian holding his drink by the bar and checking messages on his phone. Novsky thought to have a couple of drinks before heading to his room for work and was on his second shot of Jägermeister when a beautiful lady took the chair beside him. He realises that was the only chair left, and the lady had no other choice but to sit there. Dumb luck, he thinks, for this girl was an air hostess and still in her uniform. Novsky breaks the ice with a smile and a remark.

"So, straight up from the plane, right?"

The girl smiles and replies, "Yes, sir, and badly in need of a beer to wear off the tiredness from the straight 14-hour-service on air."

"Umm, let me guess, international travel, and looking at your expression, you handled either the French or the Britishers. So, a flight from Paris or London, am I right?" says Novsky.

The girl laughs and points at the waiter, "One Roy Plus strong beer, please." Then she looks at Novsky and says, "You must be definitely a Russian to hate the French and Brits, am I right?"

Novsky laughs and stretches his hand, saying, "Jovan Novsky, from Belgrade, Serbia. But yes, very close, eh!"

The girl smiles and shakes his hand, saying, "Kaamna from New Delhi."

Novsky smiles and says in a flirty manner, "Nice to meet you, Kaamna." He looks around the bar and then at Kaamna, "So, what's a good place like you doing in a girl like this?"

Kaamna says with an appreciative laugh, "Nice! That line is from the Deadpool movie, right? Looking at you, I should have figured out that a 90s joke would be on the cards."

"90s, No No No! Deadpool was 2010s girl!"

Kaamna inserts, "90s, 2000s, 2010s – all is 90s for me. I guess they never updated the slang in India after the 90s. So, it's the 90s or 2020s for me!"

"Well, ok then. But you still didn't answer my question?"

Kaamna laughs and mockingly says, "I don't enjoy sitting alone in a room, so I thought I would sit in the middle of the crowd and have a drink alone peacefully."

"Aha, and the Serbian spoiled the plan, right? Hahaha, don't worry. I won't bother you much. Can't help. I am a curious and talker type. Ask the bartender. I almost know everything about his family by now."

Kaamna smiles and responds, "No, No, Mr. Novsky. I was just kidding. It is nice to meet you. So, what do you do for a living?"

"Well, I am a Rocket Scientist, like literally! Here for some work."

Kaamna, "Oh, wow! I am guessing you went to ISRO?"

"Oh damn, And I was on a secret mission. What kind of dumbass agent am I, publicly revealing all my nefarious plans?"

Kaamna smiles and says, "You are funny, Novsky. But hey, come on, you are in Bengaluru in India and a Rocket scientist. In a city full of programmers and marketers, there is only one place for a rocket scientist: ISRO. It was just a dumb guess. Could be any other firm also, no?"

Novsky replies, "So, I can rest assured that HYDRA or its equivalent agencies did not send you, right?"

Kaamna laughs and says, "Oh, come on, 90s Avengers again! Stop it now, Novsky. Of course, not. I am an air hostess in Indie prime." She points at her shirt, "See the logo?"

Novsky, "Ya, sorry, a force of habit. I see a beautiful girl, and my flirtation circuit just gets activated."

Kaamna grins. "Damn, was that flirting? OMG. You Russians need training in this field."

Novsky, "Aww, Devojko! I am Serbian, but ya, you can call me Russian. And I am old school. What do you say? This 90s guy! All they taught us was to have remarks of Hollywood or jokes while flirting. But ya, you seem like someone born in the 2000s. You would have been bored with all that by now. But, trust me, this Serbian used to be quite lucky in his 20s."

Kaamna smiles and says, "No, no, Mr. Novsky. I think you are quite cute. These days, guys try to make a small conversation and immediately start sharing their schemes with a girl."

"That's very lazy, Devojko! Meet a girl and then start planning the schemes? What about excellent dinner, wine, long hour conversation, take a stroll, eat ice cream, drop the lady at her house and all the gentlemanly stuff?"

"Ha-ha, that's a good one and yea, we girls crave that the most on the first date, but sadly, most of the guys don't put that much effort. Ahem, Ahem, including my husband, who was too eager to take it to the next level. Hey, by the way, I am Kaamna. Why do you keep calling me Devojko?"

"Aaah, Devojko means a girl in Serbian, sorry. And, interesting to see that you are married. You look very young to be married, though. Though I am married and have got these two boys back in Serbia. Two generations next to you, I suppose."

"Yea, I got married at 22. Dated my husband back in college for 5 years, and we just clicked. Why waste time stretching this for everyday needs such as job, career etc., when we can do all that being married as well. Old school, I guess both of us are."

"I like it. I like the old-school Kaamna and her husband. God bless both of you. How long have you been married?"

Kaamna raises her glass for a toast and says, "It would be 5 years now, Mr. Novsky. And how about you?"

"For me, it would be 15 years now. And happy 15 years, by God's Grace!"

Kaamna says with a wink, "Aww, bless you guys! Does your wife know you are flirting with a younger woman in a bar?"

"Hahaha. No, for her, this would be the least trivial matter to worry about, considering the things we do for a living and our busy lives. After 15 years of marriage, it's mostly about issues and stuff."

Kaamna says, "That's nice. Issues and stuff! But, there is always more to a marriage, right, than just issues and stuff?"

"Well, of course, there is. She is my angel of life, blessed me with attention, happiness, nagging, issues, and stuff, haha!"

Kaamna laughs with him and clinks the glass with Novsky.

"So, what about you? How are things with you and your husband?"

Kaamna looks into his eyes and says, "You seem to be in a hurry to know all about me also, right?"

"Eh, come on. I am a gentleman who is…" he shows his ring on the finger, "married to Issues and Stuff."

Kaamna smiles and says, "No, it's alright. We are still as much in love as we were when we first met each other. Technically, it's over 10 years of love by now. And we try always to keep each other's back, no matter what. Though, he doesn't know that I am talking to a handsome Serbian now and I would like to keep it that way," she says and again winks at Novsky.

Novsky clinks his glass, this time with her.

Upstairs, Sharma was reviewing the data shared by Srini and correlating the same with the reference models designed for Nebula. The glitches in data were surprising enough for Sharma as well. However, he knew the entire analysis couldn't be completed single-handedly, and the last help he would need would be from Novsky. He knew Novsky would come up with his independent analysis after working with his team in Kvalitat. Sharma had already emailed the entire data to his subordinates in his team and called the team lead, Uday, to ask everyone to work overnight to make sense of all the information and come up with their views on the data. In parallel, Sharma tried to make sense of the same and provide his input. He had already heard the conversation of Novsky with his team after Novsky sent the data to his team. He was pretty sure the Serbians would leave no stone unturned to blame it all on the sensors and keep the issues in software clean.

However, little did he know that downstairs, the Serbian tech boss was least worried about the same and just enjoying the company of a young woman.

After a few more drinks, both Novsky and Kaamna get comfortable with each other and share all about their families, life, career, etc. Except that Novsky emits all the essential details of his job and primarily focuses on Kaamna's international trips and her friends' stories.

Novsky says, "It's too bad you lost your father in the COVID-19 outbreak. Those were terrible years, I remember. We unearthed a lot after the virus outbreak was over. All those corporate scams, hidden political agendas and whatnot. Many lives were lost due to a lack of preparations by the Government in their health care system. Even I had got infected and struggled for a good one month in recovery."

"Glad you recovered. So many couldn't even get a chance."

Novsky sighs and drinks from his glass. "The wounds of those years are still deep enough."

Kaamna deviates from the topic and says, “Hey, you are a rocket scientist and look like an intelligent future predicting sort of guy. Tell me, is there anything like that coming soon? I promise I won’t share with anyone. I just want to be prepared for it.” she says inquisitively.

“Oh, yea. You know what? There is an Armageddon kind of event coming up. Big comet striking the earth, and boom! It’s going to happen in just a few days. The earth will be vaporised. So, I say, you got only a few days to do whatever it is you wanted to!”

Kaamna looks at him with a ridiculed expression and says, “I was serious, dude. And what do you think I want to do before an Armageddon? Date a Serbian?”

“Well, if you want to. I know a lot of friends who like to travel to Bengaluru often?” Novsky winks at her after finishing his glass.

“Aww, you are cute. Suppressing your own desires with these so-called friends, ya. But, dude, I told you, I am happily married. Never cheated on my husband and going to keep it that way. If it were up to me to live in Armageddon days, I would book a flight right now, lock myself and my husband in a room, and spend the remaining days in love with him.”

“Aww, that’s cute! Hey, come on, for me, Albina is life. I sound flirty but have never ever crossed the line with any woman. My Albi is way too good for me in this life. However, unlike you, for guys like us, pre-Armageddon days would be a heck of a job and updating data and info to common people like you, so you can know when this world will end. And, of course, assist the Government in all their hopeless ways to get out of it. What do you call in India? Karma is the religion, right?"

Kaamna laughs and says, "Cheers to your Karma, Novsky. And also, to your issues and stuff!"

Novsky finishes the drinks and dinner with Kaamna and returns to his room like a gentleman. While returning, he is absorbed in his thoughts and memories of his first meeting with Albina. Entering his room, he takes his phone and tries to call Albina. She answers. Novsky says, "Sweetheart, how are you? And tell me about any issues and stuff?"

Chapter 5

Everything is Alright!

Sometime during the 2025s, people in their houses watched the live launch of the first manned MARS mission launched by NASA, USA. It was one of the significant events of the century. Humans landed on MARS in a specially designed suit and stayed on the base camp they set up for 1 week. The mission was a great success. It resulted from multiple innovations happening in the stealth mode by various Governments and private organisations, think tanks, universities etc. These all were monitored by TUESDA and assigned to the relevant agency/firm to take over. A manned mission on MARS was allotted to NASA and became the reason for the entire country to rejoice as they established their lead in the global space race. Little did the Americans know the world leaders cared least about that. There was another launch that happened in the hindsight of the MARS mission. TUESDA had allotted its most crucial project, NEBULA, for the ISRO launch site at almost the same time as the MARS mission. This was kept under the radar, and the media did not know of it. The only thing that was told to the media was that ISRO had launched a couple of support test satellites and space stations for MARS. However, the actual game was that all those support satellites and space stations combined to become something bigger outside our solar system, known as NEBULA. With the supersonic velocities embedded in these satellites, NEBULA was in the field outside the solar system in less than 6 months, a record even for a science fiction novel.

06 June 2031, Belgrade, Serbia

Albina is lost in her thoughts as she drives the family Volkswagen to drop Alexei to school. The morning office call was synched to her car wireless and had just gotten over. Maxim was not feeling well today and didn't go to school.

After the call, Alexei began asking about her father. "Mom, why is Dad always away from home?"

"Honey, it's his job. His work is immense and keeps him too busy."

Alexei, "What about your work, Mom? You also work but still spend time with us. Why can't dad have the same job as yours?"

Albina laughs and says, "My little peanut, everyone has different job responsibilities. Your father is working for something significant that will help every human being. He is helping the world by doing things in space, remember? Dad told you the story, right? About that space thing he made and sent away from the earth to protect the earth?"

"Oh, yes! My Dad is a hero, and he makes amazing space things. I wish he could also be with us and play every evening."

"I wish, Alexei. But you should be proud of your father."

"Oh, I am, Mom. I want to be just like my daddy when I grow up."

Suddenly, the car infotainment flashes with a call notification from Jovan. Albina picks up, puts on the car's speaker phone, and says, "Hey sweetheart, it's Alexei and me in the car on speakerphone."

Alexei shouts, "Hello Daddy, I miss you a lot!!"

Novsky, on the other side, laughs and says, "Hello, my space-fighter! Are you dropping mom off at her office and going to protect the city afterwards?"

Alexei laughs hearing this.

Novsky says, "Now, now, my Jedi knight! What did we discuss? When I go, you are to protect mom and your brother. How are you doing that job?"

"Oh, Dad. I am way ahead. Yesterday, I destroyed a colony of villains who attacked us from space. Do you remember my Light Sabre? I was fighting like Luke Skywalker, and I destroyed the Federation attack on our house," he yells in his sword-fight voice.

Albina interjects, "Alexei. Remember, I told you. No fictional stories! And Jovan, how often have I told you not to encourage him?"

Novsky laughs and says, "Albina, let the boy have fantasies and dreams! But Ok, I will calm down. Alexei, why don't you take some holidays and be a normal human for a few days till Dad returns, Ok? I will tell you about the new mission later. But, for now, you do all the human things."

Albina says, "That's right. And we will see to that when you return! What is happening, Jovi? You are flying back tomorrow, right?"

"No, sweetheart. I am not sure. Haven't booked my return ticket yet. Few things are complicated for us to digest now. Also, I am considering visiting PRIME in New Delhi from here before I return. I thought to call you guys as we had a tea break. The afternoon and evening are going to be busier."

"It's alright, Jovi."

"Listen. Are you three doing alright?"

"Yea, why are you asking this, Jovi?"

"I don't know. Just that, this time, I am kind of missing you guys."

Albina mocks, "Well, that's a new one! You are travelling half of the year and say nothing like that. Is everything alright with you? Tell me, Jovi, what's happening out there? Why did the Indians call you?"

"Yea. Everything is alright on the work side. It's just that, I guess… I also tire of all these work trips and staying away from you guys. I want to see the boys grow and experience their day-to-day developments, you know. Maybe I am getting old."

Albina, "No. It's not that. There is something else you are hiding from me. But, it's alright, you don't want to tell me now. Just don't worry about us, Jovi. I don't want you to be stressed because of us when your work is where your focus is needed the most. I trust you will solve whatever you are struggling with, Jovi! Just call me anytime you feel low, Ok?"

"Oh ya. Work is alright, Albi, it is like nothing too much to worry and it will…."

Albina cuts in, "Jovi, don't hide or lie. I know there is an issue that is stressing you out. The best way to handle it is to compose yourself and return to the job. Don't think about us right now. And call me in the evening or even late at night if you want to share anything."

"Well, you always have been a mind-reader Albi. It's true! There are things here that are a bit more stressful and unpredictable. Puts me in a bit of a mood that I can't explain. I think I have seen enough of these things in my career now and am wearing off."

Albina says, "And what about your Indian friend Ranjan? Is he stressed too? Look at him, Jovi. He is older than you and still doing all this, right?"

Novsky laughs and says, "Yea, my Indian friend Sharma. Looking at him, I can't differentiate whether he is stressed, normal or happy. His face is the same. Same anaesthetic expression, as if someone is always operating on him. I wonder how he talks to his wife, eh?"

Albina interferes, "Jovi, stop making fun of him. I know, deep down, you both have a camaraderie. Remember Nebula launch times? You both used to talk for hours and would be almost inseparable. I kind of thought something is going on between you two. Oh, and I love his family. Nidhi is so sweet, and both the kids are jovial and friendly. Really, it has been 7 years since I met them. I don't know what happened to you guys after that, with all the bullying and blame gaming. You are scientists and not politicians, Jovi! Tell Ranjan I said hi to him, Nidhi, and the kids. Now, get back to work, Jovi. Or else resign and come back here. We will open a pub, so you can drink all day, and I take care of kids and work, alright?"

Novsky laughs and says, "I will hold you to that promise. Bye, Albi. Take care."

Same day
ISRO, Bengaluru, India

Sharma and Novsky had been sitting in a conference room inside NSRC-N, Bengaluru office of ISRO, along with other ISRO scientists from Srini's team. Srini had allotted them a conference room for the morning session, where these experts could collate their individual data analysis and come up with a plan, or next steps, to solve the problem. ISRO team was also working collaboratively on the analysis and the presentation. Both Sharma and Novsky had been taking independent calls with their teams, making notes, and preparing the final summary decks, as per their understanding, before collating them together for Srini.

This goes on for five hours, from 9.30AM to 2.30PM. The pressure was enormous, and both KVALITAT and PRIME-1 teams had already been working for the entire night for the same. The guys even have their working lunch during work hours.

After 5 hours, both scientists look at each other in anticipation of the views from each other. Srini enters the room as promised at 2.30 PM to hear the collated opinions from the team.

Sharma presents the deck and speaks, "It is not what you think, Srini. The sensors are all calibrated well. There is not an iota of error coming from them. Look at this," he shows the data on the screen, "We have checked their readings against past transmission actual vs predicted and the correlation. Our sensors work in two ways: one is a predictive model basis past data and a theoretical physics model. Second is the actual data that build those models. The first one is mostly irrelevant for operational data related to the transmission, as they are only concerned about live readings. However, it serves a critical data set to provide an accuracy of the sensors and understand the theories behind the celestial space."

Novsky says, "I agree. I have checked the readings from Sharma." He takes the laptop control from Sharma and moves the slide, "Again, coming on the predictive modelling software and the data transmission software, there is no lag from our side and no error. Look at the entire data model with the error-collating models we told you about. We even checked the data for other objects, and the correlations are the same as for this object."

Sharma adds with the next slide, "If you check for the VVP and LTD for other objects, planets etc., they are all coming accurate from NEBULA when matched against other satellites database as well. There is no reason to believe that the transmission has any errors. Now the question arises, why is NEBULA picking up such erratic behaviour for this object?"

Novsky speaks. "Then there is only one suitable explanation for this, Srini. This is a proper object and not an error from NEBULA."

Srini looks at both with shock and surprise and speaks, "We are talking about a real celestial object outside our solar system with such erratic velocity and light transmission profiles. Do we know the predictive trajectory of this particle?"

Sharma adds, "That's where the mystery is, Srini. We can't determine its actual trajectory until it is at a certain minimum distance to NEBULA for that level of accurate tracking. Alternatively, we would need to follow its data for 4 more days so I could complete our predictive model. It is not following any fine structured geometric pattern. Even if we apply all the gravimetric models that NEBULA has created for the celestial objects in its trajectory, the final trajectory model would still need days to complete. You need to give us one week."

Novsky adds, "And we can even try to squeeze it before. I can also ask Polsky to divert our physicists to this project for a few days."

Srini says, "Guys, I don't think we have the one-week luxury for this. You understand that TUESDA needs pre-reads for the meeting two weeks in advance. It is the protocol. We are on a tight schedule this month now. Oh, and we must update this in TUESDA's meeting, as our shared logs state the observation date as the start of this month."

Sharma adds, "Listen, Srini. We don't want to do a botched-up job on this one. This object is unique. Had it been a normal asteroid or comet, we could turn up a predictive model in a day or for most objects, it's instantaneous. That's the beauty of the NEBULA models. They are highly accurate, and the Artificial Intelligence model keeps on learning new objects and creates accurate models on its own. But for this one, none of the predictive models are working. The correlation factors are the worst. So, we all must manually feed an algorithm for this one after analysing more data. I can promise one thing, though. We will give you presentable pitches and refined slides on this one. You don't have to spend extra time for the pre-read on this one. Until then, you can continue the business as usual for the meeting."

Srini replies, "Agree, Ranjan. But you understand my dilemma, right? This is an international summit; even the presidents and PM get the memo and minutes. This can make you lose your job if not done right. Guys, come on, I am under a great deal of pressure. So, I request you speed up your tech muscles and give me a final recommendation in the next 5 days, with weekends included. Pretty please."

Novsky smiles and says, "Don't worry, Srini. 5days it is. In fact, we will be here only and coordinate the data readings from NSRC-N directly with our colleagues in our offices. Sharma, what do you say? Won't that be faster as it would save travel time and synch-calls lag between PRIME, KVALITAT and ISRO?"

Sharma looks at Novsky and speaks to Srini, "I agree with my Serbian friend on this one. We are in Bengaluru till we present you the final analysis. I trust you can keep the office open during weekends for this week?"

Srini replies, "Alright, gentlemen. Although I don't have a good feeling about this. You know a bitter taste in the mouth about this shady object. Hope I am wrong. You guys have 5 days. We need everything by 11th June on this one. I will ensure the office is open tomorrow and the day after, even though it's the weekend."

With that, they wind up the discussion on other miscellaneous topics such as the new spare part order and presentation structure for the meeting and get back to work.

Same Day
Chikmagalur, India 6th June 2031, 1130 AM

It's a fine day in God's own country, Kerala. The village, Thirunelli, in the Wayanad district, is blooming with its glory in flora and fauna. Amongst the stretch of a coffee plantation, two North Indian girls can be spotted. One is adjusting the tripod and camera settings, and the other is identifying the perfect clicking spots for a scenic portrait of the plantations.

Zoya and Anjali have been travelling in scenic villages inside Kerala on this expedition. They had got a project from National Geographic for a piece on Kerala. Zoya was the photography expert in the duo's team, and Anjali was a writing wizard. Together, they made a fantastic combo in creating novel and exciting content in travel/tourism and wildlife, an area both girls were passionate about.

Zoya is absorbed in her camera setting when her phone rings. Seeing that Anjali is still roaming around scouting for perfect spots for the day's photo session, she takes the call for a while. After all, she and her dad Ranjan have been trying to get in touch for a while.

Ranjan says, "Hey kiddo, how are you?"

Zoya replies, "Hi Dad, am good. I am in Wayanad for the assignment I told you about. Going to send you a few pics, Dad. We must plan a fam trip here."

"Hahaha, sure, my girl. I assume Anjali and you are enjoying this assignment?"

"Yes, Dad. We are thrilled. It's a major break for us. Nat Geo is kind of a big deal in our community. I know you could have called someone, and we could have got something like that earlier, but we are very excited that they approached us after looking at our website and social media."

"I am proud of you, girl. I am sure you are going to do a fine job. So, when are you planning to come back?"

"I am thinking of staying this weekend as there are still some spots to be covered. However, this is my last destination on the trip, and I am back home straight after Wayanad is done."

"That's fabulous, beta. Listen, I am also going to be in Bengaluru this weekend. If you finish your work, why don't you come here on Monday, and we can go together back to Delhi?"

"Wow, Dad. You never asked me this, Pops. Everything alright? You are doing ok, right?"

"Arrey, why not? I thought it would be good for us to hang out here, and we could also go shopping for Mom and bro. Besides, I could use a little break here and catch up with you as well. Odd right, we seldom get to connect at home because of our work schedules."

"Your work schedule Dad. I am an easy birdie to catch. You know, Dad, I am not sure about coming from Bengaluru as I am with Anjali and don't want to abandon her. Also, unsure if she would be comfortable coming to Bengaluru. But, give me a day to think over, and I will confirm by tomorrow."

"Sure, Zoya. Just an idea, I thought."

"Dad, you sound different. Are you alright? You know, all of us love you immensely, right? Please don't mind about this one.

In case you want, I can come even tomorrow, Dad. You know it."

"Hey, kiddo, I am all fine. Don't worry about me, beta. We will catch up in Delhi and go out for dinner. It's been a while."

"Oh yeah, that's a deal, Dad!

Ranjan, "Alright, Zoya, have a good day and send me those photographs. I could use some scenic soothing on my computer."

Zoya said, "You got it, Dad. Going to send them tonight. Take care, Pa!"

With that, she disconnects the call and returns to set her camera. Anjali can spot a few areas and has already spread the markers for the tripod at various spots. Zoya thinks about the call with her dad. Though everything sounded normal, she suspected something as her dad's voice was heavy, as if he was missing her and the family. However, she knew her father's work was very stressful due to the long hours and the pressure of the deliverables. When you work for the most influential people in the world, you must be very thorough in your job. She always felt that her dad should take voluntary early retirement and either settle down for some mentorship /advisory roles or just travel the world without worry. After all, financially, they had settled well for an upper-middle-class family in India. Suddenly, Anjali interrupts her chain of thoughts. "Zoya, are you ok? I asked you to move to the next spot. Where are you lost, girl?"

"Oh, I am so sorry, Anju. I was thinking about the call I had with my dad and got lost."

Anjali says, "Oh, is he ok?"

Zoya says, "Yea, yea, he is ok and in Bengaluru. In fact, he asked me to come to his workplace so we could spend some time together and shop. Weird as he is not the sort of person who enjoys shopping and dinner, etc. He is there till Tuesday and asked if I could join him on Monday."

"Aww, that's cute, girl. Your Dad is missing you and wants to spend some time. Why worry?"

"Don't know, Anju. I sensed he was hiding something. And with the work he does, him hiding something would mean a big deal!"

"Aha, ok. Hey, why don't you go if you want to, Zoya? We will wind up the shooting by tomorrow any which way. You can leave on Sunday. We can synch up on the editing and writing plan in Delhi."

"Sounds good, Anju. Let me sleep over it. I don't want to do a botched-up job tomorrow. We won't get to come here again, right? We must deliver this by next week to Nat Geo."

"Yea, I get it. Ok, let's try for the same tomorrow, and if not, you will buy something nice for him from Wayanad and gift him in Delhi?"

"Sounds swell, girl. Now let's get back to work." With that, she picks up her tripod and mounts it in the next spot above the coffee plantation area to cover an excellent panoramic view of the valley.

Chapter 6

Just Hope we are all Wrong!

There were many terrorist organisations in the world for various causes, from religious to patriots to a few who were just interested in making money. However, PUNSAM was unique to them all. It stood for overall humanity with its famous tagline 'Longo Vivas Tempore Humanity', meaning 'Humans will live for a long time' in Latin. They had a hidden agenda of destroying or hampering everything that comes in the way of the natural progression of human growth. Starting from technological advancements in AI, Robotics, etc., to medical research to high-tech innovations in space, manufacturing and more, they evaluated each with a speculative eye, supplementing with their own theories on how this would impact the overall flora and fauna of the planet required for the human growth. They had jeopardised many events in the past.

They started their activities with the 'Great Hack of 2025' when they attacked and unlocked the loopholes of the most secure technology on the planet — The Blockchain! They advocated against its use to prevent global warming. PUNSAM team had somehow hacked into a blockchain ecosystem and did the impossible of stealing cryptocurrencies, including Bitcoin, Ethereum and many more, to a net value of $100 billion-plus. The havoc and panic caused were immense, leading to a major stock market crisis, as most high-rise, IT firms were backed by blockchain technologies. There were a few *sturdy ones who escaped the route. New regulations were placed on cryptocurrency, and the latest security patches were implemented. This made a big name for PUNSAM.*

After the hack, they send a declaration letter introducing themselves through a 'DECLARATION OF WAR' document. They used the same title for the document released after every attack. The world believed this organisation stands for humanity, so their attacks won't be lethal to human life. However, they cleared their intentions by following the 'GREAT HACK' with their first lethal attack in the same year, where they bombed an entire conference room full of corporate leaders for implementing robots in the manufacturing industries in Las Vegas, USA. They had issued a warning 3 days before the conference to cancel the same and abandon the agenda; however, the meeting was continued under the strict supervision of several security agencies, including the FBI, NSA, MI5, Mossad and even RAW. However, no one could stop the tragedy. This made the world take PUNSAM seriously and put them on every country's 'MOST WANTED TERRORIST LIST'. However, for 7 years, no one from PUNSAM was arrested, unlike the terrorists from other organisations. Despite multiple attempts and the workforce formed on this agenda, all efforts were in vain.

The intelligence agencies believed that some brilliant minds led the PUNSAM organisation on the planet, including technocrats, intelligence professionals, ex-fighters (army equivalent) and possibly even some political backing.

10 June 2031, ISRO, Bengaluru

It had been 4 hard-working days for the team at NSRC-N. Srini and Novsky had been working with the ISRO site team and their firms' remote teams non-stop for 4 days. The ISRO site team was led by the team lead, Anita Naidu, one of the best scientists and a mentee of Srini. She had been part of the NEBULA program as well. Anita had been monitoring the object's behaviour since its discovery a few days ago by one of his team members. In fact, she was the one who highlighted the abrupt VVP and LTD profiles of the object to Srini. Anita believed in discovering more and further probing the object's behaviour. However, Srini wanted to rule out the sensor and software error first. Now that the cat was out of the bag, Anita was back in action, analysing the data for the object's behaviour and running the predictive modelling exercise with Sharma and Novsky. In the meantime, a combined effort of both PRIME and KVALITAT under the supervision of Sharma and Novsky delivered the spare parts that ISRO was outsourcing from CANADA in 4 days. The flight was supervised, tracked, and protected by the national defence of both countries. 5 air force jets escorted the flight operated by a trained jet fighter from Serbia.

It was late evening, a day before the final presentation. Finally, Anita, Novsky and Sharma had concluded their work and were sitting inside the restaurant in the ISRO office with two more engineers. The conclusion was the inevitable basis of the entire analysis and data. The aura on the table was lifeless as the three of them were lost in re-looking again and again at the final data and presentation they had crafted for the ISRO. Or for the entire world, they thought. Anita Naidu was the first to speak.

"Guys, there is no chance. We can't wait for tomorrow. I am calling Srini back to the office from his home and telling him the actual story."

Sharma says, "Fair. However, I was wondering if we could again do one last check on the final analysis."

Novsky interrupts, "Ranjan, we had checked this over 5 times individually and ran it by our predictive models. Now, our team is also stunned by the last discovery. But we can't hold this information to ourselves. Though our teams respect the code of confidentiality, I doubt they can remain mum about this for even a few hours. This thing is, you know, what it is!"

"I know, my friend, what this thing is, and what the data says. If what we believe is right, don't you feel our friend deserves a night of peace?"

Anita intervenes, "One last night of peace, you can say, Sharma! There is no getting out of this one."

Sharma replies, "Well, I am not sure. We have the issue in front of us, but I am still hopeful there could be one out of a million chances that we can beat this."

Anita shrugs, "Well, I am a scientist with no family, as you both know. For me, emotions come second, and work comes first. You can blame me for being so straightforward in life, but I am the one who has got nothing to lose and clinically treat anything without impacting my emotions. However, on this one, I see nothing. It's like I am coming empty and suddenly feeling human and emotional. There is no chance we can let Srini sleep peacefully tonight when the problem needs immediate attention."

Sharma says with a sigh, "Naidu, it's your call. We guys have done enough on this, and to me, the next step is to work towards the contingency plan!"

Anita says, "Umm, maybe you are right, Sharma. One night won't hurt. We can call this night for further verification and testing of the data and inform Srini tomorrow. Heck, we can even supplement this by confirming that we have tested this an ample number of times. Let us try to rerun all scenarios, guys. Maybe, there is a one out of a million chance we might be wrong, and there is some error with the data. We don't want to be called jokers on this one if that comes out true."

Novsky agrees. "Fair point. I will communicate with my team to run more scenarios tonight."

Sharma chips in, "Agree, will do the same. Seems like this night would be our longest night, guys, for a while!"

Anita says, "I just pray to God that we find an error in our diagnostics."

Sharma mumbles a prayer, closing his eyes. His expression clearly shows that he is calling on the almighty for help. "Amen," he says.

When they return to the office, the TV news suddenly pops up with a BREAKING NEWS sign, and the host says, "It appears like there is another strike by the same organisation, PUNSAM, which bombed a plane a few days ago. This one is unique and obscure. This time, it is the assassination of an important politician, Mr. Wiseman Kelley, the US ambassador to India. He was en route to meet the Indian Prime Minister when two men in helmets riding a bullet bike stopped by the side of his car at a traffic light and blindly fired into the car's glass with their machine guns. It appears like they were carrying specialised guns with bulletproof, piercing ammunition. Both gunmen were killed on the spot in a crossfire with the police. However, it appears that the ambassador had an urgent meeting related to Indo-US relationships the same day. Only a few hours later, we got another declaration sent by PUNSAM through an email to all the leading journalists that stated the below:

DECLARATION OF WAR

Malos Autem Punire (meant Punish the bad)

We have struck again! This time to give an indirect message to a world leader who thinks and believes that everything can be bought out easily, even the laws of nature. Have we not learnt from our past mistakes? – the world wars, the economic crisis, the pandemics! You mess with the natural system and order of things, and they burst you like a catastrophe. And what happens then? The common man is affected – it's he who gets broke, injured, sick, or dies. All the decision-makers, wealthy businessmen, and corrupt world leaders will always have a safety net above them that will prevent them from catastrophes. One such disaster is on our way – again because humans have played with the natural system of the world. Mr. Wiseman's agenda with Indian PM was one of the crooked ones and a two-edged sword. We are warning the United States and Indian Govt to stop hatching schemes that will impact the common man and our mother nature.

Nothing is hidden from us. We know all about your closed room meetings. We know everything you are planning or even thinking!

It's again a warning to stop thinking on such matters/agenda, or the next strike will be a bit more adventurous.

As usual, PUNSAM stands for: Longo vivas tempore humanity.

Truly for the mankind,

PUNSAM

Anita turns to Sharma and Novsky and says, "Damn this PUNSAM with its pity agenda. I wonder what they will do once they discover what we have discovered."

Novsky says, "I agree. Who do they think they are: GODS? To tell us what's right for humanity and what's wrong? I mean, last year, they bombed an entire cafe stating that a certain someone was meeting for a hideous agenda. The collateral damage caused the death and injuries of many innocent people. And what was that statement that trended in the social media for months, Malos autem punire, to punish the bad? All their biblical references and stuff, as if they are far superior to everyone. And this impacts us guys, an organisation that is shadowing all Govt operations. I bet they know about the NEBULA and ARK project already."

Anita says, "There is nothing to worry about that, Novsky. I certainly doubt that they would even have a hint about what we are doing here. Nor would they care. Their agenda is puny. Worry about deforestation, globalisation, cryptocurrencies, and things that are bloated big but minuscule compared to the impact our projects will have. However, I just have my doubt about the Canadian shipment they bombed."

Sharma says, "I guess this is another reason to worry, Naidu. First, they bombed your Canadian shipment, and now this. I suspect they know a lot about everything and have their ears everywhere. Do you think we should..?"

Anita interrupts in between, "Mr. Sharma, don't worry! My team is vetted and tracked and constantly under vigilance until we share this news with the world leaders who will make sense of it. We took the data of your scientists also on this element and have kept it under strict vigilance with the support of our security agencies' presence both in India and Serbia. I have paid each of them a personal visit about the matter's sensitivity. I had allowed this last week only; the day you guys shared the list of your teams working under this mini project of ours."

Novsky nods and looks at Anita. "And how threatening this personal visit was for our teams?"

"Mr. Novsky, this is a matter of global security, and I certainly don't think this question is relevant here," Anita says. "However, to answer this, it was a very peaceful visit, which was a sincere request to your team members rather than a threat. If we must work on this, the last thing we need is to start something with brute force. Don't you think so?"

Novsky says, "I am sorry, Anita, it's just that I don't want our teams to be demotivated, that's it."

"Again, the wrong statement, Novsky. Demotivation is not a relevant expression in this situation, I think. It's all about SURVIVAL now!"

They left the restaurant and headed back to the NSRC-N office, where their teams were working to cross-verify everything as instructed.

Sharma excuses himself as he receives a call from Zoya. He had been looking forward to the call since the morning. Zoya arrived on Sunday to meet Sharma but ended up spending only a few minutes with him as he was called off urgently back to the ISRO.

So, all she did for one day was roam alone in Bengaluru and head back to Delhi the next day alone as Sharma had to stay for a couple more days. She was mad at her father for ruining her return trip and was not picking up his calls or talking to him in a straight mood while she was in Bengaluru. However, after reaching home and having a long discussion with her mother, she was ready to forgive Ranjan and talk to him again.

"Hey, Dad, sorry for being mad at you. I know your work precedes everything."

"No, my pumpkin. This time I am an idiot and should apologise. After all, it was me who called you here. However, I never expected things would go much out of control that I had to cancel our plan."

"It's fine, Dad. Happens to the best of us. You sound a bit stressed. What happened, Dad? Everything alright there?"

Sharma, "Yea, beta. Everything is fine. It's just that I have been sleeping very little for this last week, and with age catching up, it shows in my voice and facial expressions."

"You need to take it easy, Dad. Rajat told me about his discussion with you in Delhi. Why don't you make this switch,

Dad? PRIME-1 job is taking a toll on your health. We want you to relax and have an easier time at work."

Sharma, "I wish I could beta. However, it's not only about money and a career for me now. The things I am involved with are way too deeper than that. Someday you will understand what I stood for. Sometimes you know you are the only one who can do a particular thing, and you must do it and continue doing it. I found my calling long ago, and it's difficult to give up what I stand for in life."

"I know, Dad. But maybe you have done a lot already. I mean, you launched the impossible NEBULA thing out of space. Dad, you are a space celebrity, and the world already respects and owes you a lot. It's time you take your break and start living a life."

"Don't worry, Zoya. Things will be alright!"

"Things are alright, Dad. It's not bad at all. We are all happy. I am just worried about your overall health. Ok, promise me, when you return, we will get your blood tests done and show a good doctor about your insomniac condition."

"Done deal, Zoya! Will get back to work now. Good night, kiddo!"

With that, Sharma goes inside the office and joins the others for the final customary test runs.

Washington DC, USA

President Nathan of the United States was in his oval office in Whitehouse, currently debriefed by Chief of Staff Alex on the agenda related to his upcoming visit to Mexico for an economic summit. Next in line is the call with the Indian Prime Minister on the recent tragedy of the US Ambassador's assassination in the country. After wrapping up the call with the Mexican President, he turns back to Alex and expresses his frustration.

"Alex, things are out of control! They agitated Americans with this incident. The hate against the Government is increasing daily until we act and clarify our plans against this new PUNSAM thing. Have we got any revert from Bill on any intelligence on PUNSAM?"

Alex says, "No, Mr. President. I am afraid the entire world has nothing about them. Not even a single lead. Both assassins were hired guns and unfortunately couldn't survive any questioning." Saying this, she sits down opposite Nathan across the Resolute desk.

"Are Indians stupid or what? Why would they kill them instead of arresting them?"

"Sir, with all due respect. The attack was sudden, and the danger was that the riders had opened firing against other surrounding people, including civilians, to escape, and it appears their cops had no choice but to take them down. Though strangely, no civilians were hurt. Surprise, such professionals would miss a nearby target. The theory is they just wanted to scare people and sound dangerous to them, and it appears like it was a suicide attack after all."

"We need something quick on this. The opposition is already doing overtime on media because we could not defend our own ambassadors outside our country. And what was it they were meeting for?"

"Sir, it was related to the space agenda, especially the next programs related to NEBULA and ARK. We planned an agenda for the next TUESDA meeting to take updates on the commercial contracts and lead site for the support satellites for NEBULA and ARK projects. Mr. Ambassador must be visiting Indian PM to update on the expectations related to the meeting from our side. You remember, sir, we had the call on that last week with him as well."

"Oh yes, I do. But why would PUNSAM have an issue with this agenda? And what is the message they are giving us indirectly?"

"Sir, as with every attack, there is never a direct message given by these guys. They are a bunch of irritating and bullet-loving bastards who want to spread hate against progressive countries and companies."

"Do we know where they are based? This year, two attacks have been linked to India. Last year, I remember, they focused most of their efforts around Europe. Then a year before, they attacked us 4 times in our homeland. How can an organisation like that strive under our nose and can intercept every sensitive information and agenda?"

"Sir, we are drawing blanks here. Even the most astute security expert like Bill has worked on them for the last 5 years but has nothing. All are clueless, whether FBI, NSA, our partners across the ocean, MI6, Mossad, RAW, FSB, or GRU. PUNSAM has bested everyone on this planet regarding surveillance, tracking, or leaving any trace behind. It is now the most dangerous and feared organisation, sir. I am pretty sure they have some very important people on their payroll. We need to tread every step carefully and protect our national secrets carefully. Now with this attack, our entire agenda related to the contracts/commercialisation for satellites is being pushed back further. No one would want to mess up with PUNSAM. We have already lost interest by 10 organisations for this order, sir."

"But interestingly, I don't see KVALITAT to back out. Seems like our Russian friend is up for all the dangers. Do you find that suspicious?"

"Sir, as far as my understanding goes, PUNSAM has caused major damage to many organisations, including KVALITAT. In the last cryptocurrency attack, Polsky lost a whopping $2 billion, and it shook him deeply. I think, on the contrary, he would be in a revenge mood, sir."

Nathan nods, stands and walks towards the window. He remembers how he got there in the Whitehouse and his true purpose. He was an emerging tech billionaire who had created a Fortune 500 firm specialising in Artificial Intelligence-based software and educational products. His transition to politics was swift, backed by some very important people. Along with every successful billionaire/world leader alive on this planet in 2031, his eyes were also set on the future – THE SPACE. And clearly, he could sense a faction of people against his primary agenda. And not only his agenda but the agenda of many more, most of them affiliated with a group called TUESDA.

Chapter 7

It Breaks Out

If you think you are well acquainted with all the top agencies/ firms that would almost define the state of humanity and its future iZn 2031, i.e., TUESDA, PRIME1, KVALITAT, NASA, ISRO, PUNSAM, Governments, etc., you are in for a real surprise as you missed out a vital organisation that was set up in early 21st century with almost similar goals as the above ones. However, this organisation didn't worry about short-term objectives, day-to-day problems, or operational tasks related to various missions. They focussed more on the century rather than just a decade or 5 years, which would still be a long-term goal for someone like TUESDA. Mainly, it was concerned about the evolution of human life after 100 years. It also recommended long-term initiatives for other organisations such as TUESDA, NASA, ISRO, Governments etc. Think tanks and private organisations should focus on. They were the brains behind long-term strategies for human progress. Essentially, their work included developing theoretical mathematical models for scientific predictions, studying human behaviours under various conditions, understanding the pros and cons of different technologies, and systematically predicting the future technologies the planet should focus on. This organisation was known as SCOPE-X and was set up in Great Britain by a global treaty of countries involved in TUESDA. SCOPE-X would receive monthly updates on all the initiatives of the different organisations as well as TUESDA meetings and would provide help in terms of guidance related to various projects or even catastrophic events. However, from the reporting point of view, SCOPE-X reported directly to Bill Scott, head of TUESDA, with autonomous functioning rights under the authority of SCOPE-X.

An interesting contribution by SCOPE-X in academia was introducing a new subject known as 'Natural Order'. The Natural Order experts dealt with the deviations from the standard fixed anomalies of nature, especially those created by humans. The subject gained immense importance in the last decade post the COVID-19 crisis and the stress on the PARIS30 summit. It divided the scientific community into two with the origins of the new theories and the governing principles behind them. A significant 'Illuminati' – type faction asserted that human beings and their minds could create amazing things for economic development, and nature should fold around those changes, be it industrialisation, digitisation, space technology, human cloning, robotics and beyond. The other 'The Universe Admirers side of community' was more balanced and asserted that every development needs to be scoped out extensively regarding its pros and cons towards mother nature and the overall pulse of the Universe. Many of the latter kind became experts in this new subject known as 'Natural Order'. The subject had enormous backing from all the Governments. This subject was even introduced as a specialisation in key universities like Harvard, Stanford, Purdue, London University, University of Greenwich, Imperial College London, IITs in India, Hong Kong University, Purdue, and especially the new Keephatch University in the UK. There was once a wave of trending subjects in the early 21st century like Computer Programming, Cloud Computing, Artificial Intelligence, Robotics, Machine Learning, Blockchain, 3D Printing, Manufacturing, Emotional Intelligence, etc. However, very few people were willing to work on topics that directly impacted the planet earth, like Environmental Science, Wildlife Preservations, etc. All of this changed as post NEBULA launch, a new era of science was born. The new experts were in space technology, quantum physics, environmental science, inter-planetary science, geology and the most trending amongst all NATURAL ORDER. Natural Order studies combined everything ranging from Science, Mathematics, Data Science, Programming, Statistics, Biology, Environmental Science, Space Technology, and even Astronomy to a larger extent. To become a Natural Order Expert, one would need extensive experience in these fields and a demonstration of live projects of importance. The degree was the most challenging one to get on Earth, with only a few Colleges/ Universities offering the same.

Washington DC, 11 June 2031, post-midnight

Bill Scott, the head of TUESDA, was in his apartment sitting on his couch, reading a few manifestoes he was supposed to present to the White House. His dog was sleeping nearby, cluelessly watching a movie on the TV that was still running. Bill had a glass of single malt in his hand and was reading the reports on his tablet. He was exhausted today with many meetings and the new agenda for the month on the table for TUESDA. Since becoming head of TUESDA, his life has been a roller coaster ride. Scott, 66 years old, still single, had been already living a life of a loner but had his moments with his friends, distant family and random strangers in the bar. However, his life was now cornered around meeting scientific advisors, hi-tech company CEOs, International Government Representatives, world leaders, media etc. He hardly had time for himself. While reading the reports, he was half-convinced that he was almost done with this crap.

Bill had been planning an early retirement for the past 3 years but always pushed it further owing to some global emergency and always felt compelled to serve more. But, this time, his resolve was wearing off as things moved too slowly in this world. He had been pushing breakthrough global initiatives, including Ryan Bomb II, New Super Sonic missiles, and even ARK, for quite a while. Still, he struggled to convince world leaders, including one of his country's presidents. On the bright side, he had a lot of powers in his current roles, though he would rely on counsel and approvals from world leaders from time to time. In his current roles, various heads of agencies like NASA, ISRO, ROSCOSMOS, RAW, FBI, CIA, etc., reported to him for agendas such NEBULA and Planetary Climate project, as per alignment with their respective Governments.

Today, he had individual meetings with various council members of TUESDA, seeking their opinion on numerous projects like the Amazonian Rainforest resurrections, funds for SCOPE-X, the agenda for the next summit, and approval for ARK trials, and whatnot. Every day had been like the same for him. More meetings, agendas, and planning for the planetary transformational initiatives.

But, this year, all would be done, as he thought. He planned to announce his retirement at the winter summit of TUESDA in Geneva in October 2031. And hence, he was already in that workaholic mode as he knew it's only 4 more months to go. So, it won't hurt to work 24x7 any which way. And tonight, he had already decided on an all-night out as he had to prepare for some early meetings with the US President for some urgent matters. Sleep can wait for a day, he thought.

While he was lost in his thoughts and fantasies of his post-retirement life, he got a call from Muraly, the head of ISRO.

"What is it, my brown friend? You know, it's night-time here and one day before your time."

Muraly replies, "Hello, Bill. This matter can't wait, and I apologise. I will have to spoil your sleep tonight. I knew you would be awake tonight anyway for your big presentation tomorrow."

Bill replies, "Oh, you know about it? Nothing stays secret here in US Government, isn't it?"

Muraly replies, "Well, yea. I have some friends on TUESDA, you see. But let's get back to the point, Bill. There is something very important you need to see straight away. We all are shocked and in a state of a paralytic dilemma. Trust me, there is no doubt about this information. Our global experts, and even NASA, have tested and vetted it. Now, I must prepare an update for the Indian Prime Minister. But, once you see the report, you will know what to do. I have Srini deputed on this issue, and you can call him anytime for more information. I think it's time you call your wonder-boy from Keephatch or anyone who can help us all." And then he disconnects the call.

Bill opens the email sent by Muraly and finishes reading it. He removes his spectacles, wipes off the sweat on his head and speaks to himself, "Strange? Why do you have to give a Hollywood touch to a matter this devastating, you scientist idiot?"

With fear and stress visible on his face, he picks up the phone and dials Arjun Bhatia in the UK.

Winnersh, UK, same day

If you drive from Reading, the UK, en route to Bracknell, comes Berkshire way, where you see a lot of greenery mixed with an urban civilisation of Lower Early, Winnersh and beyond. A few miles further, you drive alongside a beautiful patch of vegetation that is part of Keephatch Reserve. The local community had been very proud of the reserve, with its lush greenery and flora-fauna. However, in 2025, a small section of the reserve was cut down despite the protests by locals. UK Government converted that patch into a small university known as The Keephatch Natural University. They wanted a separate institute in the middle of natural flora and fauna to focus on the initiatives for a "Greener Earth" and align with the 2030 goals of the 2015 Paris Summit Treaty. The rest of the natural reserve was well fenced with different entry and exit points for the University. Only the university area was off-limits, and no outsider was allowed inside, even for a casual visit. The University was inaugurated in 2027 and invited people worldwide, orchestrated by the then UK Prime Minister. Government delegates and people from private organisations were invited to the inauguration ceremony, even people from PRIME-1 and KVALITAT.

The University only invited research students pursuing PhDs in various research areas that would help the planet become greener and were hand-picked globally by the university. There was no local quota, much to the opposition of British Nationals. The comical rumour around the locals was that the University was a back-office of MI6, much transpired by the secrecy the university, its students, and professors would adhere to. Most of the students were residents and mixed very little with the locals. The professors or the head scientists followed the same suit, except for a few staying in and around the area post clearance. One such professional was Mr. Arjun Bhatia, the head of the Advanced Analytics department, responsible for analysing the historical data and creating a mathematical model for the new initiatives and research areas.

However, little did anyone know, be it the locals, the British Government employees (barring the Prime Minister and his security head), or even the press, that the University was nothing but the head office of a covert global organisation known as SCOPE-X. Mr. Arjun Bhatia was not just a professor but also the Deputy Chief of SCOPE-X.

Arjun stayed in Reading, around a 20-minute drive from Keephatch. He had a valid reason to do so. His wife Claudia was a professor at Reading University. And they wanted to be closer to their 4 years old daughter, who would stay with Arjun's parents in their house when both Arjun and Claudia would go to work. Arjun had shifted to the UK in 2025 when the Keephatch project was kick-started. For 2 years, he worked long hours to get the entire project up and running and set up relevant laboratories and facilities needed for the project. Before that, Arjun was an independent technology consultant based out of Washington, DC, US. He was the lead scientist for a prestigious global think-tank known as TUESDA. That meant he was involved in most of the significant space-tech and earth renovation projects, including our favourites NEBULA and ARK. Arjun knew Sharma, Novsky, and Srini very well. SCOPE-X was the brainchild of Arjun Sharma, though supported very well by the entire global community. Arjun held prestigious recognition and respect in the international scientific community. His research mainly focused on the major earth events, as well as space science. During his work in 2025 with Reading University for something related to the COVID-19 outbreak, he occasionally met Professor Claudia, a 30-year-old gorgeous woman who immediately connected with Bhatia on the very first day. Arjun and Claudia dated for almost a year and married in 2026, a year after the launch of NEBULA. They had a wonderful daughter Samantha, who was 4 years old.

11 June 2031, Keephatch aka SCOPE-X office, UK."

Arjun Bhatia was in his office enjoying his Americano and having a discussion with Jason, a 'Natural Order Expert' in SCOPE-X. The discussion was related to the 'ARK 2135' project. There was a recent requisition filed by PRIME-1 and KVALITAT engineers to do another Test Run for the first ARK. The ARK was designed to carry 10,000 human beings to NEBULA and come back. It was supposed to be a manned, piloted mission. The current requisition proposed deploying the first human-crewed mission to NEBULA and sending a few astronomers, scientists, and experts to NEBULA. This would be humanity's first mission to send anyone outside the solar system except the space stations, satellites, and probes. The consequences would have to be thoroughly analysed; hence, TUESDA delegated the analysis to SCOPE-X.

Jason says, "Arjun, me and my team have prepared a detailed assessment of the ARK deployment project and here is the dossier for your perusal." and transfers the 200-page document to Arjun through his tablet by swiping across to Arjun's tablet kept on the table.

Arjun, “Thanks, Jason. I will read it in a while. However, can you summarise the key observations before I take a deep dive into this?”

Jason says, “Yea, there are a few things we are concerned about, Arjun. First, the environment cycling chamber is not tested for all the extremities, and we need to understand the boundary conditions of temperature and humidity more extensively. Second, there is still a question about testing the longevity of the human body basis the specific diet on the shuttle and its potential side effects. Then, there is an entire question of the reliability tests that include stress analysis of the metal coating across the surface, the motherboard reliability, the entire electronic circuitry, A&M schedules and much more. This is not an automobile, Arjun. We are talking about a shuttle that stays permanently like this and executes functions that no machine on the earth has ever performed. Let’s not talk about the most important fact that the real normal human beings and not superhuman-like astronauts are in this one.”

“I understand, Jason. But, again, this is not the first time the earth is sending any manned missions outside its atmosphere, right? Tell me, have you made a list of all the stress scenarios and stuff that can go wrong with it?”

“Oh, yea Arjun. Believe me, when I say that my team is a group of Devil’s Advocate, we mean we are a group of Satan’s Supreme Court of Justice’s Harvey Spectre.”

“Now, that was a bad one!!”

“Sorry, I mean, of course, we have run all the boundary conditions and, above all, beyond the boundary conditions.

It's space, for Pete's sake. We don't even know what surprise it might throw us after a year, Arjun. We work a lot on our guts and experiments. This is the main reason that worries me. Of course, it's ok to do a mission like this with trained astronauts or robots. But, we are talking about sending some real normal human beings like me, the scientists-type unhealthy folks, up there and staying for a while. The proposal shows that we send 100 astronauts and 300 normal human beings and scientists to the space. How can I not freak out? This is the first real manned mission, Jason. The previous missions were the superhero missions, where trained brave Astronauts with perfect health, fighter-like attitude, years of space simulation training, in short Avengers, were sent. And now we are adding 300 people with God knows what kind of health issues, fitness levels etc., to space."

"Jason, come on, man. Why exaggerate all this? You know we will provide all of them with rigorous training and then only send them to space. Now I get your logic about the human-attitude difference, but the design of ARK is such that one doesn't even feel that they are space travelling. You know the in-house anti-acceleration chamber works well in this case."

"Glad you pointed out, mate. The anti-acceleration chamber has been tested with very few proper subjects yet. The suggestion is to test that extensively with the subjects that match the persona of the people recommended for ARK."

"And now we are talking. Talk to me about these things, man. What do we have to do before we send people to this mission? Let's not just outrightly submit a denial without properly suggesting the steps needed for approval. We are all science fans here, Jason. Don't you want your grandchildren to hear the story of how you helped in setting up the first space travel mission for all human beings?"

"Well, yea. I would love to. And that's what you will find in the report. I do not deny the proposal straight away. But there are months of testing still pending at Earth for the ARK prototype before we send it for deployment. KVALITAT and PRIME-1 have already done enough testing, and they are confident they are ready to launch. But, from where I see, they are still short on many tests, and we have highlighted those in this report."

Arjun, "Sure, that sounds good. I will run this with Sharma and Novsky once I have had a look. Anything else for the day, Jason? How is our time machine project coming up? Have you got any success? I have some accounts to be settled with 'Alfred the Great,' in the 9th century, to ban English as a primary language for teaching and replace it with the old Latin. I want to talk him through that, you know. We should get the classics back, so I could talk to you in pure Latin and say, Get ex officio meo."

Jason stares at him, waits for what he meant, and says, "Huh? a time machine. And what does this 'officio meo' thing means?"

Arjun sighs and says, "It means, 'Get out of my office'."

Jason smiles and mocks Arjun while walking back, "Damn, I wish you could read my reports with the same charm as you read the History of England!"

As Jason shuts his office door, Arjun shouts, "I heard that!"

Arjun gets back to his work and receives a call. He is utterly surprised to see the caller ID as the call is directly from Bill Scott, head of TUESDA. Arjun picks up and greets Bill, only to hear.

"Arjun, no time for pleasantry. There is something urgent to be discussed with the entire TUESDA committee, and I want your team to go back to India and find out what these buggers are up to. You have the situation report emailed to you and the backup files that your SCOPE-X team needs to make sense of. As you will read in the case file, the matter needs to be dealt with the utmost care, and I am counting on you only for this. The TUESDA meeting can't wait till the end of this month, and I am calling it for the day after tomorrow. So, you have two days to go to India, make sense of everything and present this in the TUESDA meeting. And, invite the ISRO guy Srini and his two experts, whatever their names are. Take care, my boy, and whatever happens, don't panic. This is a matter of space and science. Deal it surgically and scientifically, adding no human emotions." And then he disconnects the phone.

Arjun was perplexed by this Mission Impossible moment he had just had with Scott and smiled. He reads the email, and the report attached to it, disconnects the call holding his phone, and mumbled,

"And now, this message will be self-destructed and..." he pauses and reads it for another 2 minutes while the phone is still in his hands, and he finishes his sentence with utter shock.

"..... if you don't act on it, the entire planet will also be."

And then, he gets serious on his laptop, takes out a pen and paper, empties his coffee in the nearby sink, and returns to analysing the report immediately.

11 June 2031, Washington DC, White House

Bill briefed POTUS on his direct personal line while the President greeted some school kids at a function. There was no time for pleasantries or private meetings as the situation was out of control and urgent to act on. His personal staff had already contacted the Indian Government about his visit to Bengaluru for the TUESDA meeting scheduled to address this. All the world leaders, including him, would arrive at a moment's notice. After all, this is the only time in history when all the countries will unite to fight for one common agenda. The scientists were calling it 'THE KRAAL SCENARIO'.

Nathan thinks about everything en route to the White House. His election campaign, his proposal to his college sweetheart, with whom he is married, the first time he saw his baby girl in the delivery room, the first time he sat in the Oval Office, all the major agendas and meetings he had ever had as a President, as well as the fun he was having by using the power he had. Nothing tops what he is getting into now. And if he must savour and save these moments for eternity, he better fight for them alongside the entire world.

No time for politics. Time for action to save humanity now. Or at the least himself.

Chapter 8

We Call it 'The Kraal'.

TUESDA never calls for a meeting without proper planning. Every meeting of TUESDA was known as 'an edition'. Every edition was led by an event planner, mainly the head of TUESDA. The council included at least one world leader (i.e. it could be the President of the USA, British Prime Minister, Indian Prime Minister, Russian President, or even a Chinese Premier). Never has there been a single meeting where all the world leaders were present. Most of the meetings had attendees that included major representations from the corporate world, especially the technology companies, space research firms, government associations, and think tanks such as ISRO, NASA, ROSCOSMOS, etc. They planned the meetings one month in advance with a pre-defined agenda, preparation, and the in-meeting discipline. Any member can attend the online sessions; however, they extended the physical invites only to the council leaders, organisers, presenters, and the heads of respective think tanks. When every member is present in the meeting, they term the meeting as FULL-HOUSE, something that has happened only once or twice in the history of TUESDA. But this time, there is no choice…

13 June 2031. TUESDA Meeting: Edition MM2031-06 (FULL HOUSE)

The mood is sombre in the conference hall of NASA. All the world leaders sat in one room again after almost 6 years (post

NEBULA launch). TUESDA June 2031 edition was the most critical meeting in the organisation's history. This one is a FULL HOUSE.

Amongst the audience (both in ISRO, Bengaluru & Online) are the below:

- Political leaders including US President, UK Prime Minister, Chinese Premier, Russian and Serbian president, France Prime Minister and more.
- Indian Prime Minister, Defence Minister, Science & Technology wing heads.
- ISRO Heads & Chief.
- Srini and his team.
- Bill and his analysts.
- Arjun Bhatia and Jason.
- Prime-1 team that included Mahavir and Ranjan.
- Jovan Novsky and Polsky from Kvalitat.
- Few other military heads from the US, UK, India, China & Russia.

Bill stands up and welcomes everyone to the meeting, setting the agenda.

Bill speaks, "Welcome, ladies and gentlemen. First of all, apologies for any inconvenience caused. However, this matter required urgent attention. Hence, we preponed it, and I labelled the meeting a Level-1, equivalent to World War status priority. The full house is quintessential for this discussion, respected audience. Now, without further ado, let me share the matter for which we have gathered."

"Since a decade past the last COVID-19 crisis, we have never faced a matter that has taken precedence over every other global crisis. Now ladies and gentlemen, if you thought the world was in danger during those days, this one has a danger ratio of 1:10 million, with the former stacked for COVID-19. I can say on behalf of my ancestors and ancestors before that, that this situation is the grimmest situation humanity would have been in ever since the ice age, Stone Age or any such ages that caused mass destruction. Ladies and Gentlemen, this situation is that of an entire planet holocaust and destruction." Bill takes a breath while saying the last line.

Everyone looks at each other and Bill with curiosity, frustration, anger, and confusion.

Bill continues, "Without further ado, let me present to you our Doomsday carrier. We call it Kraal, and it is headed straight for the earth to collide with us 180 days from now. Our lead expert, Mr. Arjun Bhatia, will now take the lead and share the details." With that, Bill sits and points toward Arjun to take the matter further.

One could see the anxiety, sweat, and confusion across the room. Arjun stands up, walks up to the podium in the centre of the conference room, takes the pointer from the desk, and starts the slideshow.

Arjun, "Ladies and Gentlemen, I am a man of science but still human. What Bill said in the introduction is entirely accurate and is an understatement regarding the level of destruction he is pointing at. Per our analysis, it is not a probable scenario but a certain one. In short, without building up to the conclusion, I want to state a fact that will unlikely change at all. And that is.

The most probable destruction of this planet in the next 90 days."

This completely horrified everyone. And they started looking at each other. The murmurs in the room evolved into loud noises as everyone talks to each other, and some even start shouting at Bill and Arjun. Bill stands up, asks them to calm down and points toward Arjun to resume.

Arjun continues, "Well, I understand it is melodramatic. But there is no other way to put this. Now, let me show you our doomsday carrier." Projects the next slide and speaks. "We call it, The Kraal."

There is a pause in the room as Arjun shows a faint image of a small celestial object that looks like a stone-shaped star to the human eye but is an asteroid-type object currently transecting towards the planet earth, as is shown in the simulated pathway for the object.

Arjun continues, "With the help of the brilliant scientists at ISRO and the validation support from Ranjan and Novsky's team at Prime-1 and Kvalitat, it has been confirmed that this object, which we are calling KRAAL, is headed directly towards the earth. And it will enter our solar system in the next few days. Over 100 scientists did the image, trajectory, path calculations, simulation basis, previous motion trajectory and behaviour. Even the predictive sensors at NEBULA confirm the same as well.

Now, we all know that NEBULA is the source of truth for us when it comes to understanding any phenomenon in the Universe and the behaviour inside and outside our solar system. During the NEBULA launch, we systematically left out many satellites in their trajectory across all the planets and the pathways between them. The sensor calibration is done periodically for all these satellites and the core NEBULA. The team at NEBULA is already apprised of the situation and has taken the backup measures as well."

Bill adds, "What my colleague Arjun is trying to say in a nutshell, Ladies and Gentlemen, is that the information is 100% correct, and KRAAL will strike us in the next 6 months on our planet. Now, this is the slide that shows the effect of the impact." With that, he asks Arjun to change the slide.

The slide shows an animation of KRAAL hitting the planet earth and then zooms in on the earth, showing the rise of temperature across the impact zone that spreads uniformly across the planet.

Arjun continues, "The size of this object is around 100 km square, almost 1/10th of the moon and almost as large as the asteroid Iris. However, when it hits the planet earth, it will obliterate a continent off the planet and raise its temperature by over 500 degrees C, as per my calculations. And that too in just a few seconds. It will evaporate the entire life form on the earth in an instant. Sea will boil, and the aquatic life will be destroyed. No plants, no animals, no trees, no buildings, and no humans will be left. The only thing that might be left is sand and rocks in the end. Now, we are analysing what will happen to the core. But after we concluded the destruction of life-form part, I doubt anyone would be interested to know about the status of the earth core, and hence I will not explain further on that."

There is a long silence in the room where everyone is digesting this shocking news. Novsky and Ranjan look at each other. Mahavir is glaring at Ranjan, who does not look back at him. Polsky is numb and looking straight at Arjun in anticipation of hearing the next step.

Nathan, the US president, speaks up, "I will not react with any exclamatory question and get angry about what, why, how did we not, etc. But I will come straight to the point. Considering you all scientists are human beings and clearly understand the implication of such news, I am assuming this is not something you knew about for over 1 week?"

Bill replies to Nathan, "Sir, this is yesterday's news, and that's why we called this meeting urgently. We didn't act smart and even considered doing some backup analysis to devise a contingency plan. But we thought you should know what we will deal with in the next 6 months."

Nathan replies, "Good. My mother always told me there is no problem on the earth that collective efforts and timely action can't solve. Tell me if I can still believe her statement?"

Bill replies, "Yes and No. The solution is not that simple, sir."

Indian Prime Minister intervenes, "What are you implying, Bill? And is there any other slide Arjun wants to show us?"

Bill replies, "Mr. Prime Minister. Yes, sir, and we have one slide that solves this problem, as Arjun will share now."

Arjun shows the next slide titled, "Noah's Arc is the only means of rescue," he says and projects the picture of ARK2135 on the screen along with the first prototype picture. He looks at everyone and, in the end, meets eye to eye with Ranjan.

Ranjan smiles and so does Novsky. Polsky shakes his head and looks at Novsky.

Arjun continues, "As you all are aware, ARK2135 is operational and ready to be field-tested. This was the project we had chartered, commissioned, and developed and has been in-beta stage production since the NEBULA launch. We had planned 2040 as a full-scale demonstration launch and 2045 as the deployment of the first model in outer space to reach NEBULA. The plan was to send the first 10000 human beings at a time. We called them Shortlisted 10Ks. These people will have diverse expertise and devote their entire life to the development of NEBULA. They will live forever in the NEBULA for the continuous development of human opportunities beyond our solar system. We would time the subsequent launches every decade. And we will send young men and women every time during these launches. Hence, by 2135, we will have around 100,000 people living in NEBULA forever. They will use the means of self-sustaining after that. We are sure by then, we will have developed means and technologies to improve agriculture, water, and other facilities in NEBULA. Now in between, we had planned to create several such NEBULAs and ARKs associated with it as we advance further in science. And the plan was to explore the metals/substances beyond the earth as raw materials to create the future advanced NEBULAs. We wanted that in the next 500 to 1000 years, we would settle batches of human beings across the universe with these man-made NEBULAs that you can call a mini planet.

We designed this plan as we could not discover any life-giving planet till now. However, in the future, if we find such planets/ stars/ecosystems, the NEBULA will become the mass space stations deployed across such ecosystems, and human beings will populate those planets and start life form. Our plan was to spread humanity across the universe so that by 5000 to 10,000 years, we have multiple planets/stars/solar systems that are interconnected. The concept of countries would have vanished as every individual country will look like a small city in future, and the entire earth or other planets might look like one country. This bold vision was inspired by science fiction books like FOUNDATION by Isaac Asimov. However, we never accounted for the destruction of the planet in our vision till now."

Everyone is dumbfounded. They all thought the NEBULA was just a science experiment, a way to find weather predictions and scientific data for the different planets and maybe discover minerals, metals etc., outside earth.

Nathan says, "And whose idea was this?"

Bill replies, "This idea took its germination as a concept in the early 1980s, authorised by your forefathers and leaders of those times. TUESDA as an organisation came upfront in 2025; however, an unnamed secret society or a department in UNO had been working on this concept for long. Some of the pioneer thinkers of those times in industry, science and politics had debated for decades to come up with this plan. NEBULA was a brainchild of this vision only. I was, of course, part of this society, as was my predecessor. With time, we would have revealed this to the TUESDA leaders in the next 100 years and shown all the original documents/treaties related to this."

Nathan is shocked. The US President had no clue about this. How many such secret societies are there? Is there more to it?

Indian Prime Minister speaks up, "Mr. Arjun, assuming that what you say is true. What is it you are proposing to us now?"

Arjun replies, "At this stage, Mr. Prime Minister, we have no solution other than preponing the launch of ARK2135 in the next few months and taking 10,000 human beings to NEBULA straight away. The fate of humanity would lie in the hands of those 10,000 humans then. And…" he pauses and looks down, uttering nothing further.

Indian Prime Minister exclaims, "And everyone else dies!"

Bill says, "I am afraid that's the only option we have, sir. That or else the extinction of humans altogether." Bill prompts Arjun to speak up.

Arjun says nothing.

Russian President speaks, "Are you all out of your God damn mind? What is this? A prank? A drill? A test of our decision-making? What are you implying? This is completely ridiculous. Uprooting us out of our soil. There must be a way to destroy this celestial object. What use are the bombs on NEBULA and our entire planet? Let's nuke the entire thing up like the ARMAGEDDON movie. This is such a basic thing to do."

Bill replies, "And we will, Mr. President. Those left on this planet will do everything to save it, deploy all the countermeasures to NUKE this thing down and explode it with as many bombs as possible. But we are not sure of its trajectory until it reaches the solar system and has a 1000-mile radius of NEBULA. Until it reaches that stage, we won't know what this object is and what can make it explode. This is completely new to us as its signature does not match any planet or star ever recorded by humanity."

Nathan says, "Are you saying it could be an alien spaceship?"

Bill replies, "We have also considered that a possibility, sir. However, looking at the object's shape, it doesn't look like a spaceship, either. And we are not being judgmental about the design, but the shape is constantly changing. It appears like it is gaining and losing mass and deforming or reforming itself continuously. That's not a spaceship or a life-carrier behaviour. So until and unless we see it for ourselves, we assume it as hostile. Even if it is revealed to be a spaceship, we assume it is a hostile spaceship destined to destroy us."

Indian Prime Minister adds, "Is there a way to find out if there is any signal coming out of it? Like some radio frequency we can tap?"

Bill replies, "Again, sir. Not till it reaches the approach radius of NEBULA."

Nathan speaks up. "When will it reach the approach radius?"

Bill says, "It will collide with earth in around 4 to 5 months, and a month before that, it will reach the approach radius. It is that fast, sir."

Nathan replies, "And when do you propose our ARK2135 to leave the planet?"

Bill says, "In around 3 months, sir, as it will take 2 to 3 months to reach NEBULA."

Nathan speaks, "Mr. Bill, what you are proposing is preposterous. We can't let our fellow brothers and sisters die and have only a few of us leave the planet. We need to find a sure-shot solution. And you need to promise that the bombs will destroy this KRAAL thing. I don't want to see my beloved planet destroyed in front of my eyes on a computer when I am sitting outside the solar system. Also, ARK2135 is now officially ARK2031."

Arjun, Sharma, and Novsky looked at each other and shared a suppressed smile. The council had not even decided who would leave the planet, and Nathan had already assumed he would be one of the survivors. They looked around the table with every other leader nodding the same sentiment at Nathan as if it was clear they would be onboard the ARK and leave the planet to its fate.

Bill replied, "Sir, we will do the best of our capabilities to ensure that happens. The brightest of minds are working on it. May I introduce the project leader Mr. Sharma and his deputy Mr. Novsky, whom we have appointed to work on the remedial measures for the same? Arjun will lead the evacuation strategy with his team, while Mr. Sharma and Novsky will help prevent the KRAAL from colliding with the earth via every means necessary. Let me be clear on the evacuation plan, ladies and gentlemen. It is not yet decided who will leave the planet in the ARK as we only have a capacity of carrying 10,000 individuals on board. Hence, we will come ahead with the 10K shortlist after consulting with other dignified experts. We will look into a combination of various criteria for the survival of humanity such as education qualifications, skills, experience in handling critical situations, fitness, youth, etc."

Nathan replies, "You leave that decision to us. We will form a separate committee to nominate the final shortlisted people. I, along with other dignified leaders here, will assess this situation in a closed room and come up with the last proposal. You guys need to worry about how to destroy that thing."

The Russian Prime Minister adds, "I agree with my friend Nathan here. The short-listing will be mostly a global political decision, not a purely scientific one. However, that being said, we will make the best decision for humanity and ensure all the right people, experts, leaders, and soldiers are on board the ARK to continue the fate of humanity. This topic and this thing should not come out of this closed room. We don't want to cause panic all around the world. This is not the 2012 movie, Sir, and we cannot have mass panic and hysteria destroy our plans to save humanity. There are two priorities for you guys now. The first is deploying ARK, ensuring it is ready to travel and carry the shortlist we will provide. The second, but most important, destroy this KRAAL out of our solar system itself."

Chinese Premier adds, "Gentlemen, while I agree with my friends who just spoke on our behalf. Let me assure you and provide you with a personal guarantee. I will deploy all the Chinese resources at your disposal to handle this thing. Don't doubt our capabilities, as you do not know the scientific advancements we have made in ballistic missiles and space defence. Our defence minister will deploy the best experts for your guidance and share all the relevant material. Regarding the decision of survivors on ARK, that is a very tough, debatable, and a slightly grim topic that I, along with other Presidents, Prime Ministers, Kings and Queens will discuss and get back to you. I assure you the decision will be unbiased and only favourable for humanity."

Bill smiles at him and nods, and so does Arjun. They both know it's a political statement to assure them and have them focus only on the technicalities of ARK and the explosive device for KRAAL. It was clear from the tone and the air around the room that the survivors would comprise political leaders, wealthy businessmen, army generals, superhuman soldiers, and workers to help them carry out their day-to-day requirements, just like in the 2012 movie. Their best bet is to ensure the destruction of KRAAL.

Sharma spoke in the end, "Respected ladies and gentlemen. Regarding the destruction of KRAAL, we estimate that the number of ballistic missiles, bombs, explosive devices etc., needed is currently insufficient. We have combined all our resources on this, and I don't think we have even got 10% of what is required for KRAAL as per our estimates. In this situation, we have a very unusual request before we disperse. We would require all the nuclear bombs, explosives, missiles, bombs, etc., available in every country. These will be transported to a central location, so we can retrofit them in rockets/spaceships or even a united bomb. We have already assessed the arsenal requirement, and it appears that all the combined weapons on the earth would not match the prowess of KRAAL. But we need to take this chance for the sake of survival."

Nathan speaks up, "Mr. Sharma. We heard your request. However, this is not your call. Let our defence experts and inside council decide first. We should now call this meeting to an end so we all can get back to the urgent matters at our disposal. Thank you."

With that, the meeting is concluded, and everyone leaves the room.

Indian Prime Minister had invited all the world leaders, including Presidents and Prime Ministers from the USA, UK, China, Russia, Serbia, France, Brazil, Israel, and a few other countries, to meet in a separate conference room to discuss the next steps and agenda.

After the meeting, Sharma catches up in the cafe with Arjun and sits next to him with his coffee.

Arjun says, "Wow, Ranjan, two cubes of sugar. Really? You are not worried about your insulin, right? Should I text Nidhi and tell her about this?"

Sharma says, "Relax, my boy, and when did you worry about diet and health? Look at the paunch you are flaunting these days. Are you personally clearing the remains of the bakeries outside Keephatch?"

Arjun laughs and replies, "Been a long time, you been to the University. Why don't you come with me and we can work together there? You can bring your Russian friend along, too."

Sharma replies, "Thanks for the offer, Arjun. But, we have a lot of work here in Bengaluru only. And for your information,

Novsky is Serbian and not Russian. Plus, he is not my friend. Just a colleague on this project and competition once this is all over."

Arjun looks at Sharma. "So, you are hopeful that this will be all over?"

Sharma, "I am hopeful about many things, Arjun. Starting with the natural selection of 10,000 survivors, governments agreeing to provide all the bombs at our disposal, and KRAAL taking a last-minute detour at maybe Neptune. One can't leave the hope, right?"

Arjun says, "Then, why did you add two cubes of sugar to your coffee?" he looks straight into his eyes.

Sharma said, "While I don't deny the hope. As a scientist, I also understand the probability of survival and acknowledge that the percent probability is in the single digits. The high sugar will kill me in a decade or two, but this thing will kill me in 6 months with 90% certainty."

"That implies you have assumed you won't be on the KRAAL list of survivors. Why would you even think about it?"

"Even if I want to, I won't be allowed, Arjun. I know how these things work. Mahavir calls me and will give me a long speech about humanity. Politicians labelling us war hero before they fly. I know exactly how things will turn out and have accepted my fate. But to answer your question in totality, even if they ask me to go, I won't leave this planet, Arjun. I will fight till the end and use all the resources available on this planet to save it."

Arjun replies and raises his cup of coffee. "You are not alone on this journey, brother. Your friend at Keephatch will be with you on this."

Sharma replies, "I will raise a toast to that. But I doubt that, Arjun. Let's see the tide of events."

Arjun gets a bit confused and looks at Sharma with no response, and they both finish their coffee before returning to work.

Chapter 9

But for the Outside World

The Nebula project was one of the most ambitious projects for mankind. The plan was to have enough NEBULAs in upcoming centuries to save the entire human population on the earth by shifting them to these habitable space stations or man-made planets. This would be done till the time humans can find a sustainable environment. Or till the time Earth reboots from its loss of natural resources. However, there was a catch to the entire thing. These Nebulas were also designed to be war-ready for the future, supposedly if there is an alien encounter in the future or a division of power within humanity. There was enough ammunition on each NEBULA design to destroy another similar-sized spaceship or asteroid if such an encounter was supposed to happen. KRAAL was predicted to be much larger than NEBULA, and the entire ammunition would only do as little as a slight scratch on its surface. The scientist fraternity was totally against deploying weapons of mass destruction on such NEBULA as they joined the NEBULA team intending to design a peace-loving space station or space city that could just help our planet find the right resources for survival. However, the leadership community that comprised Presidents and Prime Ministers of various countries thought otherwise.

For the outside world, NEBULA was just another huge space station and a hub for scientists to study outer space, discover new minerals, metals, etc. They always kept ARK as a top-secret project from the common public. Anyways, with the advancements in space science and regular public updates on technologies, satellite launches, etc., the public had lost interest in the side projects like ARK or the way they pictured it. But, the KRAAL event should have been one such exceptional event, where the truth about the NEBULA, ARK, and the threat under consideration would have been shared with the public. However, prior to the departure of the ARK and the people inside it, revealing such information would cause mass hysteria and obstruct the ARK rescue mission. That's why in the last edition of the TUESDA meeting, they forbid carrying or switching on any devices, including laptops, phones, network devices, cameras, etc. A dedicated team was in charge of the security checks and appointed a special support staff before and after this meeting.

Jagat Singh, a 27-year-old male, joined the service staff team at ISRO 9 months ago. He had become great friends with the supervisor, Nakul Parekh. Both have had many parties in their room with alcohol, loud music and Jagat's happening friends, mostly pretty young women. Nakul, 47, had been married for 25 years and was in a mid-life crisis. Jagat was a welcoming distraction, and the two bonded over many topics, including movies, music, comedy, drinks, women, and cursing the top management at ISRO.

Nakul knew Jagat was trying to make a career like his, and in a few years, he was confident Jagat would also become a supervisor. There was no surprise how Jagat could maintain a rather lavish lifestyle and an interesting social circle. For Jagat had told Nakul that he worked as support staff for a media firm and occasionally supplied interesting items, rare merchandise and hosted many parties for their employees. That's how he befriended a large group of young corporate employees from his ex-employers and built his social circle and side money selling a lot of merchandise. Jagat would proudly tell his friends about his work in ISRO for the Indian Government, as it would mean a long-term job guarantee and lucrative pensions when he retires.

Or so what Nakul would like to believe!

In reality, Jagat had been a journalist with RAFTAAR Live, a controversial news channel on TV and social media that would talk about corrupt politicians, hidden government agendas, corporate scams, etc. It was often said that if anyone would tune in to RAFTAAR Live and stay online for 2 hours, they would either become depressed or stop believing in anything related to Government, economy, or humanity. It seems they had a motto to cover every negative and depressing news worldwide.

All his friends were his colleagues, including other reporters, content writers, editors, etc., trying to maintain a picture in front of Nakul for their hidden mission. In reality, they deployed Jagat to cover all the secrets of ISRO as RAFTAAR Live knew both ISRO and NASA are the leading forefront in Space Research and Space missions. And they wanted to catch up with some spicy stuff or leak a futuristic invention into space science for media. Jagat had been working for 9 months and had discovered many stories, including a few bribes taken by some senior ISRO officials from some major firms, including PRIME1, KVALITAT to name a few, extramarital affairs of ISRO employees, next cabin gossip about who is going to be promoted, etc., etc. RAFTAAR Live was creating a complete cover story, like an annual exhibition for ISRO, by the end, and Jagat was now in the 'information-collection' mode. They had published nothing on ISRO until now, for it would have blown Jagat's cover.

13 June 2031, ISRO Bengaluru

Just as the news came that the TUESDA meeting had been preponed, Jagat requested Nakul to give him one chance and be part of the support team for the big event. Well, this could be a JACKPOT for RAFTAAR Live. Certainly, there is something significant at hand. This could be a story that could create a huge TRP for Raftaar. He persuaded Nakul by stating that if some seniors in ISRO could see and remember his face, he would have a stronger chance for his career growth and could become a supervisor at an early age.

Little did Nakul know Jagat was capturing a mental image of every audience member for his storyline. Jagat was in no mood to have a long-term career in ISRO's Support staff team as he was chartering the course for a meteoric rise in the media industry by becoming the one who exposed the big scandals.

He had ironed his uniform flawlessly for the day, and his courteousness in welcoming all the guests at the door had impressed Nakul. Before the guests could enter the main conference room, Jagat, other support staff personnel, and the security team had cleaned the room properly, placed notepads, water, glasses, and pens, and checked the audio devices and video projectors, and all the assets in the room. However, Jagat independently worked on the coffee machine and cleaned it very well after placing the styrofoam cups and replenishing the coffee beans and tea leaves in the machine input cabin. And no one could notice something that he did during that time.

Jagat pretended that the dirt made him cough, covered his mouth with his hand, took out a sticker-type film from his mouth, and then placed it stealthily behind the panel while servicing the machine. This sticker was a stealth-microphone with a memory card, specially developed for spying. He could not use wireless devices as the jammers would have blocked or even caught them.

After a few hours, the TUESDA meeting at the main conference room in ISRO had ended. The leaders, guests, experts, and security staff had cleared the room. The leftovers were scrap, such as styrofoam cups, empty glasses, rough papers with notes, presentations and documents that were torn apart and shredded in the shredder. The security team swooped down the entire floor and checked for any relevant information/documents that could have been left behind before the support staff could come for cleaning. Once done, a team of 5 support staff responsible for cleaning and maintenance immediately entered the room, followed by their supervisor.

Nakul watched the entire room, followed by Jagat and others to check on the information, documents, etc., that could have been left there. Nakul was also responsible for ensuring the confidentiality of all the documents/substances left over after such meetings that were supposed to be destroyed and burnt in the document incinerator in the basement. However, it took no time for Jagat to go behind the coffee machine, pretending to check the refill of coffee cartridges, but in hindsight, he pulled out a sticker and kept it under his tongue after mimicking another cough.

As he passed the security cameras and security door control check, all the guards and machines had passed him clean. He thought to himself and chuckled, "I mean seriously, how often do you look at a man's shoes?" quoting Shawshank Redemption to himself, obviously portraying shoes as the area beneath his tongue in his mouth.

However, little did he know, his cough act in the conference room and his smile were recorded by the CCTV cameras, which at this very particular instance were not watched by just some routine security guards but by trained CIA and RAW agents who had already planned the next steps for Jagat.

Same time, Muraly's office, ISRO

Indian Prime Minister, Mr. Singh, is sitting in Muraly's office in ISRO along with Srini, Muraly, and Kulkarni, his defence minister. The meeting with all the world leaders for the KRAAL situation and ARK solution is about to start sometime. But before he entered that meeting, Mr. Singh wanted a quick internal meeting with his staff.

Kulkarni says, "Sir, we need to have a leading edge in the evacuation negotiations. Our scientists have discovered this thing, and we should be in control of the next steps."

Srini adds, "Sir, with due respect, I won't say we have entirely discovered this. The NEBULA, a global effort, actually detected it, and we were just in charge of the outsourced monitoring project."

Kulkarni looks sternly at Srini and responds, "Yet, it was us who found it first, right? You first called Ranjan and Novsky. Your team first saw it. Indian space team, Indian!" he lays a strong emphasis on the word Indian.

Muraly signals Srini with a hand wave to lie low in this discussion.

Mr. Singh walks towards the windows, looks out of Muraly's office and speaks. "Muraly, the trees have grown bigger. Pleasant garden you guys have maintained."

Muraly smiles and replies, "Sir, you should visit here regularly. Especially during the monsoon season. It looks like a paradise during the rains."

Visibly irritated, Kulkarni replies, "Respected Sir, the issue at hand is critical. So we need a game plan before the leaders' meeting in a few minutes."

Singh smiles and pats Kulkarni's shoulders, "Don't worry, Kulkarni. You will get a seat in the ARK. And we need a game plan for the games only. This is not a game but a Doomsday Scenario. This time, there is no need to be patriotic and only consider India and Indian interests. This is about humanity now. It will not be a nation against nation argument in the next meeting, but the survival of humanity against the hefty price we will pay for it. Frankly, at this moment, I don't care who goes to ARK or not. I want to hear from Muraly and Srini if this thing can be destroyed."

Muraly, diplomatically, intervenes, "Sir, as far as I know, there are <10% chances of that happening. Our team has run various simulation scenarios to predict the projected behaviour of the object we call KRAAL. I think we need more time for our assessment and analysis of the last situation."

Srini looks at Muraly with surprise. He knows Muraly is buying time for him to understand the situation, as Srini's team has already completed the final assessment. Diplomat as ever! Always interested in toplines and not micro details. A detailed report had already been submitted, and Srini regularly updated him on all emails and reports.

The genuine request at this stage was to collect all the nuclear weapons and explosive missiles in a central spot. That central spot would be the firing zone from the earth during an appropriate alignment of earth with Kraal. Act precisely on the plan that Ranjan spoke about in the meeting.

Singh catches Srini's reaction quickly and asks him, "Srini, do you have something to add?"

Muraly looks at Srini with a quizzical smile.

Srini says, "Sir, no, Sir. It's ok. All the best for the meeting, Sir."

Singh senses Srini's hesitation, comes closer to him and speaks, "Srini, I know you are holding up something. Speak directly to me. No need to be structured and hierarchical at this stage. Even if it is not relevant or dismissal worthy, speak up."

Srini takes a deep breath, avoiding Muraly and speaks, "Sir, the chances of destroying KRAAL are very less. However, they can be increased if we follow what Ranjan said in the room earlier."

Singh replies, "You mean to get all the bombs on the earth at one central point?"

Srini replies, "Yes, sir. We need to collect all the nuclear weapons, missiles, explosives, space detonating bombs, and every piece of bullet available on the planet and put that in one central location. We have only 6 months left. I suggest we estimate our global arsenal and get that transport-ready in the next few months. The first step is for all the countries to reveal this information to TUESDA so we can estimate the amount of damage we can inflict on KRAAL."

Singh shifts his gaze from Srini to Kulkarni, who says nothing but looks at Srini.

Srini adds, "I know, sir. What I am asking is preposterous. But the situation is the grimmest one. Humanity might not exist at all. What's the point of hiding behind political doors now? What's the point in confidential war strategies and secret plans of weapon development/nuclear bomb testing if we can't use that to protect our planet?"

Srini further continues, "Sir, let me explain this to you a bit more scientifically." He takes an A4 paper on the desk and draws two diagrams of earth and KRAAL side by side. "Sir, look at this diagram. On the left side, I have drawn the planet earth, and the black dots represent all the nuclear weapons/missiles/bombs locations scattered around the world, and Kraal is about to hit our planet. On the right-hand side, I have drawn the best-case scenario for us where all the nuclear weapons, missiles, and arsenals are centred at one location, which is the closest to Kraal as it approaches the planet."

Then he makes another diagram below the first diagram.

"Sir, in this new diagram, I am showing the scenario of us hitting the KRAAL when it approaches the collision alignment trajectory with respect to earth. This collision alignment point is optimal for hitting the KRAAL before entering the next zone. In this zone, even if we hit KRAAL, or it explodes or deflects, it will collide with the earth and almost destroy it. The window to leave the collision alignment point is just 4 to 5 minutes, in which we must destroy the KRAAL. Before this point or after this point, all attempts would be useless. If we hit before this point, the impact won't be the right one as our missiles would have lost momentum and a significant amount of energy in travelling time, lessening the explosion's impact.

Sir, if the missiles travelled from their current location to KRAAL, most of these would have lost their momentum and impact quotient. Also, it would be difficult to calculate and coordinate the appropriate time for each of these missiles to leave their points. However, if we have all of them in one place, we shoot all of them as one big EARTH WEAPON that carries all the might and power of our planet. Sir, scenario 2 is the only scenario where we have some chances to destroy KRAAL. As you can see, it is a very basic physics problem, sir."

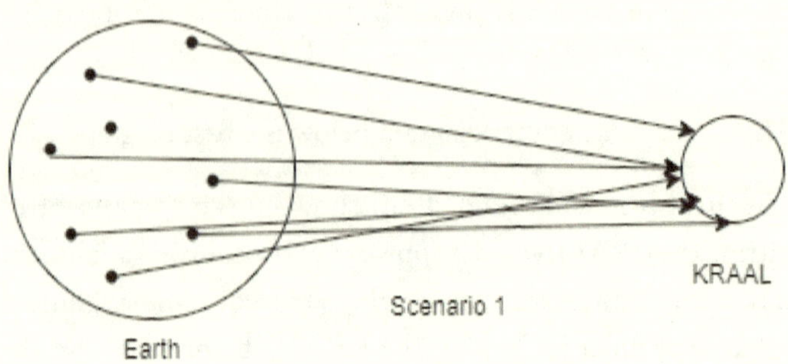

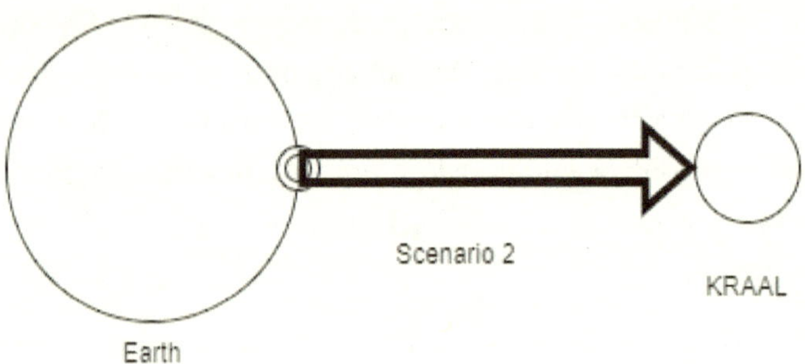

Singh, who was from a science background, grabbed the paper and replied, "Energy, eh, Srini? Use the energy of the combined system in the most optimum way. Don't let the overall system lose energy in redundant activities like travelling, coordination, etc."

"Precisely, sir," added Muraly, who realised he had been losing ground in this discussion.

Singh takes a deep breath and asks, "So where is the exact central location from where we can fire this EARTH WEAPON?"

Srini replies, "Sir, the exact location for the central point can only be determined once NEBULA detects the entire profile of KRAAL. But we need to prepare and align before that. First, we need to account for all the weapons/nuclear missiles, bombs, guns, and even a single kitchen knife hidden in all the houses in the world, Sir. Then, we make a list of all and calculate the explosion energy that we, as a planet, commandeer. Next, we calculate the optimum point basis the trajectory of KRAAL. The final decision should come in a month or two, sir. But as soon as it comes, within a day or two, all the weapons and missiles should reach that central location, sir. We would need some time to engineer the EARTH WEAPON, as well. Also, sir, there is one more angle to the complete solution. You would remember the latest innovation known as Ryan Bomb, installed on NEBULA to destroy space objects. We have assessed that the Ryan Bombs on the NEBULA won't be doing any significant damage to the KRAAL at all. But we will try to see if it can deflect the course of NEBULA. However, sir, 100 more Ryan Bombs have been installed on ARK to be transported to NEBULA. We want access to these Ryan bombs, sir. Along with the entire other ammunition. Ryan Bombs would create a bigger impact in destroying KRAAL."

Singh looks at Srini. "I can sense that you are not in a mood to get a seat in ARK, Srini?"

Srini smiles back at the question. "We will have to stay and fight, sir. However, I understand saving our species, some of us must be safe and hence we need to transport a few extraordinary men and women to space in NEBULA so that they protect and carry our legacy."

Singh replies, “Extraordinary, right! And who defines that?”

Singh chuckles and adds, “Anyways, Srini, you have made your point. I completely agree with your strategy of THE EARTH WEAPON. I will be an advocate for this petition in the next meeting. Also, from now on, I want you to be on top of everything and lead this from India. Muraly, please provide unconditional support and strategic transparency to Srini. He will report directly to me. Let’s see how the military transparency debate goes in the next leadership meeting.”

Saying this, he leaves the room for what will be the most crucial meeting of leaders in the history of humanity.

Muraly looks at Srini and says, “Congratulations on the promotion, Srini.” And then sarcastically smiles and shakes Srini’s hands.

Realising that Muraly disapproved of the entire discussion without his approval, Srini replies, “Muraly, this is not a promotion but just an assignment of a project in technical terms. Also, promotion is the last thing on my mind now. Even if I get it, now what’s the use? There is only a 10% chance that I can enjoy it.”

Muraly gives a sardonic laugh at Srini’s remark. Srini looks at the piece of paper and tears it into two pieces, separating Earth on the left and KRAAL on the right.

Same time, the ISRO compound

An unusual crowd of ISRO employees gathered around the compound outside the main conference room, where the

TUESDA meeting had just been held a while ago. A man was lying and shaking vigorously as if suffering a fit and salivating a lot of white fluid from his mouth.

His face was turning blue, and the medics had been already called on. Few employees had surrounded him. There was one employee who even tried to offer him water.

But now, the security was trying to distance all the people from him, as they worried he might carry a contagious virus that could spread.

A group of medics had just arrived wearing masks and quarantined the entire area immediately. All the employees near him were asked to wait in the garden and were surrounded by security and some more medics checking their temperature and vitals.

There were 100 medical experts stationed in ISRO at this time to prepare for the TUESDA meeting as a standard guideline in advance.

One medic checks the man lying on the ground, picks him up with the help of his partner, and puts him on a stretcher. He gives him an injection immediately to soothe his pain and replies to his partner,

"Seems like an allergic reaction to something he ate. I doubt it is something infectious or a virus. What do you say?"

The other medic replies, "What can I say, buddy? We have to follow a procedure and a protocol. After this, we got to test all these people for signs of COVID-19, H1N1, a new strain, or what not. Let's first treat this poor fella."

Both take Jagat from the stretcher, for he was the man who was vigorously shaking and unable to speak.

As they took him away in an ambulance, a RAW agent from a nearby building's roof watched him closely through his binoculars and replied to his partner.

"We have hit the target, confirmed.!"

The other agent replied, "I have never missed a target in my life, buddy, and you know it. Now, this chap is going to die in the next 30 minutes, tops. Nothing can prevent that."

Saying that, the other agent lowers his sniper.

What had happened was that as soon as Jagat had stolen the sticker from the main conference room, his activity had been picked up by the RAW agents who were watching the security for this day. A sniper had been tasked for the next step, and a mini dart-like bullet had hit Jagat just outside the building as he walked away. Before switching on his mobile phone, he had been hit by another bullet, which felt like a prick from a mosquito at once, but it had made its impact in seconds. The entire dart bullet had dissolved inside his skin and penetrated his blood. It was a slow poison that would first create a side effect of speech loss, comatose state, and nausea and then kill all the cells inside the body in less than 30 minutes.

The ISRO employee offering Jagat water was another raw agent swiftly extracting the sticker from his mouth. The sticker was a high-end microphone device that picked up the entire TUESDA conversation. The microphone was secured and destroyed immediately by the agent, along with the data it had.

RAW could not leave any loose ends to this critical meeting. Usually, it won't be that harsh, but Bill had given explicit instructions this time.

There were no questions but only execution of the order from the chain of command that preceded from Kulkarni to the RAW head.

Even though the actual leader's meeting was about to start, they instantly made one decision.

And that was.

No one outside TUESDA and the experts working on the solution should know about the KRAAL situation till they deployed the ARK.

Chapter 10

Fair or Unfair: Does it Matter?

After 2020, the world has seen its fair share of changes in the economy, health care, politics, education, and almost all industries. The cumulative rise of multiple innovations in each vertical paved the way to the rise of spectacular innovations in space technology as well. High-tech robotics, Artificial Intelligence, and the discovery of new material and low-cost energy generation gave birth to a whole new series of space crafts, AI rockets, space bots, and even an accelerated push to NEBULA's tech peripherals. Amidst all this, a new cool company came out in social networking, known as SPACE4A. This was a social network where users, entities, and scientists could post live updates about the recent events in space, create multiple information channels for education, and opinions and create a globally connected ecosystem for discussions related to space.

SPACE4A was a welcome distraction to everyone, as erstwhile social networks grew themselves largely by promoting funny videos, individual pictures, stories and celebrity news from the past. This time, however, there was a meaning attached to the feeds and discussions. And SPACE4A became a sensation when NEBULA posted all its live updates on SPACE4A on the channel NEBULA4U. The TUESDA team maintained this channel as they realised it was their door to communicate with the entire world and feed them whatever they liked. However, most of the time, it was updates and truth only. For it is not lying if you withhold sensitive information. Nebula's handle had over 100 million followers on SPACE4U and was also always part of the updates on global news channels. On 25th June 2031, there was another post on NEBULA4U with a picture of the NEBULA space station. The post read

"Around 10,000 top world leaders and experts to leave for a 3-month trip to NEBULA to celebrate the year of space and discuss future of space innovations at NEBULA (2031)." The list below included a list of people who travelled that included US President Nathan, Indian Prime Minister Mr. Singh, Industrialists Polsky and Mahavir, other notable PMs. and Presidents and all the top wealthiest people of the world."

The comments on this post were mixed, starting from 'It's time that these leaders also do some hard work and travel to NEBULA. Poor scientists have been carrying the load on them for decades' to 'What? 3 months! Are they out of their mind? They decide to have holidays and let their deputies do all the work?'

27 June 2031, New Delhi, India

Ranjan Sharma is sitting in his office after a full day of working sessions with his team, calls with Kvalitat, ISRO, NASA, & TUESDA. This was his daily routine till D-Day 1.

D-Day 1, referred to here as the day the ARK will depart from the earth with the 10,000 inhabitants or, as we knew them, The Chosen 10K! D-Day 2 would be when the KRAAL appears at the battle distance to the Earth and the Earth Weapon, or UNIBOMB would be deployed. This will determine if the earth will remain or not.

Much to Sharma's satisfaction, all the world leaders had agreed to assemble all explosive devices, nuclear missiles, bombs, bullets, or even a tiny firecracker from all the countries in one central place. The place will be called GROUND ZERO.

Scientists had predicted and betted that according to the trajectory and earth's rotation, GROUND ZERO would be triangulated somewhere around Dubai in UAE, owing to its strategic importance worldwide.

Sharma checks his clock and realises that it's around afternoon in Keephatch, UK, where the offices of SCOPE-X are. He picks up the phone to call Arjun to report on daily progress and mostly to have a general conversation to de-stress. He remembers how he and Arjun Bhatia had become very close friends during the launch of NEBULA in the 2020s. After the KRAAL meeting in Bengaluru, Arjun was promoted to the head of SCOPEX, replacing his earlier boss, John Metcalfe. After the events, John retired early and decided to spend the rest of his time with his family, physics books, and golf.

With Arjun at the helm, things were moving faster and with no bureaucratic red tape. SCOPE-X was essentially acting as the scientific arm of TUESDA. Even before the famous KRAAL meeting this month earlier, Arjun used to report to Bill regularly for all the critical updates. Bill had already instructed John to allow Arjun to connect with him directly, with no objections.

The phone rings. Arjun picks up with Ranjan on the other side.

Arjun says, "Hey Sharma, How is it going?"

Sharma replies, "Fantastic, Arjun, Can't wait to see the KRAAL and party with it!"

Arjun laughs and replies, "And all it took for your sense of humour to come back was a probable mass destruction event."

Sharma smiles and replies, "Well, first, it's a certain Armageddon event and not just probable mass destruction. And second, my sense of humour was always there for my friends. It just so happens that some of my UK friends never called and checked on me before KRAAL. You know how some people get promoted and get too busy, right?"

Arjun smiles and says, "Aaah, I see my old friend. Come on now, don't embarrass me much. Tell me, what do you need, sir?"

Sharma, "Arjun, this time, I need a personal favour from you. I know you are also in charge of giving recommendations on the chosen 10K, or in short, who lives and who dies. Am sure you are making the right judgements about the candidates that can be referred. I wanted to just recommend someone on that list. You should interview the gentleman before you make the last call."

Arjun replies, "Sharma, you don't have to ask me that. I already am considering Rajat on the list! I will try my best to get the bright young boy as a member of the delegation in the KNOWLEDGE HUB for the Chosen 10K."

Sharma replies, "You misunderstood me, Arjun. I am not even asking you to consider Rajat for that. I know that if he finds out where he is going, he will never go on board

ARK. I will convince him to join us after the news is out. The man I am recommending to you is a bright junior project manager, Arihant. He is one of the most brilliant minds I have ever seen. I am sending his CV to you as well. If there was a course that combined all the fields of science, technology, psychology, humanity, engineering, robotics and leadership, Arihant would have straight away got Summa Cum Laude. Oh, and he is on the KRAAL team and aware of the threat. He is already vetted and marked for all the correspondence and communications. Though he wants to stay and not go on ARK, I really don't want humanity to be deprived of such a unique talent. So, I would like you to consider him, and even press upon him the agenda of his survival. That means a lot to humanity."

Arjun replies, "Are you sure? Why not Rajat? Ranjan, I hope you are not trying to be great and suppress the calibre of Rajat under your greatness. I have known him for years, having counselled him about his career. I think he would be a great fit as well."

Sharma says, "Arjun, I am his father. I won't betray his wishes, too. I know he would be lifeless in ARK once he eventually sees what had to happen. If it was left to me, I would have shared the KRAAL news and recruited him straight away to fight from now only. I am proud of who he is and know he won't say no to this mission. Once D-Day 1 comes, anyway, the entire world will know the actual news of KRAAL. This would be when the ARK would have been airlifted and crossed our atmosphere. And I know he would have thanked me and been happier with this decision. Even Arihant does not want to go, but I am so glad to deny him the satisfaction of a battle and have me in his bad books for the sake of his life. Trust me, you would need him more than anyone else. He is one of the best polymaths earth has. Let's just give him that chance, Arjun."

"Ok. Ranjan. I would look into that. Also, what makes you think I am going to ARK? You know that 10K list is selected to include only world leaders, industrialists and their families, handymen to do daily chores and labour, few scientists, doctors, engineers, experts, technicians, and good-looking girls."

Sharma questions, "Why the good-looking girls?"

Arjun, "You take a guess? These women have been selected based on many parameters such as age, beauty, reproduction system analysis, general health, etc. I mean, it's shocking that these old oafs would even think of something like this. Potentially breeding these women for producing future generations is something that could be even done clinically. I feel pity now for the fate of humanity."

And then he continues.

"Take one old-world leader or at the maximum 10. Why take thousands of them? Why are they filling the seats with deputies of deputies to these powerful men and women? 50+-year-old people from some ministry that no one cares about! What will these people contribute at a granular level to the future of mankind? It's all politics, my friend. Over 50% of the Chosen 10K is filled with people over 50. Rests are some chosen people like us, experts, women and their kids. I don't want to be part of that crowd, even in the afterlife. So

I asked Bill not to add my name. Hence, I will stay here, but some SCOPE-X scientists will leave."

Sharma is silent as he understands and empathises with Arjun. "Yea, I saw your name on the list sent by Bill. Trust me, Arjun, they would need you. We all need someone like you to lead humanity in case Earth is gone."

Arjun says, "Oh ya, they need me! Why don't they need you? What about Novsky? Rajat, Srini? Anita Naidu? Nidhi? Albina, Zoya? Do humans not need them? Why?

Just because they are not some high-ranking official in a Government scientific organization, or they are not some greedy wealthy politician, billionaire, a family member of these people, or Victoria's Secret model? Is this what we humans have come to? No, Sharma, I am not joining the circus up there in ARK. Let's fight here and end the KRAAL with UNIBOMB or else humanity is done and finished anyway. In my book, the people in the ARK are not the true humans."

Sharma feels proud of his friend and says, "End to the Kraal, it is then, my friend!"

Arjun, "All the way to it, brother! Now, please email me the summary of the day. I will also do that 5 hrs from now to you." and disconnects the call with a heavy voice.

Sharma remembers his last time in Bengaluru, some 2 years ago, when Arjun had come for some work at ISRO. Sharma was part of the project as well. Both had hung out after office on MG Road, taking a stroll down the Brigade road first and then going to a lovely pub/restaurant that served non-vegetarian foods and an excellent Indian beer.

It was their favourite hangout place, known as "The Maven40". Maven served the best Keema Parathas, a personal favourite of Bhatia.

Both ordered their fair share of Parathas along with Kaleja Kebab, a delicacy of Maven. They had a strong wheat beer along with food. It was a pleasant memory for both science aficionados. Great food, excellent beer, and a somewhat meaningful discussion about everything from Bollywood, Cricket, politics, Nebula, and even the recent research by Nobel Prize winner.

However, one particular discussion that Ranjan fondly remembers was Arjun's take on "The Darwin's survival of the fittest" theory. He remembers Arjun saying,

"Ranjan, I hear you, alright! We look at the history and see all these bloody conquests, the end of a few civilisations, mass murders, wars and whatnot. All this, just so a handful of humans can seize control and rule the land!"

And he gulps down an ounce of beer in a go and continues,

"However, just look at the parallel events related to these dictatorial conquests and mad-wars. Peace is always followed through. Few humans fight and lose their lives so that an entire human generation can have a better life. Remember the agents of change in human history from Noah, Jesus Christ, Lord Rama, Lord Krishna, Mohammad, Akbar, Gandhi, Churchill, Martin Luther King, Nelson Mandela, Mother Teresa, etc. They all bought peace and new world order, bringing happiness and freedom to the masses. It's as they say in our culture in Geeta,

Yata Dharmastato Jayah!

Or where there is Dharma, there will be victory. And I mean Dharma in the righteousness manner and not just based on religion."

Sharma replies, "There is truth in what you say, my friend. But the reality is not much synchronized with this statement. We see corrupt politicians, leaders, movie stars, and celebrities getting richer and richer, winning in commerce, politics, economics, entertainment, and what not. While the righteous ones are slogging day and night from 9 to 5 and waiting for their chance to arrive."

Arjun smiles and says, "I agree, my friend, and we believe those successful people are the ones practising Dharma, and maybe we are not working or not doing something right. However, in the long run, equilibrium is attained in totality. The evil is eventually always replaced by the good."

"And after some time, the good is further replaced by the evil," Sharma adds.

Arjun laughs and replies, "Or maybe the Good turns into the evil."

"For whom? Good or evil?" asks Sharma, raising his beer glass.

Arjun laughs, stands, and salutes Sharma by saying, "Oh my Lord Krishna, your humble servant Arjuna rests his bow and arrow and will accept whatever you say as Dharma."

Sharma smiles, looks into Arjun's eyes and says, "My son, Parth, Arjun, or whatever your name is, Dharma is what I, the Lord, dictates. Sign the bloody agreement tomorrow at ISRO, and follow your DHARMA and KARMA."

With that, both friends shift the discussion to the latest movies and their family lives.

Same time, in New Delhi, Prime Minister's Office

Mr. Singh had just got a brief of the economic situation and analysis of the root cause from his aide-de-camp, Mr. Pillai, an economics expert in the finance ministry. Pillai had no clue about the KRAAL situation, as he wasn't part of the meeting at ISRO. Also, Kulkarni (also present in the room) insisted on doing so per TUESDA terms.

Pillai, however, was very confused and unable to conclude the actual reason behind this unique global crisis. The crisis was a total stock market meltdown when many top billionaires suddenly liquidated their stock positions in even blue-chip and growth stocks.

"We cannot track out why are they doing so and what instrument are they re-investing for their value growth, sir. I mean, the meltdown is so unexplainable. These are robust firms that had withstood all the past crises and are now near bankruptcy.", says Pillai.

"It seems all of them are liquidating with the same thesis like they have formed a nexus. All IT stocks have devalued to their rock bottom. Manufacturing stocks and oil & Gas have also taken a deep hit, though still floating at a reasonable value," adds Pillai.

Mr. Singh replies, "Pillai, I understand your concerns. However, don't worry about these stock market fluctuations. These are not entirely new to the world. Every decade comes a year that defines the stock market's fall and gives birth to the new economy. And each of these crises comes suddenly with no warning. Also, you can only find the root cause of the crisis when it is over, and enough data supports the actual pivotal reason behind the crash. Then, the markets always self-correct themselves. In totality, the world economy never crashes."

Pillai, a little surprised at the ease at which Indian PM was, hides his scepticism and replies, "You are right, sir! I was just curious where all this money is going. As in earlier crises, the reasons were obvious. Every time, there was a logical reason for the subsequent event, whether it was the dot-com crisis, subprime mortgage crisis, or PUNSAM's crypto hack crisis. Only this time, sir, I cannot find any logical correlation or even a remote event that could have triggered this. And most of these accounts are now confidential, as the richest people on the planet who control the stock market triggered it. If you give permission, sir, can we request an audit of the bank accounts of Indian investors who are part of that list and find out where the flow of money is?"

Kulkarni, a little irritated at Pillai, speaks, "Pillai, what are you saying? You are asking for an investigation against these innocent industrialists. It's like a CBI investigation. With no logical reason or valid grounds, we can't do this. You remember the Bank Privacy Act of 2026. Every individual has complete authority over his/her information regarding financial dealings, including bank accounts. We have already placed safeguards in place regarding the digital payment processing system mapped with the Tax details of the individuals. No one can hide the tax as and when a financial transaction occurs. Currency notes are earmarked and exchanged by individuals through tags that can define the origin and destination of these notes, which are mapped with the tax details of the individuals as well. We have reached the maximum level of financial vigilance on transactions already. So, what's the use of getting their bank accounts now? Also, these days, everyone has an incentive to pay taxes. With our reward system, the more tax they pay, the more rebates, incentives, and scores they get for future opportunities."

Pillai replies, "I agree with Kulkarni. However, we cannot trace the transactions beyond the stock market one's now. We can account for these trillion dollars disappearing from the market but cannot find where they went. It's not like they are hoarding it up with the cash in their lockers, right?"

Kulkarni speaks, "And if they are. Let them be. It's their right, their cash. You can't prosecute them because they don't want to invest. Anyway, this entire stock market concept needs a complete overhaul now."

Pillai adds, "Kulkarni, we are talking about masses of normal people who are surviving because of the stock market. And that accounts for almost everyone in the world these days. Every big company is in the stock market. They employ millions of Indians in these organisations; any impact will impact them and create a cyclic impact on the economy. Let's not forget, everything is connected."

Singh intervenes in the debate and addresses Pillai. "Very well, Mr. Pillai. We can do that. We will put surveillance on the bank accounts of these individuals. However, this won't happen just now. We are preparing for a couple of showcase projects and agendas related to our major NEBULA event, as you know. Let that even happen, and we will get to these audits. Sounds fair?"

Pillai thinks, 'The entire world is in financial turmoil, and these leaders want to do a science project for the International Olympiad. We really are doomed!' and replies, "Agreed, sir. Thank you very much." He then leaves the room, disappointment clearly visible on his face.

Kulkarni speaks, "Sir, Mr. Pillai is extra curious, and I fear he might even find out easily everything about ARK, KRAAL, and the correlation of this financial crisis. He will suspect something big when he finds out that the entire money has been smartly placed towards the fast-track development of ARK and NEBULA's peripherals. Also, he is very resourceful, sir. There are ways he can even reach out to ISRO and find out the weaker links for information. If you allow me, should I inform Bill of this situation?"

Mr. Singh looks at Kulkarni with anger. "Kulkarni, have you gone mad? Pillai is our oldest colleague, a dear friend of mine and even yours. How could you even think of eliminating him?"

"No, Sir. I am not saying we eliminate him. Maybe we could even take approval from Bill to include Pillai on our side after sharing the KRAAL news with him."

Singh replies, "No, Kulkarni, that won't be possible. You don't understand the bureaucracy involved now. The Chosen 10K list is frozen. The people who know about KRAAL are either on that list or are marked martyrs, not on the list, who are tapped and observed every second. We need to be careful. Bill shouldn't know about this. After the KRAAL event, God knows Bill has gone paranoid and is calling dangerous shots every day. Even RAW now officially reports to him under TUESDA till the time ARK is launched. We must be sensitive and resolve this with intelligent dialogues rather than bullets. I bet that if this continues, within two months, TUESDA will be more dangerous than…."

He couldn't finish the sentence when his secretary Riya rushed into the room and spoke, "Sir, Sir, you need to switch on the Television now. Please, it's urgent. I am sorry to barge in like this, sir. Sorry, but sir."

Kulkarni says, "Calm down, Riya. Relax." And with that, he switches on the Television for the news.

Aniket Mandal, a renowned Television Anchor, is on the television and saying, "As you can see from the message, it is evident that the Indian Prime Minister is hiding something and PUNSAM wants that information out. What is that? What is the Indian PM hiding? Are they planning to attack PUNSAM? Or a bigger scheme? Is PUNSAM really what they claim to be? Let's hear the message again."

And with that, they play an audio file with a robotic voice that says the following. "Hello, Mr. Singh. We at PUNSAM know what you are all up to. Hiding such important information from mankind is not proper human behaviour. It disappointed us at the level you guys have stooped to.

Also, we are conveying the same message to your dear friend in the US, Mr. Nathan. Please listen to this carefully now. Mr. Singh, Mr. Nathan, and any XYZ who was part of that meeting, you should know that you have 48 hours to reveal this information to the public. If not, PUNSAM will bomb places of significant importance in the world. Let the public decide what's right or wrong.

LONGO VIVAS TEMPORE HUMANITY."

Kulkarni looks at Mr. Singh, who is confused, angry, and scared, all at the same time. He asks Kulkarni to call Bill urgently and requests Riya to give them complete privacy for a couple of hours.

Riya leaves and closes the door, goes outside, and sends a text to an encrypted number. She then sits in her chair and smiles before opening her laptop, checking occasional emails and agenda for PM for next week.

"Malos Autumn Punier", she hums the PUNSAM's second motto before returning to work.

Chapter 11

Those Slimy Loose Ends

The past few days have been spooky for everyone who knew about KRAAL. First, the entire shock of the news, which sort of sounded like a science fiction movie like 'Don't look Up,' '2021, 'Geostorm,', etc., Then, another emotion of acting as quickly as possible to save themselves caused a bit of hysteria among these political leaders, business leaders, scientists, and defence personnel. Everyone had been trying their hands to get a seat and get inside The Chosen 10K. They were trying via power, money, their niche, valuable expertise, or some even by just dirty old politics. TUESDA maintained the confidentiality and impartiality of the 10K list as much as possible. No selected member was told beforehand. They were all supposed to be informed just a few days before the launch in a very secretive manner. They also shared that the list can change depending on these upcoming months and who contributed to what sort of discussions. Only a few members had access to the list, and they were monitored carefully. This entire event caused a lot of panic among these leaders and members. Hence, a team of psychologists, therapists, yoga instructors, and mental health professionals were hired to maintain calm and composure. All team members who knew about the KRAAL event had to go through these mandatory therapy sessions. They were monitored under a secretive camera with instructions given to members to reveal their general feelings. Most of the therapists were affiliated with TUESDA... It had been a toll-taking experience mentally for everyone.

There were a few leaks here and there, but the task force had contained them effectively under Bill. None of the members who leaked such info to their family members, psychiatrists, friends, etc., were alive, along with those to whom such information was revealed. It was as if they vanished into thin air just like that. KRAAL was not just a celestial object that could take your life after destroying the planet but also a word that could take your life if uttered anytime before it happens. The only clearance given was to high-level officials who were working on the direct solution to the KRAAL problem. And those were the core team members of UNIBOMB as well as ARK2031. Bill had been running a tight machine in a complete military fashion.

25 July 2031 (one month later) – 5 months to go.

8pm, Sharma's house, New Delhi, India

Sharma's family was gathered around the dining table after a long time. The past few months have been hectic for everyone. Ranjan was occupied in the usual "Save the world" plan (this time for real). Rajat was busy with his new product launch and had worked nonstop with the developers and product teams for quite a long time. Zoya had opted to be an Assistant Director of a famous documentary maker and was travelling extensively. Nidhi, as usual, was busy with her students' project and her book that she had just started a couple of months ago.

Ranjan had been carrying the burden of hiding the disastrous news, which had not yet been released to the public. It's only

5 months to the KRAAL event, and already the preparations on both fronts were in full swing – the ARK project, which was entirely out of the scope of Sharma and Novsky, and the UNIBOMB project, which Sharma was leading along with Novsky.

Everyone at the table was focussing on their food, and there was an awkward silence in the room.

Zoya breaks it up and asks Nidhi, "So Maa, how much time are you going to take to complete that book?"

Nidhi says, "Well, I am right now halfway there or maybe a bit more. I can wrap this up along with even editing and publish it online in like around 4 months' time if I work non-stop. However, a lot of daily work consumes my bandwidth, and then I am just too lazy after work to do anything."

Rajat interrupts, "Well, Maa, don't worry about the editing part. I will have a friend of mine do the same and save you 2 to 3 weeks of effort on their part. Just get around the main content and rest."

Nidhi laughs and says, "Rajat, you know how I do things, beta. I like to be more independent and in control of my work. Besides, I enjoy reviewing my work myself and might even correct or change the book's structure. And it's fine, what would happen if I save 3 weeks. There is enough time to do these things. I am not going anywhere."

Ranjan looks at her smiling face and gives her a smile, holding back his emotions, especially the tears, as he knows it is not true. There is a lot he has on his mind but can't share with Nidhi, Zoya or Rajat.

He composes himself and speaks up, "Nidhi Sweetheart, I think you ought to prioritise this one, yaar. This is one of the easiest times of the year with no final year projects, exams, new admissions, etc. You should take a break from the college for one month and finish this up straight away at home. Anyway, you have only one or two lectures that you can live-stream from home. I am so desperate to see how your book comes out. Maybe I might get hooked on history because of it. Do it for me, Nidhi; think of it as something I really need. Let's do this. Let me know if I can really help you?"

Nidhi looks at him and smiles, rolling her eyes with curiosity. Zoya and Rajat look at each other and smile shyly, finding it difficult to swallow that their father just expressed attention and care to Nidhi in front of them – something that Ranjan would always shy away from (typical Indian parents).

Ranjan, guessing the awkwardness in the room, laughs and speaks up, "What? Why are you folks looking at me like that? Come on, did I say something wrong? She should complete a project like that asap. You know, I once read in a blog by a famous bestselling author that continuity is the key to writing a book. If you take a big break in between, the entire momentum goes for a toss. So keep writing, stick to the timelines and wrap the first cut fast."

Rajat replies, "Sure, Dad. It must be some thoughtful writer who said that. But you should not just say it today and forget it. I think your sweetheart, Mom, would love to get your support regularly, especially on this one."

Zoya adds, "Yes, Dad, see the sweetheart's face when she hears some caring comment from you. Wasn't that sweet, sweetheart of Dad to say something like that?"

Nidhi looks slyly at the kids, "Come on, you both. Give him a breather, would you? It's between him and his sweetheart."

Ranjan interjects, "Alright, so my entire family is a bully, yaa?" and looks at each of them and continues, "See, all I am saying is this, guys! Life is unpredictable. I am not saying some voodoo stuff like you should plan daily as it is your last. But come on, God plays dice every day from above. Or maybe Nature or, I don't know, something unpredictable runs the predictability across this universe. Not a single human being has deciphered that unpredictable secret. But what a human being can do is to give their best for every breath we get, right?"

Nidhi nods at Ranjan and then tells her kids, "Did you hear what Baba Ranjan said? Do you want me to record this so you can look at it daily?"

Ranjan says, "Alright, so here we begin…"

Nidhi says, "Begin, what?"

Ranjan stands up, smiles, and says while raising his hands, "Nothing, sweetheart. Important point – Baba Ranjan is right most of the time. And today, he is just sitting across this table, graciously eating the morsels of this heavenly food, spending time with people he adores."

Zoya gets up, hugs him, and kisses his forehead, "Babaji, where were you for all these years?"

After the meal, Ranjan sits on his balcony alone, and Rajat joins him. "Dad, got a minute?"

"Yea, son, what's up?"

"Is everything alright, Dad?"

"Yes, and why would you ask this, Rajat?"

Rajat says, "It's just that today I felt uneasy at the dining table. I felt something was bothering you, and you were trying to release some stress out there."

"Well, it's just work, as usual, Rajat. And I have been thinking about spending more time with you guys now. I think I gave too much priority to work and often at the expense of simple pleasures like breaking bread with you guys."

"Well, Dad, you know that we never complain. Besides, we were always excited about your work and what you stood for, really. Also, I never felt you were not there. You were always caring for all the important milestones and problems we had. One can always do more, but then I feel it was a perfect balance. I think something related to your work is bothering you."

"No, Son. You know the magnitude of my work has always been like that only. I deal with space and science stuff all the time with problems that are too complicated and mind-boggling. It has been years, and these don't bother me much."

"Oh, so then, Dad. Why do I see in your calendar an appointment with Dr. Bringaraj, the top psychiatrist in Delhi?" He pauses as Ranjan looks at him with surprise.

"Sorry for accidentally spying on you, dad, my tablet had run out of battery, and I saw yours unlocked. Had to check the status of who won the game last night, and by mistake, I saw a calendar notification for tomorrow."

Ranjan looks at him and says, "Oh, son. Don't worry. It's standard stuff. That doesn't mean I am going through anything."

"Dad, you know you can share with me, right?"

"Yes, son. Don't worry. I am all fine. You should rest now, for you have an early start tomorrow. Good night!"

Rajat hugs his dad goodnight and goes back. Ranjan receives a text from an unknown number.

"Hi Ranjan, this is the direct message from TUESDA top protocol. We hope you know we are monitoring. Our sincere apologies for putting you in a situation where you can't share this with your family. However, you realise such a revelation won't play safe for the entire humanity. However, considering the request by Mr. Arjun, we are ready to share this information with Rajat Sharma, head of BRAINPHY, and your son, as we believe he might just be the right mind for our operation as well. Let us know what you think. Hit a reply."

Ranjan replies to the message with a NO. One could see it visibly irritated him as he tried to throw his phone angrily, but he stopped. Then he evaluated who would have told the TUESDA guys about Rajat. They surely don't want Rajat's expertise and skills but are more afraid of the fact that if Sharma tells him the truth. As they can't eliminate Ranjan, for he is the brains behind the UNIBOMB and NEBULA. Bill knew they would need him till the end. So, they were trying other ways to comfort him and buy his loyalty.

Sharma would have loved to share with Rajat something more profound than just KRAAL, as he knew the states of affairs in the world were getting more complex every day.

This has to wait. Rajat would know directly from him at a suitable time. He had it planned.

He heads back to his bedroom but gets a call from Srini on his cell phone. Anticipating that it is for Rajat's candidature, he disconnects the call and texts him, "Speak tomorrow, too tired to talk".

It was a wrong guess, though. As Srini texts back, "No need to call. Just check the news!"

Ranjan returns to his room and switches on the wall console for the latest news.

"Another attack has happened in the middle of many global events, including the recent Britain elections.

This time the attack was on a particular space shuttle outside the ISRO's Special Deploy centre, recently set up on the Mysore Highway. ISRO head, Mr. Muraly, didn't comment on the incident. However, according to our sources, the blast targeted a particular satellite launch by ISRO, and an internal mole inside the ISRO orchestrated it.

The notorious global association PUNSAM claimed responsibility for the attack and released the below statement post-attack –

"Mr. Prime Minister Saaheb, this time, it is not a surprise. We warned you of the consequences of hiding this information. This attack is a preliminary warning as a major one is coming. We give you another 48 hours to release the information to the world and tell them what's happening in space. We can reveal that too, but all the global leaders would deny the same. Hence, it should come from your end. We won't reveal this news, but we will ensure that your evil plan is kaput. 48 hours or more BOOM, BOOM!"

The reporter adds, "This is shocking, and it left the entire country startled. What important information is the Indian Government and other global leaders hiding? Does the Prime Minister have no regard for the nation's safety? Let us hear from our expert, Mr…."

Ranjan switches off the TV and takes a deep sigh.

"If these nincompoops knew about KRAAL, can't they understand that revealing such information in a panic would destroy the world with mass hysteria? Of course, everyone deserves to know it. But not revealed by a terrorist front in a manner that causes panic."

This will have to wait till tomorrow. Not something he can solve or handle. This is a matter way above his pay grade and not his responsibility. And, he felt it was something he was not even worried about. The game was much bigger than this.

The same day, the White House, United States of America

Bill is sitting with Nathan, the president, as he rushed there immediately after the PUNSAM's attack. He managed the KRAAL project with laser-sharp precision and control at every front. His network of agents included all the top intelligence agencies, including CIA, RAW, Mossad, Mi6, ISI, etc., alongside his trusted deputed decoys in various governments, institutions, companies, and space organisations like ISRO, NASA et al.

"Our decoy plan worked, Sir. We are now very close to getting a top member of PUNSAM." Bill said.

Nathan says, "This was a good plan, Bill. I am impressed. Are we sure they only destroyed the fake satellite and not anything related to ARK?"

Bill, "Yes, sir. That was the plan. To find the mole, we orchestrated the entire information flow through various channels. We then shared that an essential part of ARK's engine was tested at this ISRO's base. We have already identified the leak and the person behind it and even traced how she used to communicate with her leaders at PUNSAM. We are now observing every moment of her."

Nathan says, "Whatever you do, do it fast, Bill. We only have 48 hours, as they claimed. If the world knows about this, it would be tough to execute the ARK deployment, and no one will be safe."

Bill knew what he meant and sarcastically added, "Yes, sir, we have to do it fast as we don't want the UNIBOMB project to be impacted too."

Nathan, "Exactly, yes, that's also a significant project, but make sure you don't let the ARK project be impacted. Thank you for your time. For now, I have a meeting with the Indian Prime Minister on the same topic."

Bill leaves the Oval Office and, on the way, reflects on his thoughts in flashbacks.

A day before, Bill had allowed a sensitive piece of information to be leaked and tagged by everybody involved in the ARK or UNIBOMB projects. Even the mole was aware that she was tagged and watched out, but she was cautious in releasing the information to her leader in PUNSAM. She transmitted it through a unique device that looked like a cell phone via secured one-to-one satellite communication. Although Anita Naidu was careful throughout and was very well aware of the communication networks inside ISRO, she wasn't privy to the latest updates by Bill post KRAAL meeting. Every transmitted signal to Land Mobile networks or satellites was intercepted, decoded, and decrypted on air by a smart tracking shadow network only visible to TUESDA.

Bill thought to himself, "Ancient Latin language, huh Anita? You think you are smart, but you are still human."

After they intercepted the message, the target network address was easy to track. It was sent to someone in Greece, and Bill's agents had already tracked the person who received the message. Although they did not know whether these people, i.e., Anita Naidu and the one in Greece, were part of leadership in PUNSAM. Hence, every step was to be trodden carefully to not raise any alarming bells to PUNSAM that they were on to them.

He gets in his car and calls Kulkarni to take further updates and the scheme of actions related to Naidu and PUNSAM.

Bill asks, "Any updates? What's she on to now?"

Kulkarni replied, "Nothing yet, but we have little time left. Should we nab her and interrogate her properly to extract everything?"

Bill sighs and replies, "Too risky. We might trigger panic in PUNSAM, and they might release this information. There is only one solution to this problem: a Mission Impossible one. Find out who is the leader who commands all the dictates in PUNSAM, arrest him or her, convince him by hook or crook to answer for us, and reveal the names of everyone in the organisation. We can tip not even a single PUNSAM agent off in this entire process. It must be carried out covertly and with great discretion. And from this moment, we assume that everyone in PUNSAM knows, and no one can be trusted."

Kulkarni replies, "Fair point. Let us wait a few more hours as our teams gather everything about Anita and place dots on her communication channels. We will pick up and inform you of any suspicious we trace out."

He then pauses for a while as he receives the latest email from his connect.

Kulkarni then continues, "Hey Bill. I have received something just now. Our friend in NIS (National Intelligence Service), Greece, has already identified the man in Greece. Wait for a second. I am just reading the report.

His name is Jared Lincoln, an American CIA operative who went AWOL a decade ago. I am sending his profile to you. The name strikes any bells?"

Bill shook his head, closed his eyes, and gasped.

"Oh my God, it had to be this idiot. Yes, I know him. We have been tracking him for many years for crimes against the US government. As a field agent, I worked alongside him many years ago. He was always a bit of an idealist in an extremist fashion. He could never understand politics and was dictatorial in his beliefs and ideas. These are the guys you can't change, Kulkarni. Even with life events, counselling, or therapies. He resigned and leaked the sensitive information related to a LATAM agreement with the extremists in Columbia and joined them. He went AWOL since then, and we could not track him. I always thought he would have minted some cash and retired as an anonymous hippie lost in the crowd or on a beach house or mountains. Never imagined he could orchestrate this much via PUNSAM. One thing I am confident of is this. If he is involved in PUNSAM, he won't be a pawn. He would either be the leader or one of the leaders. So this is a good lead and surely to be acted upon."

Kulkarni replies, "So, should we arrest him?"

Bill says, "I think that would be the right thing to do. As far as I know him, he likes to be in control of whatever operation he runs. And if he is running this one, I am sure he would have a lot more information on the broader program than a to-do list assigned to him. We should nab him subtlety not to ring bells in the PUNSAM community and then use the right motivational interrogation methods for him."

Kulkarni smiles and replies, "Motivational methods, huh? Are we talking about pliers, flamethrowers, and sharp laser cutters here?"

Bill laughs. "Those won't work on him, Kulkarni. He is a hard ball for those things. Might even die and won't care. It appears that out of all people, I know one of his weaknesses, which I never acted upon owing to my good nature or, you can say to respect the ex-camaraderie we shared. But now I don't care. It's time for us to visit Lhea Lincoln, his only daughter, a renowned journalist in the US. You might have even seen her on the TV sometime."

"Whoa, this thread goes beyond what I could expect. So you are saying the daughter of the leader of one of the world's top terrorist organisations is The Lhea Lincoln, the award-winning journalist. Why would she not be so sympathetic to PUNSAM's cause? I can see a post where she outrightly criticised PUNSAM for their action."

"Well, that's what is her stance publicly. Besides, we never knew her father was involved in PUNSAM, or we would have thought about it. But this is maybe her way of hiding that fact, and maybe she even knows the truth about her father. In either case, whether she supports him or not, I know that Jared loves Claudia a lot, and this is the only soft spot we can spot right now. You tell your Greek friend to get Jared and transport him to the United States immediately. I am sending a jet to pick him up. Meanwhile, I will get hold of Lhea."

And with that, he disconnects the phone and smiles to himself. Bill loved to be in control, and this time fate had just given him a brighter chance to dismantle one of the world's largest terror groups to make a more prominent name for himself.

But what's the point of all this if no humans are left on the planet to brag about his victory? He imagined the horror of what was about to come and focused on the road ahead.

Chapter 12

Jared Lincolns Story

They said the 20th century was a century of revolutions against the cruellest regime in human history. Similarly, 21st century was the beginning of a revolution against the harsh rule of centralised governments and organisations. Or so in the exaggerated mode by the media! A lot had happened with the start of a new digitalised era, from space exploration to cloud computing to blockchain economy and then space evolution. However, the significant control of everything that mattered on the planet was under governments and big corporations. Be it Oil & Gas, Big Pharma, E-Commerce, Agriculture, Warfare, to even the identity of every human being on the planet. However, still, there was a lot of freedom for creators and the new generation of entrepreneurs to come up with solutions and a system of change for something better. However, Space Exploration was the only place where the guardrails and guidelines were difficult to cross. This was the game reserved only for the richest or the most influential people on the planet. Nebula's launch ensured it would remain like that permanently.

With the launch of Nebula, the entire space control had literally gone into the hands of firms like PRIME-1 and KVALITAT, whereas the Govt agencies were only the branded front for the same. While this was not widely discussed in the media, surely it was a matter of concern for the freedom evangelists, decentralised economy lovers, and people who resisted control. One such organisation that noticed this was PUNSAM. PUNSAM never made such claims against PRIME-1 and KVALITAT on media; however, they directly/indirectly impacted most of their operations post NEBULA launch. PUNSAM's agenda and breadth of activities included much more beyond the duo. They fought for the oppressed in Africa, jeopardising CIA covert operations in foreign countries, executing a few tyrant leaders, and even toppling a major government in a Middle East Asian country. Nothing came short of a crisis as big as KRAAL. This time, the stakes were very high for humanity. And the methods of PUNSAM were never, so to speak, peacefully. However, this time even PUNSAM was in a great dilemma. Deep inside, one of their council leaders, Jared Lincoln, knew that if such information were made public, there would be chaos and destruction around the planet. The other council members were completely against making this information public. But, Jared wasn't willing to accept the solution by TUESDA, especially the 10K evacuation plan list. So he went against the other council members of PUNSAM and created his own plan to expose the Governments. He felt they might not create an ideal list with a unanimous vote by everyone on the planet.

20 years ago

Oslo, Norway

CIA agents frequently used the old house in Gamlebyen, Oslo, for decades as a recon-point of all EU operations. It was quite an unorthodox and unheard location, far away from all the action. It was strategically placed to provide a free, peaceful place for agents to stay and connect with fellow operatives.

The house was quite spending in terms of its interior finesse, and its charming facilities included a kitchen, big standard dining rooms, a control room, independent posh rooms for agents, an interrogation room, a bar, a hi-tech operations room, a library with a bonfire, as well as a small pool in the balcony.

Jared Lincoln, a 32-year-old agent, had worked for the CIA for the past 7 years. In his tenure, he was involved in multiple operations, both lethal and non-lethal. After doing an undercover information extraction assignment, he had just returned from Munich and closed the report on the same. After that, the CIA put him on a 2-month waiting period in the Gamlebyen OSLO house.

During this time, he befriended another high-potential agent known as Bill Scott, a software engineer turned analyst for the CIA. He had his hands full of diversified assignments from cryptography, data analysis, digital watch on terror, new-age space technology, and beyond.

They never discussed their assignment, which was the honour code CIA adhered to. However, the specific generics were always up for grabs. E.g., The story of Jared's last assignment where he had to work as a janitor for a tech firm in Istanbul to extract information for a specific use case. Or Bill's recent trip to Belgrade, where he worked as an IT Engineer for a telecom organisation. The stories would often revolve around the random dates they had, interesting pubs or joints they hit, funny stories about their coworkers, etc.

It was Sunday morning with Bill and Jared sitting near the pool, having their early morning breakfast after hitting the gym. Jared had recently got an assignment to be back to

Washington DC for briefing and was in the Gamlebyen house for a couple more days.

Jared says, "5 more days, and I am out of the luxury, man. Back to the field work. Gonna miss these long talks and the hangouts here."

Bill says, "Oh, don't sell yourself short, Jared. You will be back here in a few days. I am stationed here for the central recon for EU operations for at least one year. It would be a shame to spend time with the dim-wits here and talk nonsensical stuff about politics, weather, and play Bingo."

Jared says, "Well, I know you. You won't play Bingo with these grandpas here or enjoy visiting museums for history lessons. Heard from some DC folks that your adventures are of a folk-tale galore in the intelligence community."

Bill shrugs, "Yah, no second thoughts on that one. So, what's the plan this time? Do you have any idea where you are going now? And why DC? I thought the briefing would come here directly in a Mission Impossible-style – self-destroying those Bluetooth Earphones you are wearing."

Jared says, "Naah man, this time I feel that shit is for real. Chief wants a face-to-face with me. I feel it's something I messed up, man. Don't know but have this weird feeling that this time it's not about a mission, but an interrogation, perhaps."

"Whoa, big words out there, man! I thought you did everything by the book. Any buried bodies recently been dug out?"

"Well, you know, in our work, there is always a buried body ready to be dug out. However, in my defence, there is not a single buried body that wasn't buried there for the good of the United States of America and unauthorised by the top brass. I think it's about a second-degree impact of something I did that might be up for a discussion. I have a hunch of what it is, but of course..."

"Ya, ya, you can tell me, but for that, you must kill me, James Bond!"

"Well, in your case, I will kill you and then tell you. God knows how many listening servers are connected to your brain, and the data is streamed live to God knows who."

With that, they both laugh. However, that is interrupted by multiple gunshots fired across the hall. They both take their defensive position. Jared takes a spot behind the wall separating the outside pool area from the main entrance and Bill ducks just below the wall. The wall separating the hall from the pool was half-glass, half-cement. However, the glass was bulletproof, designed for such incidents. It could also provide a couple of seconds of protection against a continuous firing even through a blaster shot-gun.

Jared whispers to Bill, "There is a gun in the mini towel wardrobe behind you. Toss me that."

However, one of the attackers hears their voice, and he shoots the glass wall towards the wall where Jared is hiding. Jared ducks and slides behind. One of the attackers wearing a mask comes forward and tries to open the poolside balcony door. However, he is halted by the gunshots fired by Bill, who was just behind the wall. Bill had managed to quickly get the gun out of the wardrobe by then. The attacker retreats and shouts something in Norwegian to his friends.

Bill speaks, "Locals or I would rather say, hired local goons by some external agency. Listen, Jared, I only have one gun, so we must share. I can see that you have a clear sight of some of these men. So, I will slide the gun to you and allow you to shoot them. You know what to do if you see someone coming in my line of sight. This one is a Desert Eagle with 8 rounds, 1 already fired. So better count them." With that, he slides the Eagle towards Jared.

Jared picks up the gun with agility and checks the armed men inside who are hiding amidst the furniture in the main hall and repeatedly shooting with their AKMs. towards the poolside area.

Jared whispers to Bill, "Bill, open the window above you. I have a clear shot from here. There are three of them inside. Two are in my line of sight. So you know what to do after my turn."

They look each other in the eye for a flash second as Bill nods in comprehension. With a swift action, Bill gets up, breaks the windowpane with a dinner plate lying near him, and ducks again.

Jared jumps into action and shoots the attacker in the head. Immediately he hears the hall door open up. Jared slides the gun to Bill, who takes a clear headshot at the attacker as soon as the attacker comes outside.

There is a silence after that shot for a while now. Bill and Jared are in their hiding positions, with Bill holding the gun.

However, the third attacker is not making any noise and is silently manoeuvring his way towards the exit door of the flat. Then, with a sudden speed, he rushes out of the door and vanishes. Jared and Bill hear the door opening and the running footsteps down the staircase in the building.

They both get up, relieved to see the attacker has fled. They both enter the living room and take a body count. Unfortunately, 4 agents were dead and 1 housekeeper. They were all senior agents with significant field experience but were caught in a sudden unprepared attack. Bill and Jared were lucky enough to get a split reaction time, take cover, and could save themselves.

Bill sighs, looks at Jared, and speaks, "We need to report this." and then tries to walk towards the security line in the operations room.

Jared stops him by grabbing his arm and looking at him, "Wait, Bill, Just wait. Let's inspect the attackers first. I doubt they are locals or were just pretending to be ones."

He inspects the man Bill had shot and tries to search for an ID and a wallet but finds nothing. Only a face. He clicks his photographs and moves towards the other body. However, here also, he suffers the same fate. Only a body, no ID, no wallet. He then looks at their guns and the make.

"AKMSP01, Serbian-made automatic guns with 100 rounds each. Who carries such ammunition? Someone who is prepared to go into a war or a mass genocide?" says Jared.

Holding the Desert Eagle, Bill looks at Jared in surprise and speaks up, "What is that to do with reporting this incident, Jared? Do you think this was a setup?"

Jared is holding AKM in his hand and looking at Bill, "Think about it, Bill. The attackers knew the place and the exact time when all agents would come out for breakfast. The attackers also knew when we would be disarmed and taken out by surprise. Now, I assume this is not external intelligence like KGB, ISI etc., but someone else. Also, they could have just bombed the apartment straight away. Maybe this was a hit planned for one of us only. And maybe one of us was a mole who leaked this info. And it would be mostly in this house only. However, the mole could be dead or..."

Bill and Jared both look at each other. Their fists clenched onto their guns, and their eyes tried to read each other. In a split second, they raise their guns and point toward each other with their hands on the trigger.

"You think I am a mole? And why not you, Jared? You seemed to have escaped the attack, too. You were also well prepared and kept your gun in the towel wardrobe. Who does that?"

"I kept this gun as a part of safety protocol, and you know I oversee the safety of all agents here. Not only in the tower wardrobe, but you can also find 10 guns hidden in this apartment in every room. Now, be a good boy and tell me who are you working for, Bill?"

"Oh, no doubt about there. I am working for the United States, man. It's you who have been cornered by the people of your own country and getting an inquiry. I bet it is related to this attack. Now, listen to me, Jared. Things aside, you are a buddy. I wanna do you a solid now. Put your gun down, walk towards the wall and let me cuff you. We will handle it peacefully. No harm will ever come to you. You know that you don't have to worry if you are innocent. Come on, man, I am just following the protocol!"

Jared, "Oh, the IT guy is speaking. However, I doubt you are just an IT guy, Bill. With that precise lock on your target and the confidence you show in your fighting skills. I think we have an all-rounder here, don't we?

But I am not answerable to you or the idiots who think I am a traitor. I have served my country with pride. Now listen to me. Maybe it's not you or me. Maybe one of the dead guys. I am a trustworthy agent with years of loyalty and field experience. Give me your gun, cuff yourself, and sit here like a good boy. I will evaluate all the agents' bodies, search their rooms, and pray to the Gods that I really find something to prove that one of these dead dim-wits is a traitor. And then it would be my pleasure to cut you off from these ties."

Bill, "That's great, Jared. Let me pass on the gun to you so you can take another headshot. Well, we have come up to an impasse here. There is no out of this dead-lock situation. I am going to slide away from this house now. Don't follow me, or I will shoot. Now, as you can see from the sirens outside, cops are already there. And if we show the signs of running and shooting, they will catch us. Let's keep our guns pointed at each other till I get out of this hall and leave you to handle the local cops. Now, don't move, or I will shoot." With that, Bill slowly walks out of the door, pointing the gun at Jared and closing the door.

Jared throws the AKM, picks up his jacket, climbs the wall behind the pool, and climbs down towards the back of the building through a pipe. The agent training had served him well in escape missions, and this was a piece of cake for him.

He climbs down the back alley of the building and jumps to the ground with a low thud so as not to alert any authorities nearby. Lucky for him, no one was in the back alley as people might have fled after hearing the gunshots. He pulls himself together and starts walking like an afraid citizen.

And then, he disappears into the vanishing crowd of Oslo as he walks away from the building where the police are escorting the residents outside the road. There was no sign of Bill anywhere in the crowd. He pulls his cap down and disappears into the crowd.

25 July 2031, Tripoli, Greece

Jared Lincoln is sitting in a bar in Tripoli having his glass of Krušovice, his favourite beer, and just finished broadcasting a message via his laptop to the Indian Prime Minister. The message was straightforward. 48 hours to go, or the truth comes out.

He would have directly transmitted the news to the world, but he knew that the world leaders would have denied and suppressed it. And hence, it needed to come from one of the most powerful person on the planet. India had risen to an eminent power in the past few decades with its significant role in the field of technology. It had become one of the top 5 nations in the world, creating impact and value for humanity. And hence, the position of the Indian Prime Minister was really important to the world. When he shares the news with everyone, it will be undoubtedly believed, and there is no going back from there.

Jared ended his broadcast via a highly secure network backed by cryptic tech. It would have been impossible for anyone to trace the origins. He had been careful in all his operations worldwide and operating other PUNSAM members.

However, the only loophole in his operation was the network connected via his agents, especially Anita. But he had no clue of that.

He walks down the road towards his home, down the alley, lost in his thoughts. Fairly confident that the entire PUNSAM plan and agenda were in place, yet blase about the entire agenda. The reason was apparent. He knew a world-ending catastrophe was about to happen with certainty. And the only chance humans have is the UNIBOMB. However, he wasn't fond of the backup plan with the ARK project. How they did the selection of 10K members was unacceptable to PUNSAM and defied every principle they stood for. In his mind, he was clear about the right thing to do. Step one is for the Indian Prime Minister to release this news and share specifics of the ARK 10K plan. Step two is for PUNSAM to release a recommended list of 10K plans and get it voted globally using an online voting tool. And then put pressure on the world leaders to accept the same. PUNSAM had already started listing the recommended members in the 10K list. Their list included a range of people from Defence, very few members of PUNSAM's team, Experts in art, science, and technology and a fair percentage of a younger generation under the age of 40 to ensure fewer medical dependencies for a few decades for the entire batch.

He knew that getting step two accepted was difficult, and he had to latch on to different tactics for the same, including a coordinated mob revolution at localised places, etc. However, he was desperately checking his notifications to see the news about the Indian Prime Minister.

As he walked, he realised someone was following him and he got suspicious. He deliberately takes a wrong turn so that he doesn't lead the stalker to his base and keeps walking till he finds a lonely spot in a corner. He assumed that the stalker behind him knew this would be action time. Jared knew any movement could stir up consequences. The advantage of the stalker following him is that Jared can't look at him and track his movement. He knew he had to be swift. With blazing speed, he puts his hand in his jacket's inner pocket, takes out his tranquilizer gun and turns around to shoot at the stalker.

However, to his utter shock, he realises that no one is behind him. He tried to look around, but there was no sign of anybody. He sighs and admits he was just being paranoid, and his senses defied him this time. However, before he could realise it, he felt a tingling pain in his neck, as if something bit him. He realises a tranquilliser shot had hit him. Before he could make sense of anything, he fell down unconscious.

All he could see while fainting was the bottom view of an RC Silent Flying Drone that took the shot. In less than 20 seconds, a car pulled around the corner; two men picked up Jared and put him in the car, ready to be transported back to the United States.

Same Day, Bengaluru, India

Anita Naidu was working in her cabin on the current KRAAL data shared by the NEBULA. It was clearly within the statistically determined path and in line with the earlier findings related to the direct collision. Every day, she would tune in and pray for some deviation, but as days passed, the data became more apparent, and the probability of impact increased.

The 47-year-old scientist had been working relentlessly for ISRO for 20 years but was recently recruited as a shadow agent by PUNSAM through one of their recruiters. It was rather an unorthodox recruitment directly done by Jared Lincoln. He had the data of Anita Naidu's escapades with ISRO and the Indian Government. Anita always tried her best to get her point approved, though frequently, she was shunned by her bosses for speaking up or advocating systems of change for the world's benefit. It took PUNSAM a couple of secret encrypted chats, calls and meetings to get her on their side after explaining the real agenda behind the organisation. And she was in. She tactfully rose in her core job at ISRO, climbed the ladder in PUNSAM, and was at a Deputy General level for the organisation.

She had been carefully transmitting the messages to Jared since the KRAAL was discovered. She even acted before, on various occasions, such as the Canadian shipment contract, which she found was orchestrated via a high-level bribe at the Government level. However, with the KRAAL news out, her entire focus was to find her way to extract the details on UNIBOMB and the 10K list. But she had been only marginally successful, as she suspected she was under surveillance. She had hacked into the live-feed of all the cameras in the ISRO facility and had been confident not to leave any trace of information leak. As usual, she did not know about the fabric behind her office's curtain, which was infused with a nano camera layer (a relatively novel invention accessible only to RAW). Her entire activities for the past few months were not only monitored but recorded and transmitted directly to TUESDA headquarters.

She tried reaching Jared twice in the morning to seek the next steps related to the plan. However, there has been no revert till now. She suspected something was wrong. She waited and kept tuned to the news on the Indian Prime Minister. However, there was no news from that end as well. Suddenly, there was a knock on the door, and Muraly entered the room along with Kulkarni. She was shocked looking at Kulkarni and immediately knew something was off.

However, she calmed herself down and asked Muraly, "Hi Muraly, I was about to release the daily report on KRAAL's trajectory. Do you want me to take you through it?"

"Sure, Anita. However, before that, Kulkarni had a few technical questions related to Nebula. I told him no one in the entire ISRO understands NEBULA more than Anita. I will leave you guys to get acquainted and will catch up with you later, Anita." With that, Muraly exits her office, smiling at both of them, leaving her with Kulkarni.

Kulkarni looks around the office and sits opposite Anita's chair.

There was an uncomfortable pause as Kulkarni smiled and stared at Anita for a while. And then he spoke, "So, Ms. Anita. About NEBULA – There are a couple of questions I want to understand as we are planning to do a significant news release from the PMO today. PM Saab Mr. Singh asked me to look into the draft. However, I want to be thorough regarding what to tell the public about NEBULA and the KRAAL. Mind if you could help me a little?"

Anita felt a bit confused. She had mixed reactions to this. At first, she assumed the Indian Government had agreed to the demands of PUNSAM and was about to release the news of KRAAL and the 10K list to the entire world.

She felt a little good about it, which means their plan worked. However, suddenly that thought was replaced with doubt. If the Indian Prime Minister had to release this news, why would he send Kulkarni from New Delhi to Bengaluru only to chat face-to-face with her over Nebula?

Suddenly, the latter thought outweighed the probability of the former. She knew her gig was up, and Kulkarni was buying time. An immediate arrest will be followed, and she suspected that there were guards or cops outside already ready to take her out.

However, she had the last chance to take her PUNSAM mobile device from her drawer and immediately release the news to the world. She had to be quick in doing that and she wasn't sure if Kulkarni would allow it.

She composed herself and played along. "Yes, Mr. Kulkarni. Tell me, what do you want to know? I rather have an exciting short 2-minute video that I recommend you watch. Wait, let me try to get that on my screen." Without waiting for Kulkarni's response, she projected her screen on a nearby monitor for Kulkarni to see and started playing the video of NEBULA.

She looked at Kulkarni, who wasn't looking at the video. Kulkarni was looking straight into Anita's eyes. And then he spoke, "Where is he, Anita?"

"Where is who, Mr. Kulkarni?" her right hand slid towards her drawer near the desk. She realised she would need a few seconds with her phone at max to release the draft news to the world.

"Don't do that" Kulkarni immediately draws out the gun and points straight at Anita. He adds, "You might not know this about me. But I was top of my class in the close-range shooting. You don't have any chance to escape. There is no one in this building right now. Everyone is escorted outside by Muraly and his team. Now be a good girl and start answering some questions. How many are you? Is there anyone in India apart from you? Anyone in ISRO?"

Anita looked at him and smiled, "Well, Mr. Kulkarni. Do you think you can stop it? We have a protocol. If you kill me and my colleague doesn't hear from me in another few minutes, they will release the news."

"Your colleague, eh? I know that's not Srini or Muraly, for sure. However, you look like a big fan of Abraham Lincoln, a visionary US President, right?"

Anita presses her lips in shock and disappointment as she realises they know about Jared Lincoln. Without wasting time, she opens the drawer and tries to pick up the phone to send the news message, but within an instant, with a loud noise, everything goes dark for her. For the gunshot from Kulkarni blasts her head. She had no moment to react and lay dead on the floor. The entire plan was a failure.

Kulkarni goes near her chair and picks up the phone she was trying to use to transmit the message. He bags the phone because it might reveal the names and stories of other players in PUNSAM.

Or would that?

Chapter 13

You and What Army?

When the news of KRAAL was broken to select world leaders and top brass from space organisations and companies, like PRIME1 and KVALITAT, many procedures were planned for the remaining members in these entities. Fabricated news was released to the world. It was shared that the world leaders have planned a peace mission that unites the entire world in space. They will carry out the mission in a specially designed spaceship, ARK. This also was a demonstration of the launch of ARK. A motivational speech was planned by US President Nathan, whose slogan of 'Surprise humanity with global unity' started trending online. A sense of pride and purpose enthused everyone who was part of this program. They felt proud to be a team member of one such mission where they will contribute to creating a historical event. The date was announced already, and there was no backing out from it. They chose the 30th of August 2031 as the ultimate day of departure from the planet. Coincidently, 10 years ago, this was the same day American troops had left Afghanistan, another mission where Bill was involved. Taliban took over Afghanistan shortly afterwards. This time, everyone was working overtime with the sheer excitement of this project, except for the people who knew about KRAAL, which included top brass and key scientists. However, these people were bound not to tell anyone this secret and were closely watched by spies. They would take these people out, even for the slightest doubt about their behaviour. And by taking out, they literally meant taking out their souls from the body.

28 July 2031, Prime Office, New Delhi

An important meeting is taking place at CEO's office in Prime-1. Mahavir, Ranjan, and an extended team have been in a working session since morning. They were conducting reviews of scenarios for the ARK and UNIBOMB projects. Also, they discussed the concerns related to sourcing and procurement of some urgent materials needed.

There was a differential distribution of emotions across the room. Out of the participants present, only a few were aware of the KRAAL situation and bound by the secrecy agreement to not speak about it. These people imposed the urgency and importance of getting stuff done as soon as possible. Then, some regular folks believe this is one of the firm's other high-ticket businesses that must be addressed on priority. Many people have already been laid off, especially those who showed lack of proactivity or a casual attitude towards these two projects. The entire organisation was working towards just ARK and UNIBOMB. They shelved every other project. There was a light wave of suspicion around the UNIBOMB as a whole agenda and why it is needed at this stage.

Rumours ranged from space attack, demonstration of a higher order of man-made weapons of mass destruction, a UN agenda to unify all nations, a scientific experiment to create something beyond nuclear weapons and so on and on.

Mahavir spoke, "Ranjan, I don't think we should wait for any more. Let's do the last tests for the system32 required for ARK. This is the final leg, guys. Let's just shoot it and get over with it. It seems all ready, as you have shown. Why do we stress test it at all temperatures and pressure ranges? We already know and have tested the boundary conditions as per our NEBULA experience. Why are you now testing them for a new profile set of variables?

Ranjan replies, "Mahavir, I disagree with this. You need to understand that space conditions change dynamically, and it has been six years already. I believe some external disturbances around the layer 5 might cause variable pressure ranges." And looks sternly at Mahavir, signalling that he is hinting that KRAAL might impact the pressure ranges around the solar system's travel zone.

Having got the point, Mahavir says, "I know you need to be scientifically accurate, but we have a deadline for the test run, right? You don't want governments and our clients to give this project to someone else? Do you want some other organisation to work for decades further into this? I am not ready to take a loss. Whatever happens, the deadline must be hit. We can't delay it even a day beyond that. I hope you understand."

Nikhil Shah, a new recruit and a thermodynamics expert from MIT, replies to Mahavir, "Mahavir, we could have skipped the tests if the ARK mission was an unmanned one. However, we can't risk the lives of the people on the ship."

Mahavir looks at Nikhil and realises that the young boy is unaware of the situation at the end and is still in a scientific mood to argue about test boundary conditions. He simply nods at Nikhil and looks at Ranjan, anticipating a solution.

Ranjan sighs and replies, "Look, Mahavir, we can try to fast-track the tests as early as possible, but you have to at least give us the budget to do this. If we want to expedite it faster, we will even get external LABS to test for us. I hope a couple of million dollars is not a problem here?"

Mahavir nods and says, "Yes, go ahead. You have full power to spend as much money within your jurisdiction on this, Ranjan. But get it done before the deadline. TUESDA will pick this unit by 18th August and make sure this is working and ready by then. There is nothing we can do afterwards. And draw up a backup plan if the test fails and start working on that immediately. I am assuming you are on to it already, Ranjan?"

Ranjan replies, "Not yet, Mahavir. The boundary conditions are a new discovery by our team, so we never expected a backup. Besides, we don't know what would be the backup for this. This is a completely new field for us. I am afraid if the test fails, we must draw up manuals on safely manoeuvring the ARK under such conditions and let's pray those conditions won't arrive."

Mahavir looks at Ranjan quizzically and with a visible irritation and thinks. "The fool knows I will be on the ARK, and he will probably die here. He cares least about the ARK and will focus his attention only on UNIBOMB. I am pretty sure he is betting on the odds of UNIBOMB plan being successful and ARK being a failure so he could get rid of me already." But he corrects his thoughts as he reveals his masterstroke to Ranjan.

"Ladies and Gentlemen, that's all for this meeting. Ranjan, can you stay longer, please? There are some budget discussions I need to have with you."

The team leaves, whereas Ranjan and Mahavir stay inside the room. Mahavir locks the room as is the norm with all private meetings in PRIME. He then pours a glass of water and sits near Ranjan.

"I know, my dear friend. I know what you are going through. Believe me, I wanted you to come to ARK with us. I don't know why you refused. You and I both know that chances of UNIBOMB are rare. Yet, you want to risk your life. However, I won't allow that to happen to my daughter's future mother-in-law and sister-in-law. They are my family, too. Hence, I have invited Nidhi and Zoya to the ARK trip. I have already booked two seats for Nidhi and Zoya in the ARK. I hope you know Arjun has already recommended Rajat to be part of the operation and join the Digital networks space initiative program in ARK."

Ranjan, sensing what's inside Mahavir's mind, "Mahavir, I request you not to break the protocol in this case. I hope you haven't told this to Shreya also, as I would be forced to report to Bill. Trust me, I give you my word. I am working full-time for the success of ARK and UNIBOMB. I want both missions to be successful. I pray to the Lord that we hit the KRAAL with the bomb and destroy it while you have a six-month holiday in space and come back to celebrate this. Let's not think of any alternate scenario. Also, I don't think they will convince Rajat of this operation. I know him very well. Space science doesn't interest him at all. He is way too busy and passionate about his work. Why don't you proceed with the plan, and we plan a nice little wedding when you guys come back, my friend." He looks at Mahavir and smiles, realising that his boss doesn't take a refusal that easy.

Mahavir looks at Ranjan disappointedly and says, "Don't worry about protocol. I haven't told about KRAAL to Shreya or anyone. She is joining me in ARK as a representative of PRIME-1 and an external communication liaison. She does not know what's happening in space and that her future husband has been left to die on this planet because of a stubborn father."

And then, after a long pause, Mahavir loses it and angrily yells at Ranjan. "Have you gone mad, Ranjan? What are you talking about? Celebrations! Do you think a bomb can destroy a celestial object just like that? You and I have seen velocity profiles and the size of the object. Even if you destroy it with a bomb, there will be worldwide destruction. Have you got a bunker inside the earth's core ready? As there won't be any place left to hide, my friend. Even if you destroy it, there are higher chances that fragments will enter inside the atmosphere and randomly hit cities, states or even an entire country. Do you want to play dice with yours and your family's lives?"

Ranjan replies, "Play dice, my friend? We are already playing dice with the entire humanity. And that too, a dangerous one. They do not know that they might be vaporised in an instant as their world leaders fly without informing anyone of the truth. And they didn't have time to vote for who will live and who will die. We just thought and imagined that there would be chaos. We never attempted to find a mid-way, peaceful one where everyone would be at least given a chance to solve this issue or maybe come on terms with what's about to happen. Think about some people. A man working all day and night to make a living for his family, imagining that one day after retirement, he will go on a trip to the Himalayas with his wife and grown-up kids. A girl who is waiting to get married and lives in anticipation every day that one day she will get proposed to by the love of her life. A boy who wants to paint but doesn't have time due to his busy schedule and has postponed that dream for the later part of his life. A poor man who is just working hard day and night to see his kids get a proper education. Dreams of billions of people, stuff they want to do before they die, people they want to be with. Are we going to deprive them of all these last moments of happiness just because the secret agenda of survival of 10,000 top leaders is of paramount importance? Don't you see the agony here? Don't you realise what I am going through every day, holding this truth along with the responsibility of the entire planet in my mind? How could you ask me to be selfish and leave everyone to their fate? Once the KRAAL is up in the space, we have only a couple of days to get around the UNIBOMB calibration and target calibration before the doom ball aimed straight at us instantly vaporised the planet."

Mahavir takes a tough stance and replies, "Our history is full of events when there is a greater good overriding the...." he could not finish his sentence when Ranjan already cuts him and says,

"Don't you give me any crap about history, Mahavir! And I don't even want you to tell me what you are thinking. I am going to only request you one thing. Stay away from my family. Follow the protocol. The organisation is no longer yours. Everyone on the KRAAL project knows about it. You have already handed the control of the organisation to TUESDA. Bill has now appointed me to lead the project, or so to speak, this company now. You have got what you wanted in return! That is yours and your daughter's life safe in the NEBULA. I suggest you stop attending these meetings also, as I assure you that nothing will happen to the ARK, and you will safely land in NEBULA. However, let me do my work according to the best interest of this planet. Else, I would be forced to report you to Bill and get you completely ousted from the ARK as well."

Mahavir realises the truth and has a bitter taste in his mouth. Only he, Ranjan and a few top brass in PRIME1 knew about the nationalisation of the organization. Indian Government had given control of this project to TUESDA. Not only PRIME1 but all the major organisations working for UNIBOMB and KRAAL, such as KVALITAT, were nationalised across the world. They gave CEOs like Bazic and Mahavir safe passage through ARK and premium treatment guaranteed for the rest of their lives in ARK and NEBULA. It was a good deal for them.

However, the downside was the loss of control. The person who used to report to him could now dictate the orders. For Ranjan, it was only about completing the work and ensuring they met the overall goals. He rarely exercised his powers and control over anyone, including his juniors. But today, he had to do that, as he realised Mahavir would not listen to him otherwise.

After a minute, Mahavir picks up his leather Italian attaché bag and leaves the room. Before leaving, he says, "Never knew you had the nerves, my friend. Alas, they would serve you only for a couple of days. I believe I am done here now. Good luck to you. Make sure you follow the protocol as well."

And he leaves.

Ranjan, lost in his thoughts, realises that it's half-past seven in the evening. Today is Zoya's birthday, and he has a few hours to get a gift for her before the party. He composes himself from his anger and leaves the office as well.

Washington DC, TUESDA Interrogation Cell

Jared was locked in an interrogation room. However, this room was different from the usual ones he had seen in his career. There is no glass around the room from where an outsider can watch the interrogation. There are cemented walls layered with acoustic foams, keeping the noise levels low to the extent that one could hear own breathing. The floor was a hardened glass floor uniquely lit by LED lights, giving a weird, surreal experience while walking. There was no camera, no mic inside the room. Just a piece of paper and a glass of water on a table and two chairs around the table. One is where he is sitting, hands cuffed behind and his legs tied up tightly with the legs of the chair. The other chair is empty, and he assumes it is for the interviewer who is about to arrive.

Suddenly the door opens, and a gentleman wearing a black dinner jacket with shiny brown shoes instead of an FBI-style attire enters the room. As he approaches the chair, Jared feels a sense of déjà vu without looking at the person. He then stares at the man who takes the opposite seat, smiles and speaks.

"Hello, old friend. We never got to finish our coffee last time in Oslo."

To this, the man opposite Jared, who goes by the name Bill, says, "That was an expensive cup of coffee and what a waste of a day it was, Jared. Oh, and by the way, you look way too fat for a person running the largest terrorist network in the globe."

Jared laughs and speaks, "Clint Eastwood called! He wants his jacket back."

Bill smiles and looks at him, "So, you were the traitor that day also in Oslo, my dear friend. I never got to solve that case, as it remained a mystery. However, now that I look at it and how you turned up post that incident, I am fairly confident you caused that."

Jared replies, "I don't have to explain anything, you moron. I was not a traitor back then, and neither I am now. These world leaders and the entire top brass involved in ARK, NEBULA and anything else you are cooking in your kitchen are the biggest culprits here in the courts of humanity. And pity that you have joined them, nay leading the entire agenda along with them. I am ashamed to have called you a friend once in my life."

Bill replies, "Oh, me and against humanity. Was I bombing the world, taking away innocent lives, destroying public properties, and disrupting economic progress? You are the king of terror, my friend, and I am glad it ends here at my hands now. I am pretty sure you are the leader of this joke that you call PUNSAM. I want you to be a good boy today and tell me the names of all your accomplices and minions."

Jared laughs, "Oh, you and what army, Bill? Where are the torture toys? The gun that breathes fire. Where is the choke pear? The judas cradle and all the toys you would have in your inventory. Do you think I will release the names just like that? And you thought I was the leader here at PUNSAM? Do you really think I am a leader type, Bill? Well, I will tell you this. We are a leaderless organisation, as is clear. Look at the way we write our love letters to you guys. We believe in decentralisation, man. The actual power lies with humanity."

Bill replies, "Oh, we have DAOs (Decentralised Autonomous Organisations) in the terror world as well. That's a good one, Jared. Do you think I was born yesterday? I will catch hold of all the people at PUNSAM. Mark my words. Each one will die a gruesome death. And then, I won't stop there. I won't tell any media or top leaders the actual truth about PUNSAM. I will get all your devices from where you release your so-called love letters. And I will release a shameless fabricated truth about PUNSAM where you kill young children, rape teenage girls, kill at will, destroy humanity and eat shit every day in your diet plan. And then I will release the name of all the PUNSAM members who will be accused of crimes so heinous, dirty and low-grade that your souls will cry at your D-day. You think I can't catch more of you?"

Jared replies, "Oh, Bill, let's be rational here. You know what will happen in some time already. Oh, and by the way, what is the date and time right now, dude? I can't see any clock or device that can tell time here. Whatever that time is, one of our members will sometimes release the news to the entire world if they have not already released it. Now stop wasting time. Call the Indian Prime Minister to release the KRAAL attack news to the entire world."

Bill laughs. "You have been sleeping for a day, my friend. What news? What member? Oh, you mean that Anita Naidu from ISRO? Yea, the last pretty picture they sent me of her had a big hole in her head before she could press the 'I love you' button on her phone." And then shows her picture to Jared.

Jared looks at it with shock, grits his teeth, yells and shouts at Bill, "Release me, you numb-nuts. Oh, please, God, please allow me to break this guy's skull immediately. What did you do to Anita? Oh no, what have you done?" and then suddenly changes his expression and starts laughing hard and continues,

"You idiot of a man, Bill. You think that if you kill my girlfriend, I will melt down and release the names of everyone in PUNSAM. You don't know how many of us are here. And we don't fear death. Death is liberation, man! We live to die. When we started PUNSAM, we died as normal human beings. We dedicate every breath we take to humanity, and everything we do is for the greater good of humanity. Do you think we have failed? Many in the group will find out what has happened and take action."

Bill replies, "Only there is one flaw, you dumb wit. Your girlfriend could not enter the kill code in her device before my man shot her. And by now, we have already extracted all the information from her device. She only transmitted the KRAAL information to you and no one else in PUNSAM, as seen from her messages. And judging by your facial expressions, I am assured you didn't send this to anyone. Also, we have your phone that confirms the same. So, I doubt you hold any cards right now. Your gig is up. Your people are scared, and it's time to end their misery. I promise I will grace everyone with an instant headshot and death within a second as a reward. Also, there is one more thing I didn't mention. I already located Lhea, your daughter, and you know the lengths I can go if you don't cooperate."

Jared looks at him with disdain, realising that his gig is over. With tears in his eyes, he speaks up. "I know you will find a way to extract the names from me. I know your methods and am merely a human and a father. I will crack, and I know of that. You might have won this day, Bill. But trust me, there is a bigger play at PUNSAM that you will never know about."

He pauses and continues, "Do you think I was the traitor that day? I dedicated my entire life to serving this country, only to realise I was working for the wrong people. However, I am not dying in vain. PUNSAM gave me the true meaning of life, and I am proud of what I have done here. I would now like to say goodbye to you, my friend. Hope we can put aside everything, meet each other in the next life and enjoy a beer like old buddies."

He looks at Bill for a moment, presses his lips and says, "Adieux, old man!"

With that, instantly, he releases a tablet inside his mouth that he had hidden beneath the large cavity of his back teeth. A few seconds afterwards, he collapses after swallowing the dangerous, heavily dosed cyanide pill he broke in his mouth.

Bill looks at this with shock as he was unprepared for this. He curses himself for missing out on the checks inside the mouth, especially the teeth cavity. He thinks and curses himself. "Had to check all the unpleasant parts of his body and his things but missed the only obvious place to hide a kill shot. I guess I am slipping with the old age."

He realises he had lost the last lead he had on PUNSAM. Now he has to either wait for the following action or pray that no one in the ARK is from PUNSAM.

Either way, the chapter of PUNSAM had to end here as he had bigger goals to focus on now.

Chapter 14

Nobody Speaks, Nobody gets Choked

As the time for ARK and UNIBOMB was getting closer, TUESDA top brass, i.e. Bill, became more paranoid about safety and security of the information. He had created a team of agents and spies by partnering with his connections in the CIA, Mossad, RAW, ISI, Chinese Secret Service and more. However, as a backup, there was another initiative within TUESDA to recruit in-house spies and analysts to monitor and spy on key important people involved in the project. Everyone was a target now, all the Government officials, PMs., World leaders, people working in KVALITAT, PRIME1, NASA, ISRO, ROSCOSMOS, SERBSPACE, etc. There were internal recruits placed by Bill in all these agencies instantly. Recruits who were trained only for such emergencies by TUESDA. There were separate teams of field spies, digital hackers, voice analysts, behavioural analysts, etc., tracking the behaviour of everyone. Calls were taken even if the target had not revealed the KRAAL secret to any outsider. Some people were just eliminated as they posed high risks with their current behaviour. Bill couldn't take a chance. Even a small deviation in their behaviours, as tracked by their behavioural analysts and further read by their psychology experts, was a good enough potential danger sign for Bill. Many people were just killed and eliminated just to be on the safer side. However, some key important people were simply pressurised and counselled directly by Bill. These included Ranjan, Arjun, Srini, Polsky,

Mahavir, Kulkarni, Novsky, and all the World leaders, including Nathan, Indian PM, Chinese Premier, etc. Everyone, including a President, King or the wealthiest person on the planet, had no choice but to report to Bill and comply with whatever he asked. Now, they had no one else to trust and bank on the human survival mission. Bill Scott had finally become the most powerful person on the planet during these months.

But you can't talk freely these days without your conversation being tracked. And even your mannerism was observed and analysed by TUESDA. Special teams had come to everyone's homes, cars, offices, and even their favourite restaurants and cafes. Bugs, spy cameras, field agents, etc., were positioned at places of importance for these people. Everyone now knew they were tracked and couldn't oppose the norms too. Even if it is a private zone in your bathroom or bedroom, you have no choice but to live telecast and broadcast the same to TUESDA. Personal life had ended for everyone, and imprisonment in the world of TUESDA had begun.

9 August 2031, Belgrade, Serbia

Jovan is watching a movie with his kids and Albina in the living room. They all seem to be in a relaxed mood after dinner. It is Saturday night and late-night snacks and movies are on a roll. However, Jovan is lost in his thoughts, especially with the doomsday scenario coming up in a few months. Every day is like a ticking time bomb, and Jovan wanted to spend every single day with his family down to the last second. He even started coming home early in the evenings as his team worked day and night for the UNIBOMB and KRAAL projects.

Over these past days, Jovan changed quite a lot. From a jovial, cheerful and a full of life man to an over-emotional, soft, scared, and a grounded personality. Albina had noticed the change but never spoke vocally about it. She assumed it was the work pressure and some office-related politics with Polsky.

However, today she had noticed that despite being at home with kids and watching a nice comic movie, Jovan was brooding, sulky and looking at the kids with keen anticipation and a suppressed smile for a long time. It's as if he is hiding something. Jovan, already drinking his third beer, didn't notice Albina looking at him like that.

Albina feared if there was a health-related matter that Jovan was hiding from her and thought to ask him about it after they had finished the movie.

Suddenly, the phone rings, and Jovan notices it's a call from Ranjan. He ignores it and puts the phone back. He just nearly misses the text that was sent immediately by Ranjan. Albina notices it and takes the phone, and tells Jovan,

"Jovi, it's urgent. Ranjan is asking to call back immediately for some emergency. I think you should take this call."

Jovan replies, "Oh, him and his emergencies. I get some beer and movie time with my boys once a week, and the world won't let me savour that moment. What could be that urgent, sweetheart? It's not as if the world is ending tomorrow." He cracks into laughter. However, Albina looks at him sternly, not amused in the least and asks him to take the phone outside straight away.

Jovan gets up, picks up his phone and calls Ranjan as he locks the balcony from outside.

"Alright, Mr. Sharma, this better be something catastrophically urgent, or I will send the UNIBOMB straight to your bedroom," says Novsky in a half-drunk tone.

Ranjan replies, "Yes, please do that. At least, I would know it is ready. Listen to me, Novsky. I have to tell you something urgently…" he pauses and continues, "Wait, are you drunk?"

Novsky replies, "When am I not drunk, my friend? It is the perpetual state of us Serbians or Russians. Now, tell me the urgency for sending a message and a call on my encrypted device. Is it something personal?"

Ranjan says, "Absorb this, what I am going to tell you, Novsky. There is a reason I used the untraceable chain to call you on your encrypted device. Some funny rumours are circulating around here in the scientific community. You would remember that there is communication between a few scientists and the core team members. TUESDA is maintaining the formal stance of letting these people go and the fact that they are locked in a safe house till the UNIBOMB and ARK plans are on the go. However, I am hearing that there is no safe house deployed by TUESDA for anyone. You get it, what I am saying?"

Novsky, unable to fathom in his half-drunken state, speaks, "Ranjan Da, what are you implying at brother? Speak clearly. I am in no mood to solve puzzles."

Ranjan replies, "It means that they are probably taken care of, and rumours are that they are eliminated for high treason against humanity. Do you get it? That's why I am calling you from this number, as I know they are watching us. Don't react or panic; I hope you are not inside your house, as we both know they bugged it. We are watched, so maintain a smile on your face already. You don't want to know where I am right now and how I am talking to you."

Novsky, trying to gather himself, replies, "I hope you are safe, my brother. What do you want me to do? I know no one is watching me as I stand here on my balcony with the only view of a big fountain wall and no one around here. The cameras and bugs are in the house only, as we all know. These idiots didn't even spare my bathroom. The feeling of living like a pig to be slaughtered is killing me."

"I understand you, brother. Believe me, I have a wife and daughter myself; it is unimaginable what we are going through right now. I wish the Governments could share this freely and not act this paranoid. For all we know, this is Bill's mastermind, and you know once the man sets his mind on anything, he will make it happen. I suspect all those kills are carried out directly under the supervision of Bill only."

Novsky replies, "Do you think Anita Naidu also was?"

Ranjan cuts him in between. "Don't take that name, Novsky, and risk anything. I just called you to take as much caution as possible. I immediately called you once my sources gave me this information. And I know how you were feeling today in our morning con-call. So, I was worried if you spoke anything with your family. You know that if you share this with them, their lives will be at stake, too."

Novsky looks back through the window in the living room, the movie is still on, and the kids and Albina share a good laugh over a fight scene. He replies to Ranjan, "Don't worry, Da. No one will know anything or suspect anything. You take good care, my friend, and thank you for calling. It's good to talk to someone on the same side. Even the Shrinks are not helping these days." he disconnects. However, he is drunk today and got in the mood to mock TUESDA intelligence agents. So, as soon as he enters the living room from his balcony, he looks straight into the wall clock where he knows a hidden camera is. He smiles, points his finger at it and makes a shooting gun sign as he walks away.

He then joins his kids and Albina and resumes the movie. A few minutes later, the family realised that a weird, foul, pungent smell was coming from their kitchen. Novsky gets up to check, and before he could enter the kitchen, he hears loud noises outside his apartment. He suspects a few people are outside the house and saying something in a muffled voice to each other. He tries to go to his room to get his gun as he has no time to lose as the kids and Albina are in the living room.

At that exact moment, there is a loud thud on his door, and four gunmen break down his door and storm inside his apartment. The gunmen were masked and asked the entire family to raise their hands and sit down on their knees. They then grab everyone in the room by pointing their guns at them and dragging them out of the apartment. The family had not a moment to react and were forced by the gunmen to go inside the lift and to the ground floor. A black SUV was parked outside the building, where the family was taken away. Before entering the SUV, Jovan notices that the entire security in the building was knocked down by the gunmen, and one of their members repeatedly warned residents through the security control speaker not to come out of their flats if they wanted to live.

Jovan, Albina, Alexei and Maxim were put in the back of the SUV and looked at each other in tears. Jovan signals to all of them that it will be Ok. They had realised if the gunmen wanted to kill them, they would have done by now. However, there is something that these people would want and that's why they are being kidnapped.

One masked gunman gives the family a bottle and forces them to drink from it one by one. They all do, and within a couple of seconds, Novsky, Albina, Maxim and Alexei fall asleep.

The gunman removes his mask and tells the driver, "Straight to the airport. The boss has already got the chartered plane ready for them. Jobs almost done, boys."

New Delhi, Same Time

Ranjan just finished his call with Novsky and comes out from the restroom of a liquor store where he went just to take this confidential call. He realises he is being followed by someone but ignores that, as he has been used to the scrutiny for the past few months by now. Ranjan is confident that the aforementioned spy could not track him in the restroom this time. He was tracked only until the time he was in the liquor store. However, the gentleman could not follow him inside the restroom of the liquor store itself. It was Friday night, and there was a tremendous rush in the store. The spy clinched his fists, unable to track Ranjan this time and miss out on what Ranjan did in the restroom. The spy prayed to the Gods that it would be an unpleasant activity he missed out tracking.

On the way home, Ranjan calls Arjun through his official phone to discuss the updates. The TUESDA call tracking software picks the call up in parallel, and the analysts listen to them for any suspicious discussion that might lead to any treason.

Keephatch University, UK

Arjun is almost packing his things after a long day and an update call from Ranjan. The project UNIBOMB is showing some early signs of success in the simulation, and he feels hopeful after a long time. Now the most challenging part is to get everything in one place. i.e. the GROUND ZERO in a desert in UAE. They had barricaded the Arabian desert with one of the largest barricades built around the planet. They informed the locals that a major minerals and oil exploration project had been commissioned here. But there had been rumours around everything, including a nuclear weapon, warzone, secret military base, etc. UAE had never seen this influx of foreign military residents and so many classified vehicles carrying CONFIDENTIAL equipment. No one ever realised that in a few days, all the nuclear weapons, bombs, missiles, etc., would be placed in the desert. Arjun had been overseeing the project with minute details and tracking every shipment himself with his team. It had frustrated him with the delays that have happened as there were many RYAN Bombs and Nuclear warheads that had not yet reached UAE and were not cleared by the countries of their origin pending a few tests.

Just as he was about to leave his office, Jason entered the room without knocking or warning and spoke, "Boss, wait for a couple of minutes, as I have to show you this."

Arjun is aware that Jason is one of the few people who have been cleared on the ARK project, is mindful of the KRAAL danger, and has also been on the watch-list. Arjun closes the door and returns to his desk, where Jason had just connected his computing disk to Arjun's screen.

Arjun replies, "What am I seeing, Jason?"

"Look at this, boss. This is the trajectory of KRAAL and the corresponding trajectory of NEBULA within the same time zones. If you notice, there is a time when we can manoeuvre NEBULA to come close enough with KRAAL to provide us with an impact radius for an explosion."

Arjun asks, "Explosion of what and with what? Speak clearly, Jason."

Jason replies, "Boss, did you forget already? Ryan Bomb!"

Arjun replies, "We have discussed that at length. Ryan Bombs are effective only for a small-scale object, Jason! We have already ordered the remaining 100 Ryan Bombs to become part of UNIBOMB. Also, the impact will not be significant enough to blast the KRAAL. That's why we got all the nukes, guns and even a damn pitchfork left on this planet transported to the Arabian Desert. How in the hell will 20 Ryan Bombs on NEBULA destroy the KRAAL?"

Jason replies, "Boss, that's the difference between linear thinking and radial thinking," he chuckles. But realises that

Arjun is in no mood for jokes as this is a sensitive matter. So he takes a pen and paper and draws them up for him.

"Alright, look at this picture. This is 100 Ryan Bombs, nukes and your pitchforks hitting the KRAAL linearly in a line and barely able to destroy KRAAL because of the nuclear bomb impact only, and the rest of the bombs are just aiding the destruction and fire inside. Now, look at this second picture. There is an object not as large as earth but fairly competitive to Kraal. I am talking about NEBULA here. Now, if we increase the speed of this object at just this precise point. And then, after a certain time beyond this point, it hits KRAAL with a particular velocity, and exactly at that instant, we activate all the RYAN bombs along with it. Then, maybe we have a brighter chance of its destruction. I have an early simulation that suggests that it will cause significant damage to KRAAL and deviate it from its usual trajectory. It will wander away from the planet earth to somewhere else."

Arjun looks at the picture with keen interest. And then thinks for a while. Jason was suggesting not to use the Ryan Bombs at NEBULA but to use NEBULA as the bomb for KRAAL.

"Hmm, this isn't a completely absurd idea, Jason. However, you realise a few things here:

1. All the bombs must be activated precisely at a particular time.
2. NEBULA's velocity and speed must be adjusted and re-adjusted for various situations as you don't know what kind of thermal and heat profile the approaching event would generate.

3. Last and the most important, it will exterminate NEBULA. So in case if this doesn't work, the ARK will have nowhere to go, and the people inside the ARK will only have a few months to survive. Remember, NEBULA is their survival strategy for the next 5 to 10 decades.

However, I see from your work that theoretically, there is a 60% chance of success per the simulations you run. This is a very higher chance of success for such an event. However, there is a 40% chance of failure and the fact that NEBULA either misses KRAAL or maybe there is something inside the KRAAL that we don't know. What if it doesn't work?"

Jason replies, "If it doesn't work, there for something mysterious inside the KRAAL, and the chances for UNIBOMB also decrease, Arjun. And any which ways we will be doomed to death if it fails there and at the earth. We have nothing left at our disposal after that. Try to understand, that if my plan fails, then the UNIBOMB will certainly fail as well. So, I recommend first hitting it with the bomb made by the combination of high-speed NEBULA and Ryan. Then post then, activate UNIBOMB a few days afterwards."

"You are thinking of the people on the planet, Jason. But, remember, we have a hope for humanity to exist beyond this event. That's precisely the reason they design ARK for."

Jason looks at Arjun. "ARK will carry an entire lot of scumbags from the planet except for you, professor. I say we give this solution its own chance for the entire humanity to survive."

Arjun looks at him and says nothing, but he gives him a sign to stop continuing the conversation on ARK's10K people. Jason realizes he is talking directly to Bill as everything inside SCOPEX is bugged, listened to, analysed, and acted upon.

Arjun replies to Jason, "Leave this on my desk. You go home now. I will dispatch this to Bill and discuss the next steps with him."

Jason leaves the computing device on the desk with a bit of discontent as is portrayed on his face and leaves Arjun's office.

As soon as he leaves, Arjun gets a call from Bill.

"So strike Nebula with KRAAL, Arjun? A brilliant plan your minion has worked out for saving humanity, I must say," Bill says.

Arjun feels disappointed as he realizes Bill was monitoring the conversation from some hidden microphone.

He replies, "I am sure you would have picked up this conversation from some microphone hidden inside some book or carpet, maybe."

Bill replies, "Don't you worry about debugging your office, my lad. Focus on what lies ahead. You know we can't take any risk for ARK and NEBULA, right? If the RYANS and NEBULAS miss out on KRAAL or make no impact, then we are doomed. Where will we go then? I suggest you bury this data right here itself and forget all about it, understand?"

Arjun pauses for a moment and then replies, "Understood, Bill. Let me send the data to the central server, so you have it in your access as well, just in case."

Bill replies, "Don't you worry about that, Arjun. You can check the computing device Jason left has already been erased. We have looked for all the documents and scientific work related to this simulation. Everything wiped off instantly except..." he pauses and says, "You know what I mean. I will always protect you, son. But you need to understand why and what I am about to do." Bill disconnects.

Arjun knew what was coming ahead and clenched his fists and closes his eyes. How could he miss this? He should have immediately stopped Jason and left the office for good before Jason could say anything. Silently, he offers a prayer for Jason. He knows his best scientist is about to meet his doom not via KRAAL but in a few moments only at the orders of Bill.

But nothing could be done now.

The next day, the SCOPEX team gathered for a few moments to observe silence for one of the best scientists who died of a car accident on the highway as he returned to his home the night before. Arjun Sharma, silent for a few moments, curses himself for not having saved him. He silently prays for Jason and to God that no other scientist in SCOPE-X starts thinking out of the box for a solution. He realises the top brass have made their mind. They don't buy into the idea of UNIBOMB and are only focused on how to survive for a lifetime living in a luxury holiday in ARK and then later NEBULA. The worst part is that many people who will not be in ARK and NEBULA support their plan. They are helping them in everything from research, analysis, construction, killing innocent people, suppressing information, and even spying on their behalf. Bill surely is one person not to be messed around. Arjun realises if he acts on anything against what's happening around him, Claudia and Samantha would be in danger. Not only that but the entire work would also be wasted if he and his family died. He needs to be alive to see the doomsday and ensure everything for UNIBOMB is foreseen properly as well.

He thinks to himself and remembers the dialogue from his favourite series, 'Narcos'.

"Only the cockroaches can survive a nuclear holocaust."

It's not a time to be brave for sure.

Chapter 15

Playing God for Everyone

When the NEBULA project was envisioned, the council had produced at least 10 NEBULAs in the 21st century to be stationed across various peripherals of space. These NEBULAs will serve as the conduit for continuing space exploration beyond our solar system. These will also serve as battlegrounds for the sustenance of humans for any catastrophic event in the future. However, no one had imagined that the time to use them would come so soon. The predictions made by the experts in global warming, virologists, scientists and futurists are that the doomsday will arrive at least after 1000 years from the 21st century. By that time, there would be enough NEBULAs around the space, and they will migrate many humans to newer planets, create new NEBULAs and keep exploring the space for new heavens. It was classic Isaac Asimov's "Foundation" coming to the actual life plan. However, the intelligent scientists missed out on one critical element of the project. Who lives and who dies in a doomsday scenarios? Who will be the first to be rescued? What sort of humans will go on exploration, etc.? The psychological and evolutionary aspects of human beings beyond our planet were the foundation of the entire subject of 'Natural Order.' But just like other new subjects and specialisations take time to develop, Natural Order was going through unprecedented evolutionary changes. Few were pioneers in the subject, including top psychoanalysts, scientists, biologists, etc. Each of them held their individual opinion towards the subject fashioned, influenced mainly by their pedigree and experience.

The first-degree program in 'Natural Order' was yet to be created, and KeepHatch University was supposed to be the first pioneer institute to offer the same. However, the entire program was overseen by the top brass in TUESDA, who recommended a different approach. They allowed only a few handfuls of vetted students to study the same. It had been 11 years since the concept was first introduced, yet there were only a few research papers on the topic. It was supposed to be a lifelong project of Arjun Bhatia, parked aside now because of the KRAAL crisis. Only a natural order student or expert would have solved the problem of human existence beyond the apocalypse, which ideally should be part of the evolution program at the ARK. It was an oxymoronic thing, a topic made redundant and dead now, thanks to the politics and individualistic agendas of TUESDA top brass. There were few supporters of 'Natural Order' though, and you already know the fanboys of the subject – Arjun Bhatia, Ranjan Sharma, Novsky, Srini and a few loyalists to these people.

11 August 2031, Durbar Square, Kathmandu, Nepal

An isolated building marked as 'New Design Architects' was located just outside the Durbar Square market in Kathmandu. To everyone in the area, it was an interior design/architecture company that led unique projects inspired by heritage places like palaces, temples, etc. All the clientele was global, and the company was strategically near one of the World's heritage sites.

The entire team was full of ex-pats, mostly with only one or two Nepali nationals. The building also had a residential floor, where the unit used to stay. There were also guest apartments for infrequent guests.

One could find a unique mixture of people from different countries like China, India, Greece, the US, the UK, Russia, Latin America and many more.

There was, however, a recent addition to the list. Four uninvited guests from Serbia – a man, a woman and two boys.

Novsky slowly opens his eyes and sees Albina, Maxim and Alexei in a small flat where it is not as cold as in Serbia. He was lying on the bed, and along his side were seated – Albina, Maxim and Alexei. He saw the kids had just finished eating the food, and Albina sat beside Novsky, trying to wake him up.

Novsky asks Albina, "Where are we, Albina? What is this place? Are you guys ok? Alexei, Maxim, are you guys ok?"

Albina, Alexei and Maxim come closer to Novsky and give him a hug and are glad to see Novsky feeling better and waking up.

Albina replies, "Yes, sweetheart. We are all ok. At first, I was scared that they might put us in prison. But strangely, these people have been awfully nice to us. They want us to stay inside and not leave the room. One of their security guards, standing outside the door, guards us. However, don't worry; we are safe and have this place for ourselves. I was waiting for you to wake up as their leader wanted to talk to you. I don't know if I should be afraid. They have given me some kind of tea that has made me a lot more relaxed. I am afraid the boys and I might have been drugged to feel relaxed. Wait, let me give you a glass of water."

Novsky drinks the water, stands up, and asks Albina to stay away from the door. He tries to open the door and sees a guard outside. The guard notices Novsky and asks him,

"Sir, are you feeling better now? Do you need anything? Some food, drink or something?"

Novsky was shocked at once, as the guard seemed awfully nice to him. Novsky replies, "No, sir. I am fine. I would like to talk to your leader, or whosoever got us here as we have many questions. You would understand, I am sure!"

The guard replies, "Sir, don't worry. You will meet her soon. Please stay inside. It's not too safe for you to be seen outside."

With that, the guard gets up and comes closer to Novsky as he asks him to close the door.

Novsky closes the door, goes back to the sofa and sits, waiting for someone to come up and explain everything.

A few moments later, the door opens, and a familiar face greets Novsky and his family.

"Kaamna!" Novsky literally cries out her name.

The lady dressed in casuals, wearing specs, greets Novsky and replies, "Hello, friend. How are you? My apologies for getting you like this."

Then turns to Albina,

"Hello, Albina! The last time I met Mr. Novsky, the only story I would hear was that of you and your boys. Let me guess, this one is Maxim, and the other one is Alexei, right, guys?"

Albina just waves at her and quizzically looks at Novsky.

Novsky asks Kaamna, "Wait a minute. What are you doing here? And who are you? I thought you were an air hostess."

Kaamna senses a bit of confusion and jealousy in Albina and comforts both by saying, "Guys, I know this is weird. First, Albina, your husband and I met in a pub in Bengaluru and just had a little chit-chat. So, relax! There is no story here. Besides, I am happily married. Remember, I told you that Novsky?"

Novsky smiles and softly replies, "How charming, Kaamna! Now that we are such good family friends, why don't we plan a dinner here? By all means, please invite your husband as well. And oh, by the way, during the dinner, maybe you could tell me who are you, why did you kidnap us, and what are we doing here?" He practically yells while narrating the last line.

Kaamna tries to calm him and speaks, "Ok. Sit down everyone. I'll tell you why you're here. Mr. Novsky, you know that your entire house was bugged, right? Like everywhere, it had cameras, listening devices, pressure sensors, temperature sensors and whatnot. We are not the ones who did it, but you already know who did it. TUESDA has now started acting as GODS deciding who lives and who dies. And you know all the stories. We just went one step ahead and started tracking some of TUESDA's activities. They think that they have moles and spies everywhere. But we are no less as well. We have been following you for a long time. Not only you, but we have also been tracking many people of key notable importance within the TUESDA ecosystem. When you flew to Bengaluru, our team hinted that something very catastrophic was coming ahead. That's why I did a reconnaissance with you. I am sorry that I bugged your phone while we were having a little chat, and you went to the restroom for a while. Since then, we have been tracking you and your activities. Now, for all of us, you have been an ideal role model, sir. Someone who wants to do good things but cannot because of someone else."

In between, Albina interrupts her, "Wait, a second. What are you saying? We were bugged, watched by TUESDA. Why? What is TUESDA doing in our home, Jovi? Is she telling the truth? Why are we being spied upon? You are just a scientist. What have you got yourself involved in?"

Jovan asks Albina to calm down and says, "Listen, sweetheart. I have done nothing. But the project I am involved in is a top-secret global project which I could not share with you yet. I am not sure if I should...." And then he rubs his head and covers his face in his hands.

Kaamna adds, "Well, Mr. Novsky. We know about KRAAL for your information. That is one reason we were studying you and assessing the next steps for this. So, when your call got over with Ranjan, we saw that the gas valve in your kitchen was automatically released. You never realised that a week ago, a few repair workers came into your house for routine A&M and had installed a lethal inflammable gas chamber in your kitchen. If my estimate is correct, they kept it inside a closet, along with your supplies. As soon as you looked at the camera, we believe TUESDA panicked. Immediately, we knew the response would be lethal. Hence, we sent a ready squad team near your location to pick you up. Since they released the gas, we had no time to explain to you and had to act like kidnappers to get you guys off from there. Let me show you what happened after we left, by the way."

After that, Kaamna shows them a picture on her phone of a completely burnt flat. It was Novksy's house, where four of them have lived happily for years.

Albina goes into shock and cries, holding Alexei and Maxim, and says, "Oh, my God. Jovi, what is this? Why would anyone want to kill us? Explain what you have done? Why did you put us all in this grave danger?"

Novsky realises it's time to act on the truth now and tells Albina and the kids about the KRAAL event, NEBULA, ARK and UNIBOMB. After he tells the entire story, there is an uncomfortable silence across the room.

Albina and the kids are in utter shock as they realise that the world is about to end. She is in utter disbelief and sits holding Alexei and Maxim close like a statue.

Kaamna replies, "Guys, I am sorry to break a family moment here. However, I want you guys to stay here inside this room only. Trust me, TUESDA has spies everywhere, including Kathmandu. Oh btw, did I tell you, you are in Nepal in Kathmandu? Sorry, guys!"

Novsky replies, "Great, this was the only city left on my to-do travel list. Pity I can't show the kids and Albina all the sights and all."

Kaamna laughs with Novsky.

Albina looks at him in disbelief and says, "How can you guys be so relaxed about it? This thing you say, KRAAL, is about to end the planet, and you don't seem that stressed out. We all will die, Novsky, and you are considering a sight-seeing excursion."

Novsky adds, "Not if the UNIBOMB works, darling. I am confident that it will work. Hold on, wait a minute. Kaamna, you didn't tell us who are you working for? And why do you guys want us safe?"

Kaamna replies, "Novsky, we want you safe as we know you are one of the few people who are our hope for a bright future for mankind. You know everything about KRAAL, UNIBOMB, ARK, NEBULA, and Space. Only a few people like you. Let's say Ranjan, Srini, Anita – God bless her soul, Arjun, and some of your team members. We've been following you for a long time. If this thing that you call UNIBOMB works, you are the next hope of humanity. You deserve to lead us into the next era of evolution. We don't wanna give the new world to the current leaders, would we?"

Novsky replies, "As if this is in your control. The current leaders are anyway not interested in the planet anymore. They are certain that we are going to die. They don't wanna take any risk staying here and evaluate their chances. Do you think they really care?"

Kaamna adds, "We have hopes, Mr. Novsky. We have high hopes for your talent, calibre and the plan you have in place. It is cruel of TUESDA and other leaders to think so low of you and subject you and your loved ones to an instant death like animals. Now, you guys are tired, I am sure. The tonic we gave you made you sleep for many hours, so we could easily get you here. I think you guys should rest. There is enough food stock in the refrigerator and kitchen. Let us know if anything is needed. Vinay, who is outside, will be your personal valet and security and is our eyes and ears."

Novsky asks, "And if I may ask Kaamna. Who are "we" and "our" in your talk? Whom do you represent?"

Kaamna walks towards the door but, before leaving, adds, "Oh Novsky, I thought you would have done your maths by now. We are PUNSAM, of course!" and then leaves the flat with a smile.

Novsky rolls his eyes over, sinks into the bed, and yells, "Oh Damn, what have I got myself into? Why didn't I become a bank employee instead of a scientist in the first place?"

Washington DC

Bill is in a meeting with Nathan, the US President and updating him on all the key events and agendas for him this week. Although not fully aware of everything Bill is up to, Nathan does not question him a single bit about his ways of working or the decisions he was making independently. Bill had Nathan bugged for security reasons as per TUESDA's New Regulations for the 10K list. So far, Nathan had been an old textbook predictable character for Bill, and he had nothing to worry about.

He had just completed his presentation on the updates on ARK, NEBULA, and UNIBOMB with Nathan when Nathan said, "Thanks for this, Bill. So, as per your presentation, UNIBOMB has a chance of destroying the KRAAL, but there is still a significant probability of failure, and we can't risk the ARK mission because of it. I want to know what the ERO is."

"Nathan, this is parked for the next week. I shared this as the discussion around this concept has already been started within TUESDA and the associated circle we have formed for the project. I thought to just share this as an agenda item for next week."

Nathan replies, "Next week, Bill. How many weeks are left on the planet? Why are you so casual about Earth-related stuff and only focussing on ARK and getting us out of here? Are you not very confident about UNIBOMB?"

Bill replies, "Nathan, my experience with scientists has been mixed for these past years. They say they are confident, but when they fail, they classify that failure as a data point and learning to be corrected for future experiments. I don't know what will happen with UNIBOMB and KRAAL. I haven't seen or experienced something like this ever. However, I know space travel already and it has been perfected to an extent that we can safely go outside our solar system. We can survive in NEBULA for at least 100 years, which is a good enough time for humanity to evolve under our leadership. So, while tactfully giving these people hope, I am not convinced about it."

Nathan looks at Bill and replies, "Fair point. We can't risk the lives of the chosen 10K people as that's humanity's last hope. I agree it is tough to explain to the people left behind that they are the chosen martyrs without consent. But then history shows that mankind has gone to extreme lengths for survival. And after this event, we will rewrite the history and would handle this event strategically in those books."

Bill says, "Exactly, Nathan. Now, the plan of action is this. KRAAL is supposed to strike the planet by around November.

We have two to three months left. The ARK's first ignition test is planned probably for next week. We will need to leave this month-end or early next month, as per our plan. Now, we can't allow the information related to ARK, NEBULA, or KRAAL to be released to the public before we all are in the ARK and safely beyond earth's atmosphere. We have decided that we will release the same information to the public by mid of September or so. Please note that sir, we will disband all our organisations and governments that we held so dearly once we leave. We will leave the earth for the remaining scientists and few world leaders who are not in the 10k plan."

Nathan says, "Go on. I sense the formation of another organisation. Don't we already have too many? TUESDA, SCOPEX, and now this one?"

Bill replies, "You guessed it right, sir. The proposal is the formation of ERO, I.e. Earth Rescue Organisation, to be led by the top scientific community and some political leadership. However, the council has already chosen who will lead the ERO and the other members working for him. It is a very peculiar choice, something I cannot fathom."

Nathan asks, "Who is this proposed leader of ERO?"

Bill says, "You know him, sir. We met him in Bengaluru during the KRAAL briefing and many more such meetings in the past. It's Ranjan Sharma, the Chief Scientist working for PRIME-1. Now, he is the CEO of PRIME-1 as the Indian Government has nationalised it. The recommendation comes directly from the Indian Prime Minister, Mr. Singh. Everyone, including the scientific community and other leaders, have already agreed. They need TUESDA to release an official order to this asap. And 'they' mean the entire community, sir, mostly these scientists."

Nathan chuckles, "Sorry for my behaviour, Bill. I had to laugh at it. The world is at the end and about to be destroyed, and now the scientists want to run it for a month or two. By all means, let them have it. If they think they can save the planet with a sure-shot destruction by some BOMB, let them take the shot. However, ensure this ERO and everything comes into existence once we have left the planet."

Bill smiles and says, "Sure, sir. Precisely my thoughts. ARK is an independently controlled spacecraft, and we will have minds to help us sustain ARK and NEBULA for our lifetime. It is sad to give these people false hope, but I am maintaining a positive stance toward this UNIBOMB and ERO thing. However, my internal team of scientific experts knows this for sure, that the chances of hitting and destroying the KRAAL are very minimal. My only fear is what if it's an alien thing. And that's actually something I had predicted as a possibility before."

Nathan replies, "What? If that's an alien thing that has detected the human life form, don't you think it poses a threat to us, too?"

Bill replies, "Not too much, sir. Few things to observe here. First, the path and trajectory seem too focussed on the earth, as if it is a missile locked on the earth. Second, as a precautionary measure, I have already asked my team to ensure that we install a combination of nuclear warheads and RYAN bombs on the ARK to the maximum capacity possible. I haven't shared this decision with anyone but a few who control the bombs. That's why there is a delay in assembling UNIBOMB right now, as the entire arsenal has not reached Dubai yet."

Nathan looks at Bill, "Boy, you are way too clever than I can imagine, Bill. I am confident that we have the right man. However, be extra careful regarding the information we hold and share. I hope you are taking incorrect parameters into consideration."

Bill speaks, "Yes, sir. And you already know about a few of them. Sadly, we had to carry out the sanctioned eliminations for the greater good. However, I am afraid the last one is an untraceable transaction."

Nathan says, "What do you mean? Have you not found Novsky yet? Why did you bomb their house if you knew he was not there?"

Bill replies, "Sir, we didn't bomb the house. It was a programmatic thing that we couldn't stop. The gas was released automatically, and the ignition trigger was activated just a few minutes after that. Once the button was pressed, we could not undo it. The strange part is how could the vigilantes find out that it was the exact moment and then they kidnapped him and his family? I am sure they want him alive to extract some information or, worse, release this to the public. It's a ticking time bomb, but we will handle it."

Nathan takes a deep breath and says, "This could be a loose end, Bill. What if he releases the entire information to the public? Everything will go waste."

Bill says, "Don't worry, sir. Of course, we will handle it with care. We have already spoken to our good friend

Polsky and Jovan's mandated psychologist. We already have created a report which says that Jovan is mentally unstable and has been acting weird for a very long time and now has disappeared with his family owing to his paranoia. In fact, before he says anything, we have already released a news piece in Serbia that reads, 'A mad scientist sets his house on fire and escapes with his family.' No one will ever believe him afterwards.'

Nathan replies, "Hmm, that's smart, Bill. I hope this handles it. What can I say! You are the man!"

They conclude their meeting, and Nathan walks out of the Oval Office. Bill sits there and contemplates his actions for a while.

He has come a long way in life, and a lot rests on his shoulder. Starting from an entry-level analyst to now the most powerful person on the planet, he had orchestrated everything perfectly for his career.

It was obvious what he wanted in the end – complete control over everything that led the 10K list to fly safely in ARK and settle in NEBULA. However, the loss on the planet would be enormous and unbearable for many on the 10K list. He is glad that he has no liabilities – no wife, no children, no siblings, parents passed away a few years ago, and he never ever made any good friends. His purpose in life was single – to make sure that the United States of America stays the most powerful country, with its full glory forever. His father had died as an Army Colonel in a war in Afghanistan. He didn't want himself to be a martyr only for his country and never bring the actual change.

He meticulously planned all his actions from the start. He knew that only a few agents and officials stood in his way to the top. The agent that posed the maximum competition was his good friend, Jared. And Bill knew he had to go out from the intelligence community. Even if it meant sacrificing a few good men in the Oslo in the Gamlebyen house. He couldn't kill Jared, though, as he was the only friend he ever had and got a bit of a soft spot for him. However, it was easy for him to frame Jared after the event by pulling some strings in the top brass. The already ensuing enquiry against Jared gave a bit of fuel to what transpired afterwards. All his plans had been near perfect, except for a few misses, especially including PUNSAM's activity and leadership, few wrong budgets calls on NEBULA and ARK, and the latest one, the disappearance of Novsky. While everything else was going as per the plan, he was curious about the disappearance of Novsky and who helped him.

But this wasn't the time for thinking about lags in his micro-management. He had to ensure that the ARK was ready, retrofitted with the backup explosive, and the 10K plan stayed intact. He had already taken the entire command for the ARK project at his hands and was not trusting this to ISRO, PRIME-1, KVALITAT, etc. Individual entities were working on smaller systems for the ARK, but the entire system integration was supposed to be done by TUESDA and SCOPE-X. Others did not even know that they secretly transported some bombs to the system integration centre of ARK. Unfortunately, some of these were supposed to go to the UNIBOMB assembly centre.

Chapter 16

Oh Captain, My Captain

By now, it would have become clearer that the most powerful entity in the world was TUESDA, with Bill holding the command lines to the battleship. However, as the KRAAL situation came near, the world leaders had no choice but to pass the leadership to a few newer entities, as they needed Bill on KRAAL. Bill Scott was the only unifying thread to all the political and corporate connections in the world. He had his eyes and ears everywhere, from governments to organisations and even some terrorist groups. Bill knew that the plan to save the planet earth with something like UNIBOMB sounded like a shot in the dark, but he was hopeful on that part, too. But his top priority was evacuating the chosen ones in the ARK to safety so humanity could continue. Even though he was working on getting everything ready for the ARK, he was closely observing and scrutinising KRAAL and UNIBOMB projects as well.

There was a separate division dedicated within all space agencies to observe KRAAL, and only a few handfuls of scientists were in that team, most of them going to stay on earth only under the leadership of Srini, as well as top officials from NASA, ROSCOSMOS, etc. Triangulating the right trajectory of KRAAL was difficult because of the limitations posed by the radio wave detection technology. It was still not mature enough to detect exoplanets and other objects outside our solar system. Nebula, however, was the closest and the most reliable source of information everyone had, as it had proven helpful in these past years. NEBULA had radio and imagery-based telescope detection that first detected KRAAL and extrapolated the approach towards the earth. Within the space community, the word of NEBULA was final, and it was certain that the KRAAL scenario would happen. Bill was the most suspicious one, though. He had asked his own personal trusted team of scientists to do multiple tests and scenarios, but sadly, everyone came to the same realisation.

Once it was clear to Bill, after thorough analysis, that a catastrophic event was more likely, he had put all his energies into the ARK project. However, he knew he would need to install a world leader that would continue pursuing the same agenda as TUESDA once they kicked the ARK project off. He was the one to propose the structuring of ERO and buying the loyalty of all ERO members towards him as a fail-safe if the UNIBOMB plan worked. He knew he could not put political and business leaders in the leadership team of ERO. Hence, he tactfully placed most scientists, authors, philosophers, and historians as leaders of ERO. These people could make the right decision under his leadership even once he was in ARK. There were only a handful of members he could now trust as he watched everyone over the past few months. He had already decided who would lead the agenda and strategically got the buy-ins from every TUESDA member and world leader. He knew when the time would come, either the planet would devastate under ERO's leadership, or if it gets saved, ERO's new leader won't care much about his position and would rather like to go back to his old scientist's life, handing over the reign back to Bill. Either way, it would always be Bill who would lead the entire thing.

Bengaluru, India, 25th August 2031, TUESDA Last Meeting: Edition MM-CONCLUDE (FULL HOUSE)

Six days to go for ARK.

They have all met again after 2.5 months. The monthly meetings were suspended completely as the council had convened on a need-to-need basis. Besides, in the last meeting, the work plans were drawn, and everyone was busy with their respective functions. They sent the agenda for this last meeting/edition with the top 3 objectives:

- Confirmation of logistics and the last ticket disbursements status of ARK to everyone on the 10K list.
- Updates on UNIBOMB and the last-minute support needed from the top leaders of the world.
- Dissolution of all the agencies (like ISRO, NASA, SCOPEX), organisations (such as PRIME1, KVALITAT which were already nationalised), key Govt. leaderships (including Presidents and PMs. of the countries) as well as TUESDA itself.
- Restructuring the new world order and power under ERO (Earth Rescue Organization). This part was a straightforward decision as nobody cared about what was left on earth. After all, most of the members in this meeting were leaving off to ARK and then to NEBULA to spend the rest of their lives, anyway.

The meeting had started at 6AM and was supposed to go till 10PM.

However, some absentees in these meetings include people like Novsky, Anita, a few rogue scientists, and a few world leaders who were not in favour of Bill's plan. They were all silenced by TUESDA except for Novsky, who was AWOL.

Srini, Ranjan and Arjun were seated together with their respective teams. Polsky and Mahavir were in the meeting too but sitting with the respective political leaders of their countries, the Russian President and the Indian Prime Minister.

After sharing the status of the final ticket disbursements on ARK, Bill announces,

"And so, ladies and gentlemen. I know you have been patient with us and co-operated well during these past few months. Now, I know everyone is wondering where the ARK will take off and where it is finally assembled.

Let me share that with you. For the past few months, we had collected all the sub-systems, spare parts, engine, core etc., for the ARK and shipped everything to one central location. That place is nowhere else but in India itself. It's not surprising that we chose the desert again, this time for this one. The ARK is currently being assembled in the middle of the desert in THAR and not anywhere else but the origins of Indian Nuclear power, Pokhran in Rajasthan. The locals in the area assumed that this was another one of India's military missions or nuclear test, and we handled the press pretty well on this one. All thanks to the Indian Prime Minister and his aide-de-camp, Mr. Kulkarni." He waves at Kulkarni and Mr. Singh, who nod at the gesture.

Bill continues, "Now, we have already transported your luggage to the ARK, and you can find that in your allocated chambers once you are onboarded. There is a reason we took your mobile phones, laptops, etc. You will now be provided with encrypted calling devices through which you can connect with your deputed TUESDA leaders on the ship for any help. The rest of the agendas will be discussed once we are on the ship itself."

He then pauses as he looks at certain people in the room who were not accompanying them in ARK and realises not to share too many details right now before they are onboard. He asks Arjun to take over and share the remaining updates and open up the table for discussion.

Arjun continues, "As Bill shared, we will have more updates related to KRAAL once we are all on the ship. Bill will be your commanding officer, with me as his deputy. We understand this is the grimmest situation of your lives, leaving many family members and friends on the earth for their fate. However, I am very confident about the plan for UNIBOMB that's led by my dear friends Ranjan and Srini here. Before I ask them to share the updates on that, I would like to ask if anyone has questions related to ARK?"

After an extensive 2 hours of questioning, debating about the 10K list and the scepticism about the ARK's survival and a trip to NEBULA, Arjun asks the Indian Prime Minister to share a few words related to logistics before passing the baton to Ranjan on UNIBOMB.

Singh stands up and speaks.

"Ladies and Gentlemen, it is a miserable moment for the entire human history. Yet, we must share a stance with the world that we are all leaving for space for a peace mission. The one and only in human history that was ever planned and perhaps the last one to be conducted, though the public won't know of the latter. It is my request to kindly cooperate with our authorities and let them assist you with the travel plans to Pokhran. After that, you will be handed over to TUESDA's special teams, which will help you with your respective batches and leads. Many of us have chosen to stay back here on the planet."

Suddenly there was shock and murmurs around the room. Everyone looked at Mr. Singh quizzically as he said the word 'us'. Kulkarni smiles, finding the gesture amusing, and looks back at Bill with his eyebrows stretched out in doubt.

"Yes, you heard right, ladies and gentlemen."

Singh continues, "I have decided to stay back and serve my country till my last breath. Although I don't expect you guys to reciprocate the same gesture. I have given up my seat for a young man, an 11-year-old bright boy named Ishaan, who studies in a Government School in a small town in Madhya Pradesh, India. When he grows up, I hope he serves humanity with his talents and gifts. I will stay with people like Ranjan and Srini to ensure peace, as we all know how the entire world will react to this news. Now, I understand you have already deputed your next successors to control your respective countries and organisations. I, however, feel that few of us should stay and still maintain balance even if it means dying here with everyone. Now, I am sure that humanity will stay and fight back, but if we cannot hit KRAAL, it is my humble request that all of you continue without us in the space with the best intentions possible. I hope you forget all the diplomacy, politics and agendas up there and work towards the sustenance of humanity and never forget our martyrdom for the cause. With that, I hand over to my dear friend Ranjan to take over and share the UNIBOMB plan."

Unlike other meetings, there was no applause when the Indian PM finished. Rather, everyone looks around each other with mixed emotions and reactions. Few clapped silently, including Ranjan, Srini, Arjun, and even Bill.

Ranjan stands up and speaks, "Thank you, Prime Minister Saheb. It is so nice of you to stay and motivate us for our cause. Ladies and gentlemen, let me share the updates and concerns related to UNIBOMB. Now, we all know that we have used UAE's Sahara desert as the pivot point for UNIBOMB from where it will be shot up in the space to hit KRAAL. Over the past few days, we have been able to get many nuclear missiles, bombs, explosive devices and even some experimental technologies by intelligence agencies worldwide. However, it is sad that few of our shipments have not been made on time yet. There is a list of shipments that were supposed to arrive from the United States, Brazil, China and Russia that were never made to the UNIBOMB sites. The shipment contains a few nuclear warheads and RYAN bombs. We would first like your support ladies and gentlemen, on this matter."

Bill stands up and replies, "Ranjan, I have had a discussion with Arjun on this matter, and we will expedite that. As of now, we have been swamped sending parts for ARK; some shipments are in transit and a bit of paperwork. Once the ARK leaves, you can take control and get those shipments fast. We have a few more months left for UNIBOMB impact, so I doubt this would be an issue."

Nathan exchanges glances with Bill, hinting we should discuss nothing beyond this, and Bill catches that in time. He then continues,

"However, something that we are curious about, Ranjan and Srini! That is the fact that you guys have not yet updated us on the KRAAL's trajectory. Do we have a live update on its location yet?"

Srini answers, "No, sir, we don't have any live camera feed from earth's satellites or the telescopes on the location yet. However, the heat signature matches from NEBULA have confirmed that it is getting closer. Once it crosses NEBULA and enters a few layers inside our solar system, we will be able to share those updates. That may be around fifteen days to a month from now."

Nathan thinks, 'By that time, we will be in the ARK, and we won't need any updates from you, duffers!'

Bill tactfully replies, "That's fair, Srini. I wish we get a much closer reading sooner once we are in The ARK. The ideal scenario is KRAAL getting destroyed so we would be able to finally come back to our beautiful earth instead of going to NEBULA."

Ranjan adds, "Yes, Bill. We hope and are counting on the UNIBOMB to work and get you guys back to the planet once it is done."

After continuing on UNIBOMB, the team shifts to the last two topics of powers, one dissolution of the current world order and the setup of ERO.

Nathan takes over the stage and speaks, "As we all know, most of the world leaders would be on the ARK, and there would be almost around 4 to 5 months when most of the decision-makers would be absent. We have hence decided to temporarily hand over the complete control of space agencies, key organisations, and even a significant political control to a new organisation setup known as ERO, or Earth Rescue Organisation."

He holds a paper and speaks, "On this paper, all of us have signed and agreed that for a period stated as a minimum of 4 months to the time it takes for the earth to be saved or recovered from the impact, we hand over the entire control to ERO and its leader. However, we hope to return to the safe haven of this planet and take up our responsibility as soon as possible. After all, we would want our bright scientists and ERO guys to also go out for holidays out to nice beaches, won't we?"

Sharma senses the politics in Nathan's speech already. He knows that this entire ERO is just to ensure that people left behind don't revolt and comply with TUESDA's bigger plan. It is just to calm down people like us not to go out in public. That's why they give us something to hold for – say, a temporary global leadership.

Nathan replies, "We have a majority vote on the President of ERO. I would call him, nay, the successor of Bill Scott and TUESDA. Ladies and Gentlemen, please welcome the new head of ERO and the General-in-command for the planet earth, Mr. Ranjan Sharma!"

This time, everyone applauds, claps, and knocks down on the table really hard. Ranjan stands up, waving at everyone without a smile or emotion. Bill looks at him with sheepish eyes, trying to read his feelings.

Ranjan speaks, "Thank you, Mr. President. I am a humble scientist who has worked all his life towards the upliftment of humanity through my work. I am thankful to each of you for putting your trust in me. But, I would request you never abandon me with your wisdom, for I will reach all of you for any advice and suggestions to destroy KRAAL and get you back to a safer earth. Also, I would like to add that I will always be working under the tutelage of Mr. Singh, our Prime Minister and the leader of our country, and would do my best not to let you guys down."

Nathan speaks, "Humble as he always is, people! Ranjan, we have full faith in you, and you can count on us for anything you need. Not only till the time we are here, but even after once we scoot off from Pokhran into the space, patch us on all updates."

Bill adds to this, "Also, I would like to say something, Ranjan. Please note that we can't release the news of KRAAL to the public. This is required to proceed with your UNIBOMB plan without distractions and chaos. Ideally, no one should know about this news, and the KRAAL should be destroyed. You should release this information only when the KRAAL is destroyed."

Nathan, sitting near Bill, whispers in his ears, "Or after we are in outer space." Bill does not react.

Bill then adds, "We need to work under complete discretion on this. Otherwise, you will have another agenda to handle: a massive global riot at an unimaginable scale. Then, you won't need a KRAAL to end humanity, but humans themselves will do it."

Ranjan nods at this and sits down. Srini shakes Ranjan's hands and congratulates him, but he realises Ranjan is not too excited about it.

Srini whispers, "Even if it is the end of the world, my friend. I would be happy to die under your leadership. Oh Captain, My Captain!"

Ranjan smiles a bit and gives a side hug to Srini.

The meeting ends positively as everyone motivates the ERO guys and gives them confidence in their UNIBOMB plan. However, everyone, including the ERO team and the 10K list, knew there was a rare chance for UNIBOMB to hit KRAAL and destroy it. It's clear that the only safe place now left is ARK.

The meeting room clears up, leaving behind only two people in the room, Bill and Ranjan. It is a sort of a hand-over meeting that Bill never imagined he would have in his life with an Indian citizen. However, these were crazy times, and anything was possible. Everything was on the table today, every intelligence agency report, every minute piece of information, codes to nuclear weapons, urban legends like Area47, Alien invasion and even military secrets of every government in the world.

Sharma realised he was talking to the most powerful man in the world, who held all the information about everything on this planet.

Sharma speaks, "So Bill, you think that Jovan Novsky has been conspiring with PUNSAM till now?"

Bill says, "Yes, and I don't want you to believe him, Ranjan, if he makes an acquaintance. You know, the call you had with him after he disappeared. And by the way, my sincere apologies for tapping you guys and putting everyone under surveillance. When you're in the position that I was, which you are in now, you will understand this. It is essential to always keep your head focussed on the big agenda."

Sharma nods in disbelief at what Bill is saying, realising that Bill knew about the call. He was lost for words for an instant, but then Bill looked at him and spoke, "Ranjan, you really think that an encrypted call would be something that TUESDA won't be capable of tracking? You have no ideas about the power of our technology, man. And by the way, it is your technology now also by all means. We knew that you guys spoke of the restrictions I have imposed on everyone and the level of scrutiny we are doing. I am sure you understand now, that it is for good only. I did nothing wrong, Sharma. Anita Naidu was a PUNSAM terrorist, and I have files on her. Not only her, I was pretty sure that Novsky was also a spy for PUNSAM. Somehow, his behaviour was off-conventional for a long time."

Sharma speaks, "Off-conventional, Bill? This is the end of the world we are talking about. How would you think anyone would react? Even I am acting numb within my family, and you also know that fact, for you are watching everything."

Bill holds his hands together and smiles at Sharma. "Hey man, I know that. I am with you on everything, Ranjan. I am not talking about you, Srini or all our good friends in the room. You do not know about Novsky, right? Let me show you a picture."

He then shows Sharma two pictures, one with Novsky and Kaamna in a bar in Bengaluru and the other with Kaamna and Anita hugging each other.

Bill says, "This girl, who goes by the name of Kaamna, is working for PUNSAM. She is Anita Naidu's sister and has always tracked you guys from the beginning. Anita was dating the leader of the group itself. I am sure of that as Jared, the man in question himself, confessed to it. Not only that, I have pictures of Anita meeting Lhea, Jared's daughter, for lunches, dinners and what not. I suspect a bigger game at PUNSAM, and you need to be aware of these bastards. They are not able to spread the panic as we have been carefully tracking them and denying all the false rumours and controlling media for now."

Sharma looks at everything in disbelief and buries his face in his hands. And then speaks, "Oh my God, Bill. If what you are saying is true, I have already been subjected to a lot. Jovan knows way too much about KRAAL, ARK, UNIBOMB and NEBULA. If he is a PUNSAM agent, then we have a lot to worry about."

Bill puts his hands on Sharma's shoulders and speaks, "Ranjan, you don't have to worry about anything, my man, till I am there. Even in ARK, we will both be each other's eyes and ears. I have been watching you since the beginning. Though you might say my right hand in the scientific community was always Arjun, it's you who I admired the most. The man with all the composure, knowledge and rigour, you are the only person I can trust with a responsibility like this. But, we have to work together on this, you understand? You know, we can't let ARK go in the hands of the rogues. I suspect there will be a last-minute foul-play by PUNSAM for the ARK project, and they will then release the news to the world. We have tripled our security at Pokhran and provided Z-level security to everyone in the 10K team and you. However, there is one thing I don't understand, Ranjan."

Ranjan looks at Bill and asks, "What is that, Bill?"

Bill replies, "We gave you a chance to be in the ARK along with Novsky, who I understand didn't take it because of his associations with PUNSAM. But why would you not take it up or not even allow your family to be safe? Why are you subjecting yourself to this martyrdom, man?"

Ranjan looks at Bill and replies, "Bill, I have a huge family. Brothers, sisters, their brothers and sisters, their wives and their families, friends and friends of friends. And I am a religious man who believes in the afterlife and everything you would have heard about Hindu mythology. I don't want to be in a place where I go up in the courts of God and cannot meet eyes with all these people. If you have to take me, I am afraid I might need over 500 seats because of my extended family. But, if we do that for one person, we should do it for everyone. Hence, I stayed back."

Bill smiles and speaks, "For all I know and the extent I trust you, I am sure you will knock that bastard KRAAL out with your UNIBOMB. The doomsday won't come, my friend. And once this is all over, invite me to your 500 people's party too, man. Would love to have some Indian spicy food and the local drinks you guys serve. Now come on and join me for some of that great food while we can have it on an actual planet," he chuckles.

Ranjan laughs at Bill and the irony of his situation and gives Bill a high five before they leave the room for dinner.

The same day, New Delhi

Rajat is in Shreya's apartment helping her pack her things as she has to leave with a few delegates to Pokhran for the ARK Peace Mission. Over the past few days, the couple had bonded a lot and decided that they would marry once Shreya was back. Of course, Mahavir and Ranjan knew it was a long shot and only a pipe dream for these kids. Shreya would not have gone to ARK had she known the actual story, though Rajat would have asked her to go. Shreya was, however, suspicious of the new changes, especially after the nationalisation of PRIME-1 and Rajat's father taking control as its new Chairman.

Rajat speaks, "For a 4-month trip, you are packing very light, love!"

Shreya says, "Ya, they have a very limited luggage allowance. Besides, we are getting a standard uniform and an allocated ration quota per person. Dad would have tried to superimpose his powers to allocate more for us, but then this time, the competition is not with some start-up cofounders but the kings and queens of the castles around the planet."

Rajat says, "And what's this entire thing about? No laptops, no mobiles. How will we talk then?"

Shreya, "After today, honey, we won't be able to speak for the next 4 months on a phone or laptop. Every call will be made to the space pods we have, and there is a unique request that you will have to generate after calling favours with your father. He is amongst the only few members who may maintain contact with us. So, lucky us, we would talk to each other."

Rajat, "And you think it would be easy for me to call my father for this ya? Do you know he tried to recruit me for PRIME-1 recently? I was like, now when it is a semi-government organisation, you want me to join. I wasn't even joining when this company was a private limited. Gutsy ask that was!"

Shreya comes closer to Rajat, kisses him and hugs him. "I am going to miss you, honey. Just don't worry about me. I am worried about you. How will you live for 4 months once I am not there? I hope you don't fool around with other girls. Remember now, we are almost about to be married."

Rajat replies, "As if I have ever fooled around with anyone, Shreya. I am just not very sure of this ARK thing, Shreya. How reliable is this, and why are they doing this sudden manned mission? And why is your father risking your life also in it?"

Shreya replies, "Come on! We are living in the time of space revolution, honey. Do you remember how many trips our teams have taken in space for NEBULA repairs and other things? You haven't gone to space, and that's why feeling scared. My father and your father have made short trips to many planets and NEBULA, and you know that. It's not as if I am going to the Bermuda Triangle. Every day, many people go to space. Last year, a couple got married in the space. I wish I could have taken you if you had agreed to work for us when asked."

Rajat folds his hands and replies, “Please, Shreya, don’t over-exaggerate! Everyone you are talking about is astronauts and scientists. I am concerned because this is carrying inexperienced human beings. Anyway, you go take a trip and share the pictures with me once you return. Also, bring me some rocks, minerals, or maybe some ether, my Jane Foster!”

Shreya kisses Rajat, saying, “Ok, Thor! Don’t you go rogue now and obey what Odinson commands, alright?”

Rajat bids goodbye to Shreya and leaves for his house. He did not know he was seeing her for the last time, and there was rather a larger rock pointed straight to his planet. He wouldn’t have questioned or doubted anything happening around these days. His mind was occupied with the thoughts of his marriage planning and his life with Shreya these days.

Chapter 17

Les carrottes sont Cuites (The Carrots are Cooked!)

Over the past few months, scientists working on the ARK have designed proper procedures, methods and protocols for residents before onboarding, during as well as post the launch. They decided that 5 days before the launch, from 26th August onwards, there would be batches of people who would be taken to Pokhran and examined for medical and fitness purposes. Already the training program, diet schedules etc., had been shared with these residents two months ago, which they had to follow rigorously. Some even lost weight for the first time, some improved their sleep cycle, and some continued the way it was. However, physical fitness and proper mental health were given utmost importance for these residents, irrespective of how privileged these people were. TUESDA's team and their families were given a different preferential treatment because of their importance in the mission and were already trained on all the procedures. They decided that many members would arrive without their families in Pokhran before 28th August, and their families would come from 29th August till 31st August morning. The take-off was planned for the 31st afternoon at 3PM Indian Standard time. They did this to keep the suspicion of the media low. Also, most of these members from the 10K list had to go directly into the sleeping chamber, for which the demarcation was done separately.

He was preparing an Indian sumptuous breakfast for his wife and daughter today. After all, Sundays must be perfect after a week's long, hard work. The weather was a breeze today in Reading, UK, with light winds, a pleasant drizzle, and sharp sunlight cutting straight through the droplets. Samantha was playing in the garden, and Arjun could see her through the kitchen window. Claudia was setting up the dining table and preparing the dishes for breakfast.

In a few moments, Arjun comes out of the kitchen to the living room with the spread of the day, Indian delicious Parathas, *aachaar* (Indian pickle), curd and tea. This was a typical Punjabi breakfast and a favourite of Arjun's father. He fondly remembers his parents and the time he spent with them till they were alive. Unfortunately, he could not even be with them during their last moments. Arjun's parents died in a car accident in India while he was staying abroad in the United States for his work. A regret that he carried forth throughout his life!

He comes out of his thoughts and calls Samantha to go inside. However, even after calling her 2 to 3 times, she doesn't respond. Arjun goes outside the garden and sees Samantha looking up at the sky. He runs closer to Samantha without looking up and picks her up in his arm.

"What are you doing, my sweetheart?" Arjun says.

Samantha replies, "Dad, look up. There is an amazing light breaking through the sky. Are the aliens coming?"

Arjun laughs and looks up while saying, "Aliens, ya. How can aliens…."

And with that, he realizes with utter shock. The sky was almost torn apart completely with an exceedingly bright light that could make anyone blind.

Suddenly, the birds are flying, scattering from one tree to another. There are noises of traffic and car honks that can be heard. Cries and shouts replaced the sounds as he realised the sky was tearing apart and the bright light was getting closer.

He could feel the temperature rising even during winters in the UK. It felt as if he was in an Arabian desert. Claudia comes running from behind and comes closer to Arjun and Samantha.

They all look up as suddenly an enormous ball comes down, rushing towards Arjun's house and destroying the entire house behind them with fire.

Claudia and Samantha yell out and start crying while Arjun tries to hold them both together.

He looks up again, and instead of running, they all just stand still as if they were spellbound by some force. Within one second, multiple fireballs come down to hit the planet, and Arjun closes his eyes, realizing it's their last moment. He hugs both Claudia and Samantha and says, "I love...."

And with that, he wakes up from his bed, sweating terribly and realizing it was just a dream. He sees Claudia sleeping on the side of the bed with Samantha in between them. He kisses Samantha on her forehead and runs his hand through Claudia's hair to feel his family.

He realizes it was a bad dream. After all, he was not in the UK but in Gurugram, India (near New Delhi), waiting to go to ARK. He gets up and goes to get a glass of water. He recalls the past events. Even though he didn't want to be in ARK, Bill had convinced him otherwise. There was no choice for Arjun in this matter. He realized Bill needed him up there. Bill had baited Arjun by providing extra seats for Claudia and Sophia. His nightmares had been increasing day by day as well. In the end, he gave up for the sake of his family and joined Bill on the ARK. Since then, he could not meet Sharma or any other scientist face to face. He largely kept to himself and focussed on the work and his family.

28th August 2031 0930AM, The Leela Hotel, Gurgaon, India

Arjun had been staying with Claudia and Samantha in The Leela for the past week. He had told Claudia that they would go to ARK as a part of the global peace mission. Only a few select people could take their families and kids, notably a few politicians, world leaders and influential entrepreneurs. Claudia agreed to it as she realised it would be a lively environment to meet around so many bright minds. She and Samantha could spend a lot of time with Arjun. Besides, Samantha always wanted to go to space, which would reflect greatly in her life experience journal. Arjun, however, had to leave this morning itself to Pokhran. Claudia and Samantha would leave in the evening with other families, including the wives and kids of other members.

However, right now, the family was having a post-breakfast conversation inside the room itself. Arjun had asked for it, as he wanted one last earthly meal with his family before they departed for space for good. Of course, Samantha and Claudia did not know what would happen.

Samantha asks, "Dad, would we get a pizza in the space on weekends?"

Arjun laughs, "A Pizza, girl? We would be lucky to even have a bread toast there. We will have special healthy food, as directed by the excellent doctors over there in the spaceship."

Claudia adds, "Now, don't be greedy, Sammy. You have had enough fun during these holidays, haven't you? It's time to have the real adventure of our lives now. I want you to work on your experience journal from today itself. Capture all the feelings before going to the spaceship and continue afterwards in your journal, OK?"

Arjun asked, "How are you feeling today, Sammy?"

Samantha says, "I don't know, Daddy. I am excited but I am also afraid. Maybe I have watched too many movies. I will miss my friends too. But the best part is that I will see space and stars and jump in the spaceship with no gravity." And raises her hands with excitement.

Arjun laughs and says, "Yes, Sammy, we will all do that together. And don't worry, we will be back soon to meet your friends. Now get your packing done, honey. I will see you on the ship itself." With that, he hugs Samantha as he finishes his breakfast.

Claudia notices Arjun, who is tearful and asks him, "Babe, are you ok? You seem to be overburdened with something. What's going on? I know it's a lot to ask. But I feel you aren't too excited about this ARK Peace Mission."

Arjun replies, "There is nothing like that, Claudia. This mission is vital for all of us, not only me. We should be able to show the world that we can unite everyone peacefully. Space travel is a means for people to look at the earth from the outside and realize it is one unit. Look at the guest list. Every world leader, the richest people on the planet, these expert scientists and top brass of every organisation are travelling along with their families in it. There are over 1000 families here, and we are lucky to be a part of them. It's just that I am the deputy commander of this mission, and there is a lot of work on my plate. So, it's really the stress that is showing up on my face."

Claudia hugs Arjun and puts her head on his chest and says, "Why do you trouble yourself this much, Arjun? You don't have to work this hard all the time. Let's take a big holiday after we come back from this mission. Like, let's just vanish for 5 to 6 months in a peaceful place and spend some time together, just the three of us. And, don't worry about this mission on the spaceship. You have us with you every day up there, and we sure know a lot of ways to cheer you up."

Arjun holds Claudia tight in his arms and sheds a few tears without letting Claudia notice. "You are right, Claudia. I don't want to be away from both of you for even a moment now. I hope I am not asking too much by dragging you from your normal lives and taking up in the space." He knew he didn't mean the last part but still wanted Claudia to be comfortable before leaving.

Claudia looks at Arjun and says, "It's not a bother, sweetheart. I see it as a long vacation myself. The only part I am not too excited about is these 3 day-long waiting periods from now. Why do you have to leave now along with everyone else to the pods inside the ARK? And why can't we leave with you right now, or you leave with us after a few hours?"

"It is for the safety of everyone, Claudia. I am trained in space travel and have been calibrated mentally and physically to handle the stress of acceleration and deceleration. Although the chambers inside are force-neutral, you still won't feel anything. But we want everyone else to be put in the sleeping chambers till the entire lift-off, and you will go for preliminary tests and other formalities for tomorrow. But, don't worry, I will come and get you guys to show the entire spaceship and our rooms there once the lift-off is done. You are going to love it. They are really something."

Arjun realises he has been lying through his teeth for a long time now. He realises that Claudia will never forgive Arjun once she knows the truth. Claudia and Samantha would be on their own, up in the space, and he won't be able to face them again. But this was a risk he would take up for the safety of his wife and the daughter. With that, he leaves the hotel, leaving behind Claudia and Samantha, who will come later in the evening on a separate flight.

While on his way to the airport, he looks around all the Indian people walking, driving, and eating on the highway, clueless that an end is coming soon. He mourns silently for the fate of the people he is leaving behind. However, he knows he can't do anything now.

"Les carrottes sont cuites"

The Carrots are cooked!

The same day, Durbar Square, Kathmandu, Nepal

The vibes at PUNSAM's base didn't feel too much of an aggressive kind for Novsky and the family. Luckily, they were at the intelligence base, not Nepal's military training base. Albina and the kids had also made peace with their whereabouts after learning that PUNSAM saved their lives and this might be a safer place for them to stay. Also, knowing that the world was about to end and there was a slight chance of UNIBOMB succeeding, they started looking at the brighter side. PUNSAM had given them hope that there was a plan to save from all this and that they had been lucky to be together as a family in these dangerous times.

In these few days, they learnt a lot about PUNSAM. First, it poses as a terrorist organisation, but it rarely killed innocent people barring few collateral damages that added to the gruesome tag behind its name.

The environment at PUNSAM was pan-global, pan-peaceful here. Many people came from various backgrounds and all around the world.

Jovan had got acquainted with many members at PUNSAM as they gathered a lot of information related to KVALITAT deals, the questionable corrupt deals that his boss had done without his consent, the thinking behind ARK, TUESDA protocols, etc. He observed that there was no reporting hierarchy in PUNSAM. It appeared like a very flat organisation with no reporting circles.

He learned they have been funded well by some wealthy people worldwide and even backed by a few political leaders. One thing he was clear on was that he won't be able to resume his everyday life back, as TUESDA was hunting him and his family. There is no place safer on this planet except under the PUNSAM network and protection. This was the only organisation with that level of muscle power, brains, and resources to match TUESDA's prowess.

Kaamna had become a very dear friend to Novsky's family and even bonded well with Alexei and Maxim. She was the emotional support they needed and a comforting factor. They were now safer in PUNSAM's shelter. She insisted that Novsky becomes part of PUNSAM and fight for the right cause against TUESDA's nefarious plans to destroy mankind. PUNSAM was very confident that if they could expose TUESDA's hidden agenda and the top world leaders who backed those for their benefit, the entire humanity would understand the actual image of PUNSAM. They were not a terrorist entity but a revolutionary organisation that wanted to make this planet a better place to live.

Kaamna and Novsky were having a working lunch session after the detailed briefs shared by Novsky.

Novsky asked, "Kaamna, I am worried here now. We all know that an extinction-level event is upcoming, and here we are researching notes like reporters. It's like college days when we would all brainstorm together and research to write a white paper on something. I thought PUNSAM believed in actions. You know, blow up the villains and win the way type, eh?"

Kaamna smiles and replies, "Well, we don't believe in violence until, unless it is absolutely needed, Novsky. We are rational, scientific and truth-seeker sorts here. If something can be done with peace, we would always, till our last breath, resort to that. However, the few bombings, assassinations, etc., that we carried out were paramount. Our council leaders planned and sanctioned those events, as otherwise, there would have been major losses to the world economy or mankind. Even there, we proceed with the utmost caution not to do any significant collateral damage. So far, we have been most successful in doing that. Remember the plane crash with your Canadian consignment? Well, no one died in that crash. Both the pilots were members of PUNSAM and had escaped with parachutes way before the crash. They are in one of our safe-houses, probably preparing for their next mission."

Novsky, visibly surprised, speaks, "Ahh, I never thought of this possibility once the news was out, but I am glad they are safe. Although I disapprove of your other bombings and assassinations. An eye for an eye makes the universe blind, Kaamna."

Kaamna replies, "Wow, a Serbian quoting Gandhi. You certainly have read your history books very well, Jovan. I know you won't approve of our methods, but we have no other choice left but to resort to them. No one will hear our pleads, letters and peace marches anymore. Entities like TUESDA only open their ears when they hear a bang and a blast."

Novsky says, "Well, there is no arguing about that. Tell me, how did you join PUNSAM? You were not born into it, right?"

"Well, it was two years ago, around September 2029, when we were approached by a top council member of PUNSAM," says Kaamna.

Novsky interferes and says, "We? You mean you and your husband?"

Kaamna replies, "No, Novsky, me and my sister. You have met her many times already. Her name is, I am sorry, was Anita Naidu and she used to work for ISRO, Bengaluru till a few days ago. I am assuming you know what happened to her?"

Novsky was in shock and said, "Anita was your sister! Oh damn, now I can connect all the dots. So that's how you guys came to know about KRAAL, NEBULA and ARK, right?" he pauses and says, "I am sorry for interfering again. So how did you meet the PUNSAM leader, and where is your husband in all this? You are married, right?"

Kaamna smiles and says, "Yes, Novsky, I am married even though my husband is not with me anymore. And before you think anything else, the matter here is that of life and death. He is no more in this world now. May God bless his soul. Actually, that's the reason we got connected with PUNSAM.

She adds, "Three years ago, my husband was killed in a wild goose chase in Delhi. He was an investigating officer in the NIA (National Intelligence Agency). They were working with the ATS team in Delhi for a suspected terrorist attack that was about to happen. However, within a few days, he disappeared, leaving no trace of his whereabouts. His team, me, his friends and his family searched for him for many days. 3 months after, his body arrived in a body bag, and they asked me for identification. It was the most horrifying and the worst moment of my lifetime." She pauses and Novsky holds her hand and pats it.

"After his death, I started inquiring about his mission and other things he was looking into. My husband Aman used to tell me a lot about the corruption poisoning ATS and NIA and how his work was hampered daily by that. One day before his disappearance, he was drinking a lot and blabbering about someone in Government. The latter was making things tougher for him and his team. I noticed little about the depth of his concerns and why he behaved differently that day. I thought it might be some usual work stress that was making Aman sulky that day. However, the next day he went to the office and was supposed to go for some field work and never returned.

We all tried to enquire about him at all the places, from his office, spoke to his colleagues and superiors, even complained formally via an FIR, and tried to speak to some political resources we had. And then, even when it was confirmed he was no more, I didn't stop there. I wanted ATS and NIA to investigate the matter more deeply, but they all said it was an accident. They said some locals fished his body out from a nearby canal. They discovered him in a small village in Uttar Pradesh, some 100 miles away from New Delhi. They said they did not know what he was doing there as he wasn't assigned any case recently. However, me and Anita Didi, my sister, suspected foul play as nothing was making sense. Why would he travel all the way to a small village for no reason? We pressurised and pressurised but were dismissed by all authorities, and even the local police in Delhi and UP refused to help us further. Some even tainted his image by putting baseless labels on him like maybe he had an affair, or perhaps he was involved with the local mafia, maybe he took some bribe and didn't do the deed, etc. etc."

Kaamna takes a deep breath after saying all this, heart still heavy and eyes moist.

Novsky holds her hand and speaks, "I am sorry, Kaamna. So, when we met at that time, your husband was not alive, I assume. I can understand and imagine how you would have felt having lost the love of your life. And that too in such a mysterious way. Did you find out what happened to him after all this?"

Kaamna speaks, "Not till a very long time, Novsky. One day after coming from the NIA office, an American slipped a note in my sister's wallet." He said, "I know what happened to Aman. Meet me at Boris12 Cafe in Hauz Khas at 5pm."

So, Didi and I went there. And that's where we met for the first time, one of the council leaders of PUNSAM, Jared Lincoln. In fact, the entire cafe is owned by PUNSAM only and used as a meeting spot for our agents, apart from entertaining some infrequent guests.

That day, no one was in the cafe except me, Anita and Jared. He told us what had happened to Aman.

Long story short, Aman was investigating a promising lead that could have proved that it linked a renowned politician in UP to terrorist activities in India and abroad. He was directly linked with multiple terrorist groups and moved money, weapons, and import-export approvals through his business and other local support. Jared told us it was that same politician who got

Aman killed in the same village where he met his informer. The worst part was that local authorities, police and even big shots at CBI, NIA and ATS didn't tell us anything about it. Jared mentioned that many top leaders in the Indian Government and these agencies are aware of the association but had turned deaf ears while serving the 'Greater Good' agenda."

Kaamna continued, "This didn't gel at all with Didi and me. We wanted to expose everyone involved in this scam. We wanted to go to the media and organise protests and rallies against this cause. However, Jared told us it wouldn't matter, and that won't be the right way to avenge Aman's martyrdom. Then he shared with us about PUNSAM and what it stood for. He shared his story as well and asked us to join the cause. In the first meeting, Anita connected with Jared's belief and PUNSAM's long-term goal of serving humanity with truth and peace. In fact, later on, as we joined PUNSAM, they both bonded really well and started seeing each other as well.

However, I knew if I had to really honour Aman's sacrifice, I had to look beyond the small pawns involved in that scandal and instead go for the bigger goal. The goal for which PUNSAM stands and the end-game we planned for all such crooks. Anita and I went through rigorous training provided by PUNSAM in a village in Ireland. You might recall that if you had worked closely with Anita. She had taken a 3-month break for a family emergency in between from ISRO. When we returned to India, they had trained us efficiently in hand-to-hand combat, close-range shooting, guerilla battles and whatnot. Our first assignment was a revenge assignment only. We had silently eliminated all the assassins of Aman, including the aforementioned politician. After that, I was involved in many other missions as well.

At PUNSAM, we had thought of something much bigger this year, but then the KRAAL news came, and everything came standstill. Since then, we have investigated KRAAL, ARK and everyone related to this. As of now, our agenda is to ensure that humanity survives and justice be done to the people running away from this planet without properly fighting for it. All the corrupts, selfish men and women, brutal two-faced people who have bought themselves life at the cost of few who deserved it for humanity's sake. We don't want to go to ARK. All we wanted was that the selection criteria be justified. But, sadly, we could do nothing about it. Now we want the UNIBOMB to be given the proper priority, and everyone on the earth knows what's coming ahead."

Novsky asks, "Then why don't you guys tell everyone about ARK, KRAAL and the 10K mission and UNIBOMB? Tell the humanity about this chaos, this madness, the unjustified selection of people on ARK and everything."

Kaamna replies, "We could have told all this. We have deeper connections in media and even politics. However, all that would be nothing, as TUESDA and other world leaders would dismiss such revelation as an urban myth. Something like UFO sightings in Roswell, etc.

However, our council at PUNSAM was also divided into two – one wanted the world leaders to reveal this, and the other wanted this to lie low as otherwise, it would be madness all around. However, Jared went rogue and independent with Anita, as he belonged to the former school of thought. They asked the Indian Prime Minister to share this news with the media. However, before they could pressurise them into doing that, TUESDA killed Jared and Anita. The new council at PUNSAM held this information for now. The rumour in PUNSAM is that maybe at the last moment, another unit at PUNSAM will secretly sneak in a few people in ARK. We have many units now in PUNSAM, each disconnected from the other for our members' safety. Only the council leaders know about every member."

Novsky says, "I am sorry about Anita, Kaamna. Do you know who the new council leaders of PUNSAM are and where are they right now? What do they want? Everyone is about to die, and you guys are just doing search and rescue operations?"

Kaamna smiles. "Exactly our dilemma, Novsky. We have been asking the same question to them. However, we get the same answer always. We need to wait for the right time. We get instructions from them in a coded message; all we must do is execute them. This might sound hierarchical, but the council is the last word at PUNSAM. In the past, our success is only due to wise leadership by our council leads, and we trust them blindly now as well. However, truth be told, I am not scared at all. I have lost all the family I had in the past few years. So, dead or alive, I don't care. But I really want the martyrdom of Aman, Anita and Jared not to go to waste. I have full faith in the leadership at PUNSAM, and I know they are thinking of something better for humanity only."

Novsky thinks to himself, feeling sorry about KAAMNA. He felt that maybe she is putting her trust in the wrong people. People she has never met as well. Perhaps the council leads of PUNSAM are considering safeguarding themselves as a priority. Maybe they would be the ones who will sneak inside the ARK along with other people, who knows. He knew he and his family were safer for a few months, thanks to PUNSAM. But the initial gratitude would be replaced by what was coming to them in a few months – the ultimate end, which gave him sleepless nights for months.

Suddenly KAAMNA gets a message on her encrypted phone. She leaves the room and tells Novsky, "Pack your stuff, Jovan. We have to leave urgently for New Delhi in the next hour. Our plane is ready. The plot will develop further from there. I have a feeling we might meet the council leaders this time."

Jovan looks at KAAMNA with anticipation and leaves to return to his room to fetch Albina and the kids.

Same day 0930 PM, Pokhran, Rajasthan

Arjun had arrived in Pokhran and was on the ARK as he led all the training, preparations, calibration and testing of the space shuttle. However, he missed Claudia and Samantha and waited eagerly to catch up with them after the take-off on the 31st.

Bill was on his base after having a debrief meeting with Nathan on the procedures at ARK. For the past 2 days, Bill had been involved in the ARK, preparing for the launch procedures and overlooking the entire site and base preparations. People were admitted inside the ARK in small batches after their medical examination on the site and provided training and tour for the next hour or two. This was a time-consuming process, and hence Bill wanted to be involved personally in overlooking the preparations. After all, there was nothing left on the planet earth for him to do now. The remaining batches will be onboarded on ARK the next day so that they can fly off on the 31st per the schedule. The entire thing was carried out confidentially and no media was allowed to cover the event. Few journalists had disguised themselves to cover the whole thing, but in the end, every media person was caught off by TUESDA agents, killed and buried in the desert.

Bill knew that this would arouse suspicion in the back-offices of these media people, but he cared least about what they will report on the event now. Already, the media was buzzing about the entire questionability of this whole mission. There was a series of news floating around the need for this peace mission and why the media was not allowed to cover this. There were already rumours and speculations in media going about various scenarios like the discovery of life beyond earth on mars. Some even speculated that these leaders wanted to capture the land on mars first before anyone else or claim rights to some rare mineral discovered on a planet or an alien invasion. Few even mentioned a potential doomsday scenario. Bill had sources in the media to keep the reasoning balanced and skewed more away from the doomsday scenario strategically, though it was not labelled as an out-of-agenda item.

Bill was consumed by his thoughts when a knock outside Bill's room and an agent from TUESDA walked inside. The agent says, "Sir, sorry for barging in at this hour. However, I have alarming news."

Bill looks at him and asks him to speak. Agent replies, "Sir, many of our members in the 10K list are missing. Many have not arrived in Pokhran. Some are missing from their designated hotels in New Delhi, Jaipur and Chandigarh. We are trying to trace the vehicle's GPS and the security escorting them. But shockingly, we cannot reach anyone till now. Around 1000 people are missing, Sir."

Bill looks highly frustrated and agitated. "How can they be missing? Did you ask Indian PM to look into it and check where they went? They were supposed to be on separate routes, right? Are you telling me that some planes also disappeared in the air?"

The agent looks embarrassed and says, "Yes, sir, precisely this. Some planes have also disappeared as well, sir. And some cars too. We don't have any leads now, sir. As you know, all our agents are now busy in ARK preparations."

Bill pauses for a moment.

The agent senses the anxiety in Bill's silence and adds, "Sir, there is further to it. Arjun's wife and daughter, Claudia and Samantha, have disappeared from their hotel as we planned to get them for today's evening travel to Pokhran. The security said that there were agents dressed like TUESDA's agents and got them out of the hotel early in a black SUV."

Bill looks extremely agitated and bangs the table with his fist. He dismisses the agent and picks up his phone to call Nathan and inform this news. Nathan picks up the phone and, before Bill can say anything, yells, "1000 people, Bill. How can they vanish into thin air under your nose?"

Bill replies, "Sir, how did you know that? Did an agent come and inform you?"

Nathan speaks, "News, my friend, and it's not any news. The only news I hate as it comes as a declaration by those bastards again."

Bill says, "PUNSAM! How can PUNSAM be involved? We got Jared and already took care of him. Wait a minute, sir..." And he starts his television to watch the news.

The TV reporter was debating with another senior retired Indian intelligence agent at the occurrence.

The reporter said, "It is shocking to find out that PUNSAM would go at this length and kidnap some of these world leaders and declare a formal war. Do you really believe what they are saying is true? Conspiracy at this highest level. We can't believe it….."

Bill switches the channel and searches for the source where PUNSAM's original declaration came. He finds a channel that reveals the PUNSAM's accurate statements and looks at it with shock.

He replies to Nathan on the phone, "Sir, it's time. Please board the ARK right now. We might leave any hour now."

And then he disconnects, gets ready and speaks to himself, "The carrots are cooked and might be over-burnt if we wait!

Chapter 18

If you Just Smile.

By now, you would have figured out that TUESDA and the other chaps in the world had one primary hobby – creating new organisations with abbreviations that sound super cool. ERO was one of them – called Earth Rescue Organisation. The idea was floated in the meeting at ISRO on 25th August 2031, and they made Ranjan the head of ERO. The team had quickly worked out the organisation's details, including its goals and strategic objectives (one of which included 24X7 support to ARK for its voyage) as well as team members of ERO. The team members of ERO were picked all around the world, and they flew to India at a day's notice and started working ASAP with Ranjan. These included key directors, scientists, army veterans, political experts, business leaders, medical professionals and even educators from around the world. Bill wanted ERO to have the best brains available in the world to carry out its agenda. The charter of ERO was valid for 4 months, after which TUESDA will pass a strategic order to continue or stop the organisation. They strategically chose the office of ERO to be the PRIME-1 office only as provided by Mahavir. This was because PRIME-1 had all the capabilities, including space monitoring stations, equipment, controls and even a private airfield from which even planes, jets and missiles could be launched. Ranjan was acting chairman of ERO and the sole decision-maker. The only other person who had the power to influence Ranjan's decision was the Indian Prime Minister because of the land in which the ERO operated. However, behind all this, Bill knew secretly that ERO is nothing but another puppet organisation of TUESDA. He was confident that Sharma would only act on his orders based on his meetings with him.

28th August 10:00PM, Pokhran, the Launch site of ARK

The rush and chaos inside the ARK are visible. After the notification message was sent to all, everyone was just rushing towards any pod available inside and getting themselves in it. Bill had just sent the SOS message to everyone and urged everyone to leave anything they were doing and rush towards their designated pod. However, without any concierge coordination and guidance, people were just going to any pod they would find available.

They repeatedly echoed the inside announcement in the ARK every minute,

"60 minutes to launch

59 minutes to launch…58 minutes to launch…"

Arjun tried calling Claudia and Samantha but could not connect via any phone or communication device on the ship or with him. In parallel, he guided the residents inside towards their allocated pod and tried to get the launch protocols started for the ship. He could not get in touch with Bill as the notice came abruptly. He knew Bill would be at the command centre of the ship controlling everything from there. But he could not get there, as Bill had instructed him to help everyone settle down and prepare the engineering team for the launch.

Bill had already entered the command centre and controlled every minute detail of the launch. He had been texting everyone in charge of the launch protocol, Arjun for Engineering, Clyde for the Medical team to supervise and monitor the residents, Kulkarni for the security part, ensuring only the people with designated passes enter the ship and controlling the external security of the mobs that will pop up.

The anxiety and worry on Arjun's face were clear as he was half-heartedly doing his job of guiding his engineering team, repeatedly wiping the sweat on his forehead, as the worries of not seeing his family increased for him every minute.

Finally, after a few minutes, he could set things in motion, rushed towards the command centre, and caught hold of Bill. Bill is talking to one of the command-centre executives and looks at Arjun as he enters.

Arjun speaks while panting. "Bill, what is this? Why have we preponed this launch two days in advance? We have just finished mock drills and had to do a lot before we take off, the medical tests, mentally preparing people for the next steps, proper see-off of other people on the planet, handover to ERO, etc. Also, on a separate note, where are Claudia and Samantha, Bill? I cannot find them."

Bill puts his hands on Arjun's shoulder and speaks, "Arjun, calm yourself down right now," and lies further, "Claudia and Samantha are in their chambers already put to sleep, Ok! I handled it personally as I had already got them on the afternoon trip, and they arrived here just on time with a few others. However, we must leave many other family members as they are still in transit. Now, look at this! PUNSAM had already brewed things out." With that, he points toward the screen and asks the operator to show the news.

The news was on, and the reporter was talking while the line read below the "BIGGEST DECEPTION IN HUMAN HISTORY." The aerial shots of the ARK were shown from a helicopter far from sight as any copter near the ARK was shot down by TUESDA's armoured drones. A very unclear image of the sight was being projected in the night along with lights covering the entire scene, and a reporter was talking about the biggest story in human history ever.

He adds, "As you can see, this peace operation was nothing but rescue and flee operation masterminded by TUESDA, all world leaders, businessmen and politicians. There is an imminent threat striking the earth and the first thing these leaders did was to get them out of the planet and leave us at the mercy of God or the last hope of striking the KRAAL with UNIBOMB."

Arjun looks at Bill in shock. "How come they know about KRAAL, UNIBOMB?"

The Indian reporter further adds, "The organisation we thought was a terrorist turned out to be the one who were fighting for humanity. PUNSAM has revealed the dark side of TUESDA and these world leaders and how they kept the entire planet in the dark about KRAAL, NEBULA, ARK and UNIBOMB. We now know that KRAAL, a large celestial object, is about to strike us in the next 2 to 3 months. Thanks to TUESDA, now there is no world leader strong enough left to calm humanity and lead fiercely and destroy the KRAAL. We are happy to inform you that the Indian Prime Minister decided not to leave and stay with us here to defend till his last breath. Sadly, we can't say the same for other countries whose leaders have already fled. Let me reread the PUNSAM's revelation.

THE STORY OF BETRAYAL AND TRUST

Humans,

We would like to inform you with deep regret that your own world leaders have fooled and duped you all. The ones who have been feeding you with false information, false images of the people in their network and false assurance of the fact that WE ARE ALL SAFE.

We at PUNSAM have discovered through our confirmed sources, informants and channels that 3 months from now, in December (or even late November), a heavy celestial object will strike the earth and the life as we know it will cease to exist. It will evaporate the planet instantly along with any living form staying on or inside the planet. This was discovered a few months ago by ISRO and some other top scientists from companies like PRIME-1 and KVALITAT. They did the revelation to TUESDA and every world leader. They started working on two plans. One was to destroy this with a globalised effort of creating the most potent weapon ever wielded by mankind known as UNIBOMB and the second was to get 10,000 people away from the planet in a special craft known as ARK. The ARK was meant to carry 10,000 worthy individuals from the planet with skills, talents and the biological make to help humanity prosper beyond our age. However, what was done by these leaders was shocking. The real-life staging of '2012' and 'Don't look up' movies. First, they decided they could all get on ARK, and mind it, these are old men and women in their 50s and

60s and some even in the 80s. Then they decided they would carry a handful of young men and women who are fighters, workers, labourers, engineers, and beautiful women, people not decided basis merit and the value they would bring in the sustenance of humanity, but to serve them for their comforts till their lifetime. Last, they formed an organisation known as ERO, Earth Rescue Organisation and got them access to all nuclear weapons, bombs etc., which are deployed in a desert in UAE to be called UNIBOMB. And they added a pinch of salt to that. They even extracted some vital nuclear bombs, armaments, etc., that were in UNIBOMB and got them installed on ARK for their second layer of safety. What would you call this entire plot, humans? We gave them many warnings and threats to reveal this, but they didn't. We knew if we had told this earlier to everyone, no one would have believed us, and TUESDA would have projected another agenda in their self-defence. However, we are now showing you select footage of some key people who are part of this project and confirm this. We will also show you the actual images of ARK and the order letter where the evacuation plan was discussed.

The reporter continues, "After this, they showed us the real interview of one Mr. Jovan Novsky, the brains behind KVALITAT and the architect of NEBULA and ARK."

The interview of Novsky continues with Kaamna interviewing him in a mask. Novsky reveals the entire plan and shows the actual images and footage of ARK, NEBULA and the government signed orders on evacuation. He reveals how the selection of the 10K list was all fake and then further reveals the murders and executions carried out by TUESDA to protect this secret. He also shows how his family was attacked but then saved by PUNSAM.

Arjun looks at this with horror and looks back at Bill, who had already stopped watching it minutes ago as he was busy preparing for the launch.

Arjun grabs Bill and says, "Bill, what is it? Were you planning to kill Novsky? When was I gonna be informed of this? And why are we doing this? Let's do this the right way. Let's not get PUNSAM to win this battle and get all humans on their side. We discussed how ERO will step in, calm the public, and prepare them for the battle slowly, piece by piece. Now the cat is out of bags. How will ERO handle the rest of the mission? There will be chaos and mutiny all over the world. What are we supposed to do now?"

Bill speaks, "Arjun, I have already spoken to Sharma and the Indian PM, who released their communication just a few minutes ago. Check out the news again." With that, he tunes in to another channel where the update came.

The news report said,

"After the PUNSAM's deadly revelation on the betrayal of trust, we have got the latest remarks and comments by the Indian Prime Minister. Let's look at the official email sent to all the media channels. It says:

This is to inform everyone on the planet that they should not believe whatever is being said by PUNSAM. Please don't panic. There is no imminent danger here. PUNSAM is trying to hijack the most vital mission of peace for humanity, and we should just not get our minds into speculations at this stage.

As we know it, the earth is and will always be safe. We deny any information related to KRAAL or fancy terms you would have heard. In fact, to put you all at rest, tomorrow at 11 AM IST, we will do an official address by the Indian Prime Minister and share the next plan of peace mission and the steps taken by us to control PUNSAM's terrorist activities. Please stop believing in this terrorist organisation known as PUNSAM."

Arjun looks at Bill and calms down slightly. "Do you think this is supposed to calm down the public? This sounds so made-up and bureaucratic. PUNSAM showed the details of ARK, Novsky's video and what not?"

Bill speaks, "We have monitored the activity around the world. Road protests and riots are happening right now, and a lot of public property destruction, etc. But nothing we can't handle. A significant proportion of people still believe in what we are saying and not in PUNSAM's shady depiction of events. Sharma will have a huge role to play. Only before the D-day strike event, on the day we will shoot UNIBOMB, and if it fails, will we inform the people about the end event. That would give them 2 to 3 hours to be with their family and spend the last time together."

Arjun looks at Bill with such shock and disgust that he speaks. "Are you out of your mind? Spend last time together. Are we not going to reveal the truth even tomorrow?"

Bill says, "Are you kidding me? And not give a chance for UNIBOMB to work? If we tell them tomorrow, they will just destroy everything on the planet already. And possibly some mob will go to the UAE desert and scrape off every bomb from UNIBOMB and figure out how to come in a space shuttle to NEBULA already."

Arjun says, "Ok, now you are being fictional!"

Bill says, "The point is, let the peace and harmony be the way it is. Let's divert them to other issues like some Bollywood couple marriage, some scam in Russia or the US or some major currency crisis or heck, let's even give them a recession in the stock market. We don't want the UNIBOMB plan to fail, right? Let Sharma give enough time, focus on the real work, and not handle these stupid global riots and events. He is a scientist and not a political mastermind. Now, don't waste my time and be with your engineering team during the launch and start the protocol."

Arjun nods at Bill with a bit of disapproval and runs towards the engineering section of the spacecraft to be with his team members.

New Delhi, same time

Sharma was in his office today and had decided not to go home. He had informed his family that he would stay in the office for one week because of the progress of an important peace event. There was a protocol defined by TUESDA in which they could not contact their families for 3 days before and 3 days after the launch of ARK. This was for the safety of the entire operation. The entire building of ERO was secured, and they had installed network jammers. The security was a mix of agents of TUESDA, independent security agencies, Indian soldiers, the Army and even some freelancers from the US. This was a very important base for the ARK operation, as ERO will help monitor the launch and control any support needed by the ARK in the future. TUESDA decided that ERO was the one instead of NASA or ISRO for this operation, as ERO was a far more global entity owing to its members' nationalities. They chose the ERO members at the last stage; many of them didn't know each other. Sharma had a tremendous task ahead of him in getting the work from people who didn't even connect well with each other but only answered to Bill or their world leaders.

At precisely 10pm, he had got a quick call from Bill.

Bill says, "Sharma, my friend. I hope you are doing good. I have to inform you that because of some unfortunate circumstances, we have to take off from ARK right now in the next hour. There is a mob directed at us that will not stop at any cost. Our sources are showing the mix of some citizens, members of the underworld, rogue armed forces, etc. that are coming here to stop this operation at any instant. Now, the memo you and Indian PM released was helpful, but they still want control here and ask questions. We don't want to be here and unnecessarily halt the operation and handle them. Believe me, we can, but the outcomes can go in any direction, and I am in no mood for casualties now. Wish you all the best. Message me if there is any concern. I will see you live on the command-centre field now."

With that, he disconnects, and the only thing Sharma said was "Hello Bill" at the start and "Okay Bill" at the end of the call. He realised and presumed that this was the sort of conversation Bill enjoyed mostly, as Arjun had told him many times.

With that, Sharma walks to the ground command centre of ERO, where many analysts, scientists etc., were gathered. They connected everyone on the video with large screens that displayed the video of the command centre at the ARK.

Engineers were getting instructions from their peers regarding the protocol to be followed. All calibrations were done. They, anyway, were prepared for the mission in advance. Even before the KRAAL event announcement, the ARK was tested for launch by a team of scientists, including Sharma and Novsky. Sharma knew that the launch would be successful, and his team is efficient enough to handle the relay commands for the launch. Even the team on board ARK was trained; some of them were scientists with whom Sharma and his team had worked for quite a long time.

Bill is talking to his team members while Sharma watches the commotion on the screen. He observes the discussion Arjun had with Bill over his discontent over the entire urgency of the operation. He also watches Arjun rushing towards his engineering bay after being assured falsely by Bill about Claudia and Samantha. Sharma and his team had scanned the entire ARK spaceship, including the key members, and there was no sign of Samantha and Claudia.

Sharma felt a bit disgusted about Bill and how he lied to Arjun, but he knew he couldn't say anything to Arjun, as it would compromise the complete operation.

He takes a seat, takes off his spectacles, puts his hands on his face, and watches everything in front of him with various camera-feeds live telecasting everything around the spaceship. The show goes on for him. He was so baked mentally that he ignored all the voices, put headphones on his ears, and tuned in to the song.

It was his favourite classical song, "Smile" by Jimmy Durante. As the song starts, the entire scene unfolds in front of him.

'Smile, though your heart is achin'

Smile even though it's breakin'

When there are clouds in the sky,

You'll get by."

Bill stands in the middle and observes every team member on the spaceship and is on a constant call with his people around the spacecraft. Engineers are all running here and there before the launch to get everything in place. Medical staff rushed towards the pods, calibrating each pod with a particular temperature and taking the vital readings of every guest in the pod.

"Light up your face with gladness

Hide every trace of sadness

Although a tear

Maybe ever so near."

He watches the residents, some tucked in the vertical chambers in the pods sleeping and some seated in the visitor lounge seats, wearing belts. The latter are the ones who want to witness space travel and are the ones who might be called for any help. He sees the emotions on everyone, a touch of anxiety, hope and a bit of relief that they are being saved from imminent destruction.

"That's the time you must keep on tryin'

Smile, what's the use of cryin'

You'll find that life is still worthwhile

If you just smile."

Then he watches the readings of various instruments as shown on the instrument panel LEDs. All parameters under control, internal humidity, temperature, pressure readings, the initial thrust of engines, all sensors, server uptime, etc. He then fixes his eyes on the only screen he thought was worth focussing on. The countdown timer begins.

"10

9

8

7

6

5

4

3

2

.....Project ARK is a Go," says the command centre.

With that, ARK was launched into space successfully, and there was a bit of clapping by a few naïve scientists who did not know about KRAAL and what the real purpose of ARK was. One could see the video streaming of people inside the ARK, all strapped in their seats and experiencing acceleration while awake or asleep. Two faces showed very little anxiety about the flight – one Mr. Bhatia and the other who orchestrated this entire thing at his fingertips and Sharma's immediate boss now for the next 3 months, Bill.

Sharma closes his eyes as the song ends,

"If you just smile."

Inside the space station ARK, they set the clock to 0 at precisely 2300 hrs IST on 28th August 2031, known as Day 1 Space-time for ARK from now on.

Chapter 19

That's What Makes you that Guy!

It was mandatory in every space travel mission to have a group of medical officers and doctors on the board. The entire journey would take a toll not only on the mental but emotional health of the residents as well. With ARK, though the residents were given enough training for a month or two, they were still amateurs compared to the trained astronauts and space scientists. They onboarded a large group of medical officers and doctors on ARK to serve the rest. A huge medical bay was created with a lounge, check-up rooms, and even an operation theatre for emergencies. Many of the residents were old and needed regular medical treatment for one or two ailments. The entire bay was called The ARK Clinic, but it was like a mini-hospital inside the spaceship. Many argued that the clinic's scale was way too large for a spacecraft, and had it been travelling with the fit astronauts, space scientists etc., only one or two rooms would have sufficed. They equipped the entire ARK with many thermal sensors and diagnostic points across the spaceship where people can test their vitals such as heart rate, blood tests, fever, X-rays, etc. All the vitals of every resident were captured in one place and analysed by full-time operators on the job. The report would be auto-generated and shared across the ARK leadership, presided by Bill. Not only that, there were a group of trained behavioural scientists and psychoanalysts who would observe anyone on the deck, watch out for any simulative aggressive or non-linear behaviour and do the right intervention. They tested the entire residents before the commencement of the flight for viral infections and possible communicable diseases (e.g. Coronavirus, flu, HIV, Hepatitis, Monkey Pox, H1N1 and whatnot). Every resident marked as Alpha was exempted from the medical test before and after the flight. These people would not be sleeping in the pods under sleeping gas but would be active in supporting the launch, monitoring it, observing it, etc. These were fairly experienced people who already had explored space before, and their bodies had been used to space travel. Bill and Nathan, amongst others, had in the past travelled to the Moon Station for a few meetings. Everyone else marked as Beta had to undergo medical tests before and after the launch and entry into the cruise zone for the spacecraft.

28th August 2031, Greater Kailash, New Delhi, 1130 PM

Claudia and Sophia wake up in a comfortable room inside a posh guest house in GK-2, New Delhi. Claudia checks on Sophia and hugs her after touching her head and face. She kisses her head, and they both cry, hugging each other. Then, she stands up, realising that someone is behind her.

Novsky is standing along with Albina. Claudia is a bit relieved to see the familiar face of Novsky, as Arjun had mentioned a lot about him and even had a video call with him once during a birthday celebration. Albina walks towards her and holds her hand and introduces herself. Claudia and Sophia look at them with surprise when the door opens, and Kaamna enters.

After offering her a glass of water, she sits down near Claudia and speaks, "Hi, sorry to have you both moved here like that.

However, we were instructed to do so. Don't worry about any side effects of the sleeping pill you got inside the car where we picked you up. We had to give you that for your own safety reasons. Let me share a few details with you on the truth about what's happening."

She then tells Claudia the entire story about PUNSAM, KRAAL, ARK, NEBULA and how TUESDA conspired and got the 10K list, excluding the worthy individuals to serve their personal agenda. Claudia was hearing this all with surprise and utmost shock when she realised Arjun was also part of the plan, even though his heart didn't want to be in it. PUNSAM had been tracking Arjun for long, and they had an idea about his disapproval towards everything TUESDA had been conspiring and that he couldn't do anything because he was worried about the safety of Claudia and Sophia.

Claudia speaks, "Oh my God, I don't know what to say. I cannot believe anything that you are saying. Why would Arjun hide such a big thing from me? I have always supported him in every decision of his."

Novsky speaks, "Claudia, the way I know him, he would have guessed that you won't sign up for being on board at ARK but face the same fate as the rest of the planet only."

Kaamna adds, "Yes, our agents also confirm the same. We have people who monitor the chatter and the key psychological analysis of everyone we tag. Our suspicion was the same as well. He hid it from you and Sophia because he feared you won't be on board with him. But we were disappointed in him as we thought he, out of all the people, would leave no stone unturned when it came to saving the planet. But, well, the pressure of one's family and the potential thought of risking the life of your own little daughter might corrupt the best men in the world. So, no hard feelings out there."

Claudia looks surprised at Kaamna and says, "What are you talking about? Hard feelings for what? How does it matter now? He has already fled the planet along with everyone else. He didn't even care to search for us and was busy fulfilling his duties. Why would you believe he would be worried about us and not only him?"

Kaamna replies, "No, Claudia, our sources have confirmed that he was eager to see you guys on the ship and would have deboarded if he had known that you have not made it. He was falsely assured by Bill, his boss, that you guys are on board. And that he had no time to check or react, as they only had a few minutes to go. Bill somehow confused him with another lady and a daughter of a similar age group and showed camera footage where they wore masks and slept inside a pod. Arjun assumed from the distant picture that it was you guys and carried along with the launch activity. We have one inside agent already on the ARK, a very successful businessman turned politician from Israel."

Claudia sighs, looking down and then holds Samantha, who is looking at everyone with a half understanding of what's happening.

Kaamna concludes, "You might wonder that we wanted both of you to stay with us and face the doomsday destruction. However, our plan was quite the opposite. We wanted to get hold of Arjun many times and get him to a secure location. However, the TUESDA's security around him was always super intense. He was monitored by Bill regularly, too. It would have been a suicide mission. However, our leaders wanted you guys to be on the earth only and be very positive about the UNIBOMB plan. They feel that you deserve a normal human life amongst everyone else and not some artificially constructed space life on ARK."

Claudia looks at Kaamna and quizzically adds, "But if UNIBOMB is successful, then people on ARK could also come back to the planet and live a normal life, too. Why don't you admit you wanted us to die with everyone else and not get preferential treatment? Now, wait!" she pauses and points a finger at Claudia and adds,

"Before you speak any further, Kaamna, I would like to tell you that this would have been my decision, too. I would have chosen to stay with Samantha on the planet and die with everyone else rather than be in a space pod watching this planet come to tatters. So, don't get me wrong, I am thankful, but you don't have to sugar-coat your intentions. I get it, live like humans, die like humans."

Kaamna smiles at her and mutters, "So, our guess and Arjun's predicament was right. If you had known the truth, you would have refused to go to ARK."

Claudia replies, "Definitely, not only that. I wouldn't have allowed him to go to ARK too and rather spend these last beautiful gorgeous moments with us, friends and relatives. I am shattered that during the last days of our lives, we don't have Arjun with us. And I am even feeling worse for him and terrified now what would happen to him when he finds the truth that we are not there?"

Novsky speaks, "He will find that out in just a couple of hours as the ARK gets into a stable orbit now."

Samantha looks at everyone, sits on Claudia's lap, hugs her, and speaks, "I miss Daddy. He should not have worked for these bad people, Mom."

29th August 2031, 0130 AM IST (0230 hrs, Day 1, Space-Time)

The ARK is launched into space effectively and gets inside the stable zone, crossing the Earth's atmosphere from the launch phase to the cruise phase. Arjun seems a bit relaxed now as his major work is done and comes to the regular maintenance and issue resolution stage only at the Cruise stage. He will have to get to the action a few days before the commencement of docking with NEBULA (which is a few months from now).

He is excited to see Claudia and Samantha and heads to the pod where he was told they are. As soon as he reaches there, he finds the pod is empty and is being serviced by a space housecleaning staff. She tells him the occupants have been called for a medical check-up in the lounge area along with other travellers.

He runs towards the lounge area and sees a lot of visitors seated in the lounge and many inside various medical rooms waiting for their turn. He walks toward every row and corner and even glances inside each medical room (perks of being the ship's second-in-command). However, he cannot find Samantha or Claudia anywhere. His worry and anxiety kept on building every minute he could not see them.

Then he realises that the information about residents and their 24/7 tracking is done at the command centre by the

TUESDA security teams under Bill. He rushes towards the command centre and catches hold of an operator doing the head-count and synching the medical data of all residents.

He checks with him the status of residents Claudia and Samantha. The operator tells him they are not marked present since the flight's start. Arjun gets anxious, asks the operator to move away from the computer, and starts scanning himself. He finds that only 7000 people could get inside the ARK out of 10,000 because of the last-minute fiasco. They left most of the family members behind, especially those in transit. Many family members who had arrived early were, however, able to get inside. Arjun's eyes are welling with tears, and his entire body is trembling as he stands and looks around to find Bill in the central command.

Bill was seated in his commander/captain seat and discussing with the ground team at ERO with Sharma on a video call on various earth-related updates. Suddenly, he sees Arjun coming to him, and he walks towards Arjun with authority and looks at him with firm eyes, waiting for Arjun to speak. He can see Arjun, red-eyed, full of tears, glaring at him as if he had found his bluff. As soon as Arjun approaches Bill, he shouts and yells at him.

"Bill, tell me you were not lying when you said Claudia and Samantha are on the ship."

Bill doesn't reply to the question and keeps looking at Arjun straight in his eyes for another few seconds. Arjun grits his teeth, looks away from Bill, wipes his tears, and then comes closer to Bill, pointing a finger at his chest.

"How dare you risk my family and leave them on Earth to die with everyone else alone without me being there with them? I told you my only condition to come to ARK is if Claudia and Samantha are coming. And you agreed to it. Why couldn't you wait for an hour or two so everyone could have arrived on the spot, and we could have left together?"

Bill looks at him and replies, "Arjun, what do you think I was doing before? I was tracking only Claudia and Samantha from the entire lot that was left behind. I would have waited for them or bloody flew a chopper or a high-speed jet if I could have traced them."

Arjun looks at him with shock and says, "What do you mean, trace them? They were in that hotel Leela in Gurgaon, right? So where are they now?"

Bill says, "I found out from my sources that they left early in the afternoon in a black SUV along with agents who posed as TUESDA agents. After that, there is no trace of where they went. This is like the earlier abductions by this group, including Novsky in Serbia. You know who I am talking about – those PUNSAM bastards."

Arjun is shocked, puts his hands on his face, and says, "Oh my God. How could the terrorist get hold of them, Bill? Where was our security when they got into? How could your guys be such idiots? Oh my God! My wife and my poor little daughter at the hands of the terrorists. Please tell me they are safe, Bill. Did you get any revert from them?"

Bill says, "Nothing, but the ERO has been tracking them. We already had the edible GPS tracker inside their body, which works on their pulse. Don't worry; there is no side effect of that, and it is perfectly untraceable. After Novsky's case, I got it installed for many of our people. We have confirmation that the tracker is active, which means both of them are alive. Also, we have a precise location of their whereabouts. We will act on the intelligence soon. The team at ERO has been informed. However, you need to buy us some time until we have sorted out other matters. I want you to be calm about this. I assure you I will get them."

Arjun looks at him in disapproval and shouts, "To hell with you and your assurances! What is the use now? They are on earth and will die with everyone else in a few months." With that, he holds Bill by his collar, and Bill fights him back and pushes him away. Two security guards run and grip Arjun in their fists.

In retaliation, Arjun shouts at Bill, "You are a monster, Bill! A complete monster. You killed many people only to ensure that your power and agendas are protected. You have no sense of morality or humanity left in you. So many people are left behind just because of your inability to act and stand up for humanity." And then he looks around the command centre and yells at everyone.

"All of you! All of you are cowards and selfish people. The only thing you care about is your life and nothing else. You have no sense of morality, you have no…." Bill interrupts him in a harsh voice.

"Oh, come on, Arjun. Spare us your blame game. Morality, humanity, selfishness – if that's what we are, then you are the one too. You could have stayed back on the planet, along with many others who knew about this plan. I offered the tickets to everyone, you, Sharma, Novsky, many scientists, Prime Ministers, and others. You took the chance along with everyone else on the deck. You also only cared about your family and your safety. Your best friend Sharma is back on the planet, about to die with his family. Why didn't you do the same, and what are you talking about, morality, humanity? Do you think I wanted you because you are the only expert here? No, I wanted you because I cared about you and the other team members. I knew you guys were one of the best and gave a chance to everyone to be with me. That stupid Novsky was slipping, and I had to make a call to eliminate him. But that was to assure the safety of everyone else on the ship, including you. Now, stop all the whining and settle down like a man. We all have left our families, friends, and relatives back on earth and yet continue this journey."

Arjun looks at him with anger and spits on the floor near him. "To hell with you and your fake speech, Bill. All you cared about was power, and you wanted people who supported you on this. This is all bullshit. You wouldn't have blinked an eye on deciding whether to help my family. Everything is a number, asset, or plan for you. None of you, insensible people, deserve to be here. I had selected so many great human beings who could have been crucial to the survival of mankind. Those were the people who would have built a better society in space. And here we are. Left with fools, money-minded, power-hungry people on the deck. Such bloody irony!!"

Bill paces towards Arjun, punches him in the face, and speaks, "Enough!" And asks the guards to take him away.

The guards put tape on Arjun's face and drag him away into a cell.

Bill resumes his call with Ranjan, who was watching all this drama from his screen. Bill speaks, "I am sorry, Ranjan, that you have to watch this. But I am sure you understand my decision's rationale and why we must leave many people behind. If this launch had been delayed, it would never have happened as time was of the essence. I am pretty sure we would have been in an actual war with an army of mobs, and the damage would have been on Indian soil. Also, there wouldn't have been any ARK left afterwards."

Ranjan replies, "Understood, Bill, though I don't agree with this completely. I think you could have had a diplomatic discussion on this with everyone and resolved it. But then, it would have taken a lot of time and possibly delayed the launch. While there can be many arguments against what you did, I don't judge the decision taken. After all, you have far more experience in such stuff than me."

Bill replies with a laugh, "Such stuff? Do you mean the doomsday scenario stuff? Yes, yes, I have a lot of experience in this. Have saved hundreds of species from another planet. Anyway, you tell me, how are things back at ERO? You mentioned the Prime Minister's address to the world that's about to happen in a few hours, right?"

Ranjan replies, "Yes, Bill. PM Mr. Singh will address everyone worldwide at 9AM IST sharp. The agenda is to basically calm everyone about the suspicion of ARK, the doomsday scenario and put the claims by PUNSAM to rest. We have also sent a copy of the speech to you in advance. Our stance is the same:

this is a peace mission, and PUNSAM is just trying to play a blame game against the world leader as they want to obstruct human peace. We are also adding the fact that PUNSAM has secretly sent us a demand of 20 Billion Dollars recently for releasing the government leaders and their family members as abducted by them. This will further add fuel in public against PUNSAM, and they won't heed their warnings and this KRAAL doomsday scenario event."

Bill smiles and replies as he looks at the copy of the speech himself, "Very well done, Mr. Sharma. I see you have acted as a genuine leader already. You shouldn't be a scientist. When our UNIBOMB plan becomes a success, and we return, you can expect a leadership role in TUESDA itself."

Sharma replies, "Thanks, Bill. I think I will stick to science. The politics and strategic games aren't my strong point. I am doing what you have instructed me to – precise clockwork rollout of your doctrine, Sir."

Bill replies, "Hahaha, that's good, Mr. Sharma. You will reach heights in your life. We will watch the PM address at 9AM IST, around 1000 hrs of Spacetime, Day 1. I will release the announcement in the spaceship immediately for the same so that we are all tuned together for this. We will play this announcement across all the screens in the spaceship, and the audio will be relayed across every section of the aircraft. Tell Mr. Singh to add some motivational touch to his speech to boost the morale of everyone on the planet and provide confidence. Everyone here would also love to be assured that our dear friends on the planet earth are not anxious about what's coming." He sets his clock at the alarm for 9AM IST, or 1000 hrs space-time. He then relays a notification, a voice message inside the space deck and mail to every resident about the PM's address and that they should all be listening to that.

Nathan watches Bill as he disconnects and speaks. "Pity what happened to your dear boy, Arjun! I see you have found yourself a new student for Bill-101 with Ranjan." Bill chuckles at Nathan on this.

"Everything is going as per the plan," Bill speaks. "Now, if this PM can address and calm everyone on the planet, that would be the last masterstroke, and we will set things in motion for the next few months. Otherwise, it would be a pity, as the chaos in the world would be unsettling. That would further impact the support ARK would get from ERO in due course of their journey, as ERO will be occupied in handling the fiasco on Earth."

Also, he secretly wished that he was wrong for this decision and that UNIBOMB would become a success. Either way, he and his people are already protected in both scenarios.

ERO Office, New Delhi, same time

Ranjan had just concluded his call with Bill. He felt bad for what happened to Arjun but couldn't do anything. While he was lost in his thoughts, someone sat behind his chair and placed a beer bottle in front of him.

He observes and sees Rajat holding another beer bottle in his hand behind him.

Rajat speaks, "Cheers, Dad. The peace mission is successful. You had been working way too hard for months. I thought before the PM address tomorrow, I should come up and grab a beer with you. These guys allowed me today. Seems like I am a big shot now, the son of someone really important, ya."

Ranjan smiles, looks at Rajat, grabs the beer, and clinks the glass with Rajat. He realises Rajat feels proud of his father as he is part of leading a peace mission of top world leaders in space. But he does not know about doomsday, the end of the world, and that a few thousand world leaders deceived the entire humanity.

Ranjan speaks, "Thanks, son. Yea, these guys allowed you because I said so. I thought it would be great if you could visit me from time to time here and maybe one day convince your mind to join us."

Rajat laughs, "Dad, you are playing the reverse recruitment philosophy here with me. A couple of months ago, I convinced you to join our firm, and here you are now, poaching me from your future employer."

Ranjan laughs and drinks another sip of beer.

Rajat asks, "An important event tomorrow, Dad! The PM speech and all. So happy and proud to see you rising so fast, even in a Government-led setting. Now I understand the reason why everyone wants to work with you. You indeed are one of the top thought leaders of this century, Papa. I wish I could be half of what you are. You are a genuine hero, Dad."

Ranjan laughs. "You know what you get for being a hero? Nothing. You get a pat on the back, blah, blah, attaboy. You can't go home on time. Your wife and kids all miss you." And starts laughing, quoting his favourite Die Hard movie dialogue in front of another Die-Hard fan, his son.

Rajat gets into action and asks as a response to the dialogue, "Then why are you doing this, Pops?"

Ranjan replies, and Rajat joins him in unison, "Because there's nobody else to do it right now, that's why!"

And with that, they both finish their bottle of beer.

Rajat burps. stands up and concludes, "Dad, that's what makes you that guy!" he winks at him back and leaves as he knows Ranjan has a long night before the main event.

Chapter 20

Speech, Speech, Speech, Speech!

There was an old saying, "Whoever controls the media, controls the mind". It has been true for centuries for now. Anyone who controls the source of public information would influence how the public will react. Over the past years, TUESDA has been successful in one of its most important projects: complete control of global media, including news, social media, and networks such as NEBULA4U, newspapers, and everything that provided news. PUNSAM knew this fact, which is why they knew it was pointless to release any information to the public before the crisis was at their hand and TUESDA inaccessible. Hence, the declaration of betrayal came at an opportune moment when TUESDA won't have time to activate its media arm to undo the impact. However, Bill also provided the same power and access to ERO. ERO had unlimited access to all the media networks, radio frequencies, agents, reporters, influencers, etc., and could get a global re-confirmation on any story they want people to believe. The plan was already in place for the same. After Indian PM's address, ERO will activate its media contacts and start spreading the false claims and declarations of PUNSAM and caution everyone to beware of this heinous terrorist organisation against mankind. All the press releases, social media updates, video stories, and channel stories scripts were prepared overnight and ran past Bill and Sharma in the loop. However, Sharma was much more of an FYI than a decision-maker here. His entire focus was to ensure the execution of commands by Bill as well as provide ground-level support to ARK as much as possible. Indian Prime Minister was glad to some extent that India was playing a significant role in this event of crisis and had become a central hub for the entire command of operations. From the discovery of KRAAL to the creation of ARK, the launch of ARK and then the ERO setup boosted the country's morale. Mr. Singh was actively monitoring the UNIBOMB plan along with Sharma and hoped humanity would survive.

However, everyone knew that the probability was decreasing as each day came near to the KRAAL event. Yet, in these last moments, one could ensure that people can live without worrying about being dead in a few months. Hence, Indian PM needed to put people's minds at ease and ensure subsequent media coverage supports the same as well. There was already a list of scandals and important events scripted for months to come. This would provide enough distraction to the world and ensure ERO can work towards UNIBOMB and silently destroy KRAAL. However, that was a pipe dream, according to Bill. He knew from the data on KRAAL that complete destruction of the object was impossible, and there would definitely be significant damage that would happen on planet earth.

29th August 7AM IST, 0800 hrs Spacetime, Day 0, THE ARK

The night was pretty long for some people, especially Arjun, who was awake in a prison cell inside the ARK. He had been uncontrollably crying for a long time inside, repenting over his decision to trust Bill and, more so, agreeing on the idea of boarding ARK. All he wanted was to be with Claudia and Samantha the whole time, from the beginning. He remembers a few years ago when he was offered this job in the front.

He thought working in SCOPE-X for more important agenda items for the world would provide him more time for his family. And it was correct for a few years for him till the work started building more and more. After working for NEBULA and ARK for years, he wanted to focus on planetary problems such as global warming, education, agricultural innovations, etc.

He had promised Claudia that he would spend more time with her and Samantha. He had so many dreams as a husband and a father. He wished he could spend more time with Sammy and teach her his favourite musical instrument, the flute. He wished he could go on more holidays with them, especially to the Alps, which he had been pushing for a long time.

But, all that was left now was his solitude, a meaningless life ahead and no reason to live for. If Samantha and Claudia didn't survive the holocaust, he was as good as a dead man as well. He kicked himself hard for not double-checking Bill's lies and not personally confirming on Claudia and Samantha before boarding. He kicked himself for having accepted the fact that he should arrive early in the morning. He kicked himself for having accepted he should be on ARK and would have rather lived these past months happily with his family and fought for survival.

But nothing could be changed now. His only hope was for the KRAAL to be destroyed by UNIBOMB, and he could return home to Claudia and Samantha. He had decided that he would quit everything if that happened and would only live for his family after that – no career ambition taking precedence over his life, no work taking importance over his daughter, no one's orders taking over his wife's wishes, and no decision that would keep him away from his family.

Away from the prison area, in the lounge, there were a group of people rejoicing over the fact that they would survive and were having drinks and enjoying light conversations as they were relaxed and excited about what was ahead. Many of them were quoting that their life would be like 'Foundationeers' from Isaac Asimov's Foundation. They would often quote Bill as their "Hari Seldon" and empire to be the group of world leaders and ERO as a collective that was left behind with the vain hope of survival via UNIBOMB. In that group was US President Nathan, who was having a drink with a 25-year-old Hollywood actress and boasting about his influence and control over mankind in the future. He was talking to Mindy Chase, the Hollywood sensation and a former Miss Universe. He had got Mindy on the ARK at his own expense and influence, claiming that she was a leading authority in art and was important for the re-colonization plan. However, most people knew the real reason behind getting Mindy. It was mainly for his personal reasons rather than for the fate of humanity.

Inside the control station, the Hari Seldon of the group, Bill, is again connected to the ground station with Sharma, head of ERO.

Sharma says, "Bill, I understand what happened that night with Arjun and you. But it's time you put that aside and try to convince him to rejoin his role in the ARK as its Deputy. No one except him knows how to handle this thing in crisis and even during the docking with the NEBULA. In his absence, I am afraid there is an imminent risk in the journey. His engineers and your experts are good, but no one has the depth of experience he has. I have worked with him in the NEBULA launch, and I can vouch for that. We have travelled to space together in the past also."

Bill replies, "Sharma, my friend. I also agree with you. However, I feel he will be the biggest danger to ARK rather than an asset in this current state of mind. Besides, I don't worry about the issue resolutions, etc. Our team is good, and we also have remote support from you and ERO, who are as good or even better than Arjun. But, don't worry, you leave Arjun on me. As the days pass, he will slowly realise there is no point in lamenting over the past, and he will move on ahead. You should worry more about Indian PM's address and ensure that everyone on the planet calms down afterwards. I have asked some of my best people in PR, media, security, Governments, etc., to corroborate all the facts that Mr. Singh will be sharing. The reaffirmation and confirmation from some of these top people would mean a lot for mankind. I am pretty sure all the heat will go away. It's just that some work must be done at clockwork precision."

Sharma replies, "Bill, thanks for that. Frankly, that is one area in which I have no experience and I will rely completely on you and your team. As far as Arjun is concerned, I fear he is very attached to his family and quite an emotional man. In case you want, I can speak to him. I am pretty sure there is a panel in his prison cell with which I can connect to him post your clearance. Maybe something from an old friend might soothe him more than what's coming from a superior. Besides, I have constantly been getting updates from our security team on Samantha and Claudia's whereabouts. We have traced them, and in a few hours, we will pick them up from the location where PUNSAM is hiding them."

Bill's eyes widen, and he says, smiling, "That's interesting, Sharma. If our ground team has become this efficient, I am glad. Or maybe PUNSAM has been slipping away for quite a while. Ensure you eliminate all these terrorists holding back Arjun's wife and daughter. I have already met one of their leaders and know the kind of people they are by now. There is no point in capturing them. No one will speak anything; besides, there is nothing you can get from them now. Just give a shoot-at-sight order for these idiots but ensure that the girl and her mother are safe. After that, you and Arjun should have a call together. I don't think before that it makes any sense."

Sharma doesn't reply to anything and takes a deep breath after hearing this from Bill.

Bill senses the pause and diverts the topic. "Ranjan, we are patching the current data from the ARK on its trajectory profile, engine performance, medical stats, etc. Please confirm and sign off on that as Day 0-1 data point check vs standard specifications. Do share with us if there are any gaps and suggest remedial measures for corrections as well. We will tune in another two hours to hear the Indian PM address in the world. After that, let's get on a quick call to reconfirm the entire PR and media strategy to be executed. Don't worry. You have my help and support 24/7, even if I am not there," he disconnects after saying that. Bill then stands up, stretches his entire body, smiles, and looks everywhere. He was the man of control, liked everything in control, and wanted to control everything.

0855AM IST, South Block, New Delhi

Inside the PM office's Media Address room, cameras, lights, and microphones have been set up already. The entire team was gathered and waiting for PM to come out of his office. Many people gathered, including his security staff, advisors, his National security advisor and the replacement of Mr. Kulkarni, as well as many internal party members. This gathering was supposed to be only for the planning after PM's address. They did it to ensure that the communication is relayed everywhere.

Everyone was tuned in to their televisions, mobiles, tablets, laptops, etc., for this critical address. Claudia, Albina, Novsky, and Kaamna were tuned in to the Television in the standard room of the GK-2 guest house in Delhi. They got the notice from PUNSAM's leader to carefully watch out for this address and draft another memorandum if needed and a declaration supporting more facts against whatever Indian PM had to say.

At ISRO, Srini and his team members tuned in for formalities sake to watch what Indian PM could say to calm down the chaos created by PUNSAM. However, their main agenda was to capture if there was any activity or action required by them post the news come out. ISRO, NASA, and every top space research centre in the world were supposed to release a parallel communication corroborating the evidence to support that there was no danger and the ARK mission was indeed a peace mission.

At ARK, Bill had asked everyone to tune in to this important release to ensure that all the world leaders and influential people on the ARK could also activate their connections on the planet and support the claims made by Indian PM. It was supposed to be a perfectly orchestrated opera that would run in the next 5 minutes.

In New Delhi, at Sharma's residence, Nidhi, Zoya, and Ranjan had woken up and tuned in to the Television today along with breakfast to watch out for the news. They knew that Ranjan's name would be mentioned as the peace mission's head and the presiding officer for the project in space.

At ERO, Sharma had logged in to his laptop as he switched on the television across him to watch the Indian PM's address.

The time was ticking. Everyone waiting. And...

9 AM IST

At precisely 9AM IST, the Indian Prime Minister walks inside the media room, takes a chair, and starts the worldwide address to humanity.

"My dear brothers and sisters across this lovely planet. This is the first time a world leader is addressing not only his/her nation but the entire mankind. But with the false accusation and revelations happening all around by dangerous, anti-human organisations, they leave us with nothing but to organise such an address."

Bill smiles as he hears this start. Everything is according to his plan, and this will soon be in control. The PM continues.

"Over the last few months, we have been preparing for a very rare and unique missions in the history of humanity. The ARK Peace Mission is one of its kind and designed to unite all the world leaders in one place, away from this planet and into space. The agenda is simple. Everyone lives together under one roof, with a common agency presiding over the security and monitoring the health of the residents. The intention was for everyone to get together, discuss issues of vital importance, prepare tactics to handle global terrorism, leave all the enmity behind, and work towards a better planet. Many of us stayed here to ensure the normal running and operations of the key institutes that run our humanity, governments, businesses, etc. If this mission is successful, we will watch the beginning of a new era for humanity. This mission is presided over by an Earth Rescue Organisation or ERO. The name is inspired by our key goal of rescuing earth from hatred, terrorism, and other evils corrupting the planet. The head of ERO is Mr. Ranjan Sharma, the erstwhile Chief Scientist Officer of PRIME-1 and the NEBULA inventor. He is one of the top Indian scientists and now a global leader of this mission, working in New Delhi for the same."

With that, the photo of Ranjan Sharma and a mute video of him delivering a lecture in IISc appear.

Nidhi, Zoya and Rajat are elated as Ranjan's picture comes on the television.

The PM continues,

"Unfortunately, one of the terrorist organisations got hold of this plan and started creating false evidence, kidnapping various scientists, government leaders, and people involved in this plan. Then, by force, they asked those people to lie and create a fictional story of some world destruction event. My dear brothers and sisters, please don't believe in their science fiction lies and get scared by…"

Suddenly, the lights go off in the PM office and restart again. The network is rebooted, and the entire telecast is disconnected. Everywhere across televisions, the Internet, and social media live events, the telecast is interrupted, and a whizzing sound and a black background appears.

There is a mad rush in the media office of the Indian PM. The Indian PM is perplexed by his support staff. He yells at his advisors to solve the problem immediately. They all are tuned in to the TV and suddenly watch the screens come alive.

A silhouette of a man appears in a dimly lit background. It shocked everyone. This certainly was not an Indian Prime Minister.

The coffee mug from Bill's hand drops, and he stands up and immediately asks his people to dial everyone in ERO and the Indian Government in parallel. He was running across the ARK's command centre from one base computer to another to find out where the hitch had appeared. He had complete access to the background networks for the event, after all.

Everyone in the world is shocked at this hack. It was undoubtedly a hack, for the silhouette appears to have a voice after 20 seconds of pause.

The man speaks, "Hello, World!" And then chuckles, "I am sure the programmers and the engineers get this reference."

And then he continues further.

"Yes, of course, we are PUNSAM." A smile is visible on his face after he says this.

Bill is shocked and sinks into his chair in the ARK. Arjun is in the prison cell and is shockingly watching this live telecast as the man appears. He realises and feels as if he has seen him before. Of course, by now, Bill's eyes caught the person's silhouette, recognized his proper voice, and realised who he was.

So did Mahavir.

So did the Indian PM.

So did Polsky, Shreya and Mahavir on ARK.

So did Rajat.

So did Zoya.

And so did the man's wife, Nidhi, as the man's face emerged in the light.

Ranjan Sharma's face appears in the full light on the Television as he continues. "Yes, we are PUNSAM!" he says and pauses.

Everyone is shocked looking at it.

The Indian Prime Minister cannot believe his eyes as he sinks into his seat. He asks his NSA to immediately go to ERO's office to make this arrest. But, despite an attempt by the PM Media office and other engineers from various channels, they cannot shut down the telecast. It seems like Ranjan had veto control over everything today. After all, he was the head of the ERO.

Tears come out of Nidhi's eyes as Rajat and Zoya watch this in shock.

Kaamna looks at the television with shock. She was watching the head of her organisation now.

Ranjan continues, "Who am I? Well, I am nobody but just a scientist. One who has devoted his entire life towards the progress of mankind with his work on space technology and planetary science. I have done nothing but work for others as I believed in those people. These others included the top world leaders, businessmen, secret organisations claiming to be working for society, and many Government organisations.

I believed in them for a very long time. Their doctrine, vision, value statements and agendas sounded pure, impactful, and noble to me. So, I listened to them and believed in their doctrines.

I am Ranjan Sharma, the one our respected Prime Minister, Mr. Singh, mentioned. I head ERO and am aware of the entire truth about ARK, NEBULA, and KRAAL".

With that, he pauses for a minute and keeps looking at the screen. The entire world is watching this in shock as the panic rises. The stock market immediately takes a nosedive with that statement. Everywhere there is chaos. This single minute proves to be a deadly one for humanity.

Bill is holding his head and is feeling annoyed, angry, and irritated all at the same time. Though he knows that nothing else matters, as he is far away from the planet. Now the only challenge is to reinstate ERO's head, get new staff, etc. His work increases for some days again. He had already texted his agents to eliminate Ranjan Sharma immediately inside the ERO and waited for the result.

Ranjan continues, "However, don't worry about anything. We have things under our control."

Bill's jaw drops. Arjun, inside the prison, looks in shock and excitement at the TV. The entire world pauses and is glued to the screen, causing no further panic.

Ranjan speaks, "Let's just capture the highlights, shall we? Now everyone here on this planet knows the state of scientific advancement we had with NEBULA in 2025. We installed the massive space station or a space city in the outer orbit of our solar system to capture critical data on various planets, new solar systems outside ours, constellations, and even possibilities of life beyond our world. We have accurately been able to predict many global phenomena by the power of NEBULA and its child satellites across our planet. We connected all these child satellites via a peer-to-peer network of satellites across the path between earth and NEBULA. This is how NEBULA can get a very accurate data for planet earth and all the planets inside the solar system. Now, this comes with another superpower – information and data.

Not only is NEBULA able to track all the weather-related information but also to read every encrypted information on every other satellite in the entire solar system. This means anything and everything on the internet, anything connected to any satellite, radio waves, and so on and on.

In short, anyone controlling NEBULA would control everything on the planet. And as they say, with great power comes greater responsibility. The responsibility to protect this planet and not destroy the very essence of humanity.

However, this didn't happen.

The power went to a central commanding authority that started using this information to benefit a certain faction of world leaders – people, whom this authority considered the supreme power. They then destroyed the pure democratic notion that exists in the world today. The data was freely shared for a price amongst these powerful men, so they took many decisions based on this. They thought so, and other scientists did not know what they were up to. But every time they logged in, I got a copy of the log, and we followed up with the event that transversed post that. It wasn't difficult to connect the dots and find out what happened and why? That's precisely one reason PUNSAM created its own satellite port not connected to NEBULA, and it was certainly possible, as many of us were involved in this project. Let's not talk about data security for now. After all, how is that a big problem? Let them read our data and take some calls on that.

Right?

No! The problem is not just reading the data but acting on that for their selfish interests.

Be it price-fixing, selling the data to the rich to make them richer, killing a few innocent people who are obstructing the path of success for these men, snatching the independence from a few people who are fighting for it, or even mass-murdering a section of society as they pose a threat for the existence of these powerful men and women.

Feeling betrayed?

Come on, I have not even started the actual story yet. I mean, this is all alright and sort of acceptable, right?

But now, let's move past these issues of data-stealing, corruption, and all the things that perhaps are like daily sob stories for you in the media. One corruption case arises, the media talks about it, the fire is on for some days, and then it extinguishes as something else of importance kicks in.

But killing innocent people regularly is not acceptable. I had been watching so many people, some even close friends, becoming victims of corruption, losing their life savings, and opportunities, or even being buried in the sand in the desert. One would think that even after so many wars, dynasties, revolutions, and world wars, we would have realised the importance of peace, democracy, and freedom for humanity. However, the more powerful a person gets, the blinder he or she becomes to the ordinary folks.

Allow me to reveal the biggest dictatorial ruler in the world today. Someone who had been ruling this entire planet with no one knowing about it. You might have heard this name many times – TUESDA, The Unified Earth Space Discovery Agency. This unified global agency was meant to streamline all the international efforts toward space exploration. However, its inner agenda was much more twisted than that. By controlling space exploration, they indirectly also controlled NEBULA and hence all the information of every country, government, finances, banks, social media, sentiments, and every confidential information that existed online. This way, they controlled the actions of every Government, business, organisation, or any entity of notable importance. Many countries have been active members of TUESDA and their so-called council meetings. What was supposed to be a meeting where only space exploration and scientific advancements would be discussed turned out to be a convention of these world leaders to unite under a banner and carry out their nefarious agendas."

The Indian PM is watching this as his security advisor, who whispers in his ears, interrupts him, "Sir, we have lost contact with the security. Apparently, we cannot arrest Ranjan as none of our agents is reachable, and whosoever we sent to arrest them is untraceable. This seems bigger, sir."

It shocked Indian PM as he understands the sheer power of PUNSAM and its leader, Ranjan Sharma, now. He tunes in to the TV again.

Ranjan continues,

"And now why are we here? We could have tolerated their corrupt agendas and the crimes they have been doing for decades. But, we realised these parasites will not only corrupt humanity but eventually obliterate our existence on this planet. To explain this, I have to tell you the long-term goals of NEBULA and ARKs.

Many years ago, we discovered our planet is plagued, and the fate of humanity is in danger. The Global climate crisis and global warming are real! Ladies and Gentlemen. And it will surely destroy this planet in a few centuries if we don't act. We searched for life beyond earth for many years but found nothing. Hence, we decided to build special space stations or man-made planets called NEBULA. The first one is already out there, as you know it. Then we created small space carriers known as ARKs. The purpose of these ARKs was to carry human beings from earth to these NEBULAs. The plan was to get everyone out from this planet in the next 400 to 500 years and out on these self-sustaining man-made planets. Trust me, there is no other solution to save everyone. If we don't do this, our innocent great-grandchildren will have to pay the price of our sins against nature. The scientists worldwide working on these projects knew the reality and grimness of the situation.

However, these so-called world leaders, corrupt businessmen and prophets don't care about the future of mankind but their personal profits only. And they delayed the launch and development of multiple ARKs and NEBULAs as far as possible. Instead, they focussed their energies on creating missiles, bombs, and nuclear bombs to show their prowess or destroy anyone who did not obey them. We tried a lot to reason with them over the years, but without success. We realized there is no other option but to uproot them off this planet."

Ranjan takes off his spectacles and presses his eyes, and continues, "With an agenda of cleaning the world of corruption, evil plans of influential people and serve humanity with true dedication and commitment via scientific advancements, a group of people like me came together under a similar agenda and started PUNSAM with the motto,

Longo vivas tempore humanity or Long live humanity.

PUNSAM is a short form for Punarjagran Samhita or the Code of Renaissance.

For the past 10 years, I, along with my peers at PUNSAM, created an organisation with members worldwide. Some of us are political leaders, businessmen, scientists like me, educators, teachers, security advisors, army officials, police, religious leaders from all religions, and many more. We cause no damage to anyone innocent and only work towards fighting against evil and corruption. Three council leaders, including me, devised a mastermind plan a year ago to uproot all the evil together. No one in PUNSAM other than us three was aware of this master plan. This was crucial for the execution of the plan as we could not even trust our own for this. However, luckily for us, everyone in PUNSAM acted along with the best faith as expected when they faced the threat of the grim news ornamental to this plan. Allow me to get my other two colleagues who will explain the plan."

Kaamna sits with Claudia, Albina and others, smiling and beaming with the excitement of what will come next. Suddenly a camera person walks inside the room and points the camera towards Novsky, who gets up and sits in a separate chair away from others and gets ready.

They connected the camera to a live feed, and Novsky looked at Albina and Kaamna and winked at both of them. Kaamna is shocked and smiles at Novsky, for she realises he is one of the council leaders at PUNSAM. Albina still cannot fathom what's happening.

The camera rolls, and the image of Novsky appears on the TV.

Novsky speaks in his Serbian accent, "Hello everyone. I am Jovan, a scientist working for a corrupt organisation led by a corrupt person named Mr. Polsky, another evil mastermind on this planet."

At the ARK, everyone looks around Polsky, whose jaw drops as he looks at Novsky on the camera. Bill is visibly angry and looks at his security head with disgust.

Novsky continues, "Trust me, people. There are many more like me who are part of this pure and sweet organisation started by my dear friend Sharma from India, known as PUNSAM. He approached me a few years ago, and we started working on projects that would expose corruption and evil to mankind. One year ago, we came up with a plan. A plan whose smaller sections were masterminded by the scientists and strategized well by various masterminds from the military, secret agencies, security advisors, and even world leaders who are part of PUNSAM. Well, much on the members later. First, let's share the plan to put your mind at ease. The plan was simple, and my colleague will explain this."

Suddenly the camera stops rolling at Novsky's end. There is a slight pause on the TV, and then the face of another gentleman appears.

This man was seated in his office at ISRO, Bengaluru.

Srini's face lights up as he speaks, "Everyone, I am Srini, the third council leader of PUNSAM. Continuing from where Jovan left, getting rid of this corrupt crowd, one by one, was near impossible. We scientists always believe in uprooting the root cause of the problem and clean the system to operate efficiently. We decided to bring all these criminals, corrupted and evil leaders, under one location and eliminate them then. And so we hatched a plan."

Bill stands up from his seat and is trembling with fear as he realises what's coming next.

Srini continues, "We at ISRO injected a virus in the mainframe of NEBULA along with its child satellites and other independent disconnected satellites via the help of many supporters. We created a fake celestial object on the system with a very real-looking trajectory and a visible image that changes via an algorithm. We created KRAAL. Every one of you has already heard about this name in the so-called Fake Declaration by PUNSAM as per the Indian Prime Minister."

Sharma takes over and speaks on the TV, "We organised urgent TUESDA meetings and called everyone in one place. We told them about an extinction-level event and showed them data that looked very realistic. Many of our agents, like one Ms. Anita Naidu from ISRO and an ex-US marine Jared Lincoln, did not know about the plan. We instructed every PUNSAM agent to act in good faith as they all assumed this news was real. We are so proud of them as they acted in the good faith of humanity as expected. However, we lost many of our good people, including Ms. Anita and Jared, who lost their lives to protect the faith of humanity. Their sacrifice will not go to waste. It was a mistake on our end. We didn't expect TUESDA to go to this extent."

Kaamna looks at the screen with visible anger on her face against TUESDA.

Sharma then continues, "The most troublesome part was to convince the head of TUESDA and the most important person in this story. Let's call him Bill, which is also his real name." He chuckles at that.

Novsky picks up from there, "Convincing Bill was the tricky part. However, one of our non-agents and a wonderful friend, Mr. Arjun Sharma, believed in us. He bought into the entire theory as well.

We knew him well and had a complete idea of what sort of data would make him believe in the reality of such ELE. I even had to sacrifice a few talented team members in this process."

Inside the GK-2 guest houses, PUNSAM had kidnapped two more members who were supposed to go into the ARK. Arihant (the engineer recommended by Sharma) looks at the screen, quite shaken and full of tears. Ishaan, a poor young boy of 11, whom the Indian Prime Minister had nominated, stares blankly at the screen.

Srini speaks, "After Arjun was convinced, getting to Bill was not that difficult. We had speculated that there would be a subsequent meeting where they would decide the fate of humanity. The only solution to this problem was to deploy the ARK project and shortlist 10,000 members for the rescue. We had betted on them getting the entire filth of the planet on that 10K list. And that's what happened. They tried to bury this news under the carpet and sold the 10K seats to all the non-worthy corrupt politicians, businessmen, criminal masterminds, autocrats, and diplomats."

After that, Ranjan, Novsky and Srini explain the entire sequence of events, from the discovery of KRAAL to suppressing this news in media, UNIBOMB, TUESDA, killing anyone who posed a threat to leak this information, etc.

Ranjan says. "We lost many innocent people and even a few PUNSAM agents in this process. Mr. Jared Lincoln was not only our agent but the founder of PUNSAM as well. We won't let the lives of martyrs and millions of innocent people to go waste. "

Srini adds, "And then, as expected, TUESDA got the entire trash of the planet in one place and docked them in a funny-looking aircraft we call as ARK, and went outside the planet for no reason. There is no KRAAL Bill. It was a joke we played with you." With that, he laughs at the camera as if making fun of Bill.

Everyone on the planet is amused at this, but they do not know what's coming ahead.

Ranjan then reveals, "In summary, what we have is a group of 7000 people, out of which 90% are corrupt politicians, businessmen, and world leaders. This we are 100 % sure."

Ranjan then reveals the UNIBOMB plan and the location, and its purpose.

He then says, "And now, for the last part. For the first time in human history, we have a unique advantage. We have a spaceship full of 7000 people, which comprises mainly the most corrupt, selfish, and dictatorial men and women on the planet. We have a unique opportunity to uproot the evil from this planet once and for all. And once they are gone, we can implement the long-term agenda of saving humanity by building more ARKs, NEBULAs and securing our future.

Not only that, we will destroy every nuclear bomb, dangerous missiles, and explosives on this planet. As we have combined everything into UNIBOMB, which was meant for KRAAL.

There are a few wonderful exceptions, like Mr. Arjun Sharma and others. My only regret is that we would have to sacrifice these few good people to uproot the evil from the planet. And not only that, my own to-be daughter-in-law is on the ship."

Shreya looks stunningly at the screen with tears in her eyes. Mahavir grits his teeth at Sharma's betrayal. Rajat was numb and shocked at what his father was saying.

Bill is completely shocked looking at this. Nathan rushes toward Bill and asks him what is happening. Arjun is in the prison cell and laughing his heart out at the paradoxical situation this has turned into.

Everyone is shocked at this new avatar of Ranjan.

Kaamna seems to be beaming with excitement, but after looking at Claudia, she calms herself down as she realises her husband is in the spaceship. Claudia is watching the entire thing with surprise and shock.

Ranjan continues, "You guessed it right, people. We will use UNIBOMB to blow up the ARK and destroy the entire evil from the planet. Well, not entirely, but still a very significant part of evil. After all, every system needs a REBOOT once in a while, especially when the virus has impacted the system."

The Indian Prime Minister is desperately trying to call Ranjan to stop this madness.

However, the ERO office is exceptionally well guarded by PUNSAM's agents and is holding so many hostages already. Turns out PUNSAM was much bigger than what they had expected.

Bill calls every one of his agents on earth and tries to do anything possible.

Nathan yells at him, "Bomb this guy straight away. Get on to war with India if we have to. Call the Indian PM and tell them we are doing it." Bill is connecting to the security heads at the planet but hears Ranjan's voice and pauses.

Ranjan continues, "You cannot prevent this, Bill. The cat is out of the bag. We could have got you back and held you prisoners, but you would have escaped and gotten back into the same place."

With that, he pauses. The camera zooms on to him as he says,

"This is PUNSAM's ultimate message to humanity. In a few seconds from now, people around the UAE will see a few missiles go up. These are nothing but all the missiles under the complete UNIBOMB plan. The plan was to use such missiles to destroy the KRAAL, an object that was supposed to destroy the planet, and we had to kill it before it could kill us. There is no difference in the mission, even now.

The new KRAAL is The ARK; the flags have changed the colour, but the mission remains the same. Protect humanity and this beautiful earth at any cost of anything and any evil that destroys it.

And without further ado. He presses a button at his desk and says, "LONGO."

Novsky comes on screen and says, "VIVAS."

Srini says, "TEMPORE."

Ranjan says, "DE HUMANITY."

And then, in unison, they say, "REBOOT!"

Instantly, many missiles are fired from the UAE desert, directed up towards the space with their coordinates locked onto ARK.

The entire world watches this scene with shock. A few, including PUNSAM, and many common people started rejoicing and dancing happily in their homes, outside the streets where they were gathered to hear this and were jubilant at this last act of PUNSAM.

Indian Prime Minister sinks completely in his seat, takes off his spectacles and sheds a few tears. Nothing could be done now.

Rajat, Shreya, and Nidhi are in an abysmal shock, watching a good father, a good husband, and a peaceful man carrying out such a devastating act against the enemy.

Claudia bursts into tears and is uncontrollable as she runs towards NOVSKY to stop him. Novsky looks at her but moves his face away. Kaamna rushes towards her, holds her, and tries to calm her down.

On the ARK, Arjun seems to be the most elated man inside his prison cell, waiting for the missiles to hit and destroy everyone on it. He closes his eyes and whispers, “I am coming to you, mom and dad!”

At the control centre, everyone is shocked, trembling, shouting, and crying for help. The loud shrieks are visible as ARK counter-reacts with a shaky accelerated jitteriness once it detects the incoming missiles heading towards them.

Bill is completely numb as he sees a ball of fire from the big screen heading directly towards the ARK. He walks towards his chair and opens up the drawer of a nearby table, pulls out a bottle of whiskey, pops it open, and drinks as he watches the show unfolds.

He smiles and then says, “Well played, Sharma. Good to meet an adversary of my worth.” And then waits patiently.

The incoming missile alert is sounded, and the entire ARK is glowing with red lights and a sounding alert. “Everyone, please take your seats, incoming missile alert. Incoming missile alert, Brace for Impact, Brace for impact, Collision detected in the next 30 seconds, 30..... 29..... 28....

Sharma switches off his TV as the screens everywhere in the world are flooded with the scene of the footage inside ARK, the live feed of missiles heading towards the ARK, and the countdown converging to zero.

A new era had begun. The world won’t be the same place ever after this.

PUNSAM had rebooted the earth.

www.ingramcontent.com/pod-product-compliance
Lightning Source LLC
La Vergne TN
LVHW041012150826
845672LV00001B/66

9798887049281